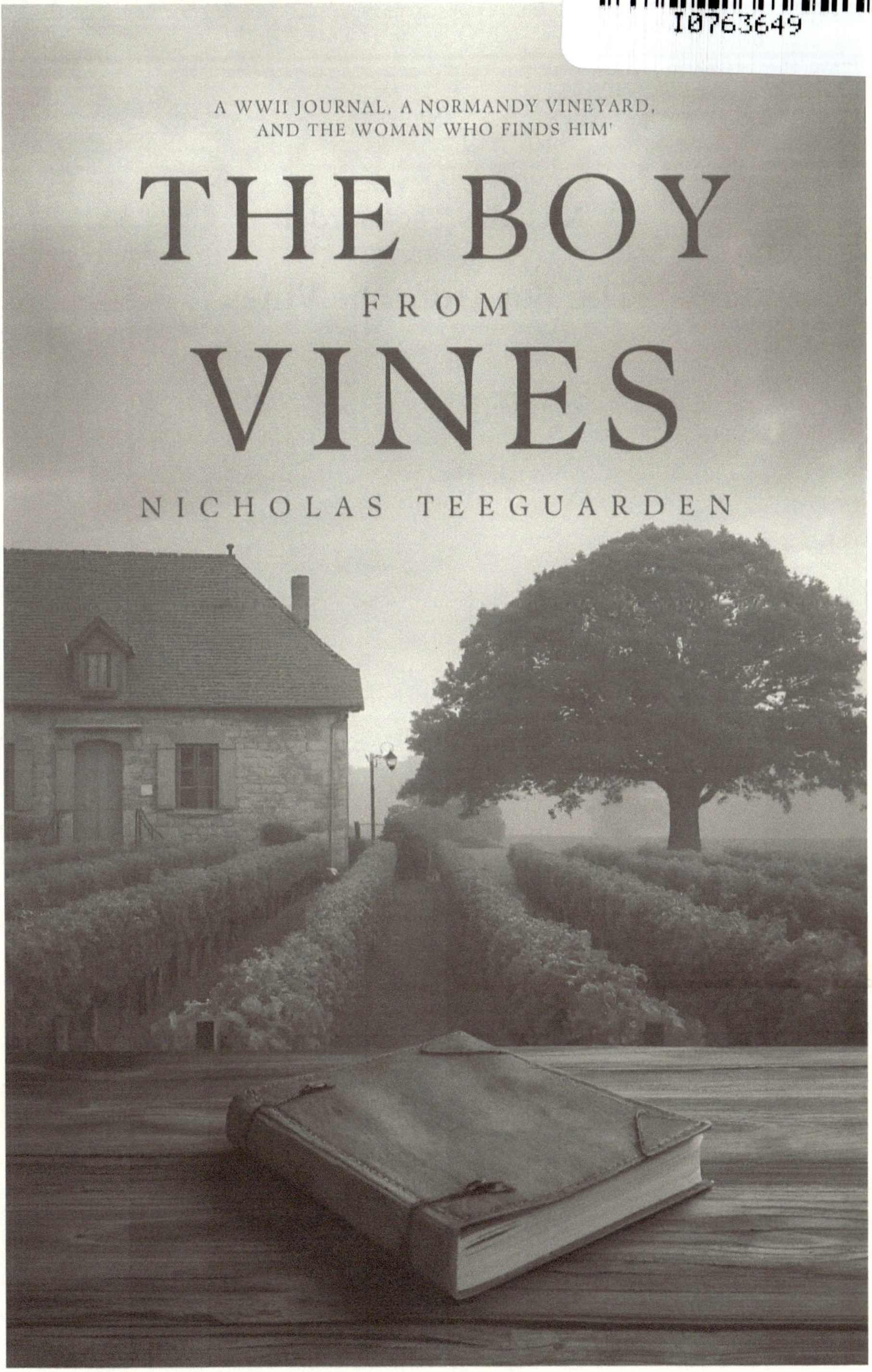

A WWII JOURNAL, A NORMANDY VINEYARD,
AND THE WOMAN WHO FINDS HIM'

THE BOY FROM VINES

NICHOLAS TEEGUARDEN

Nicholas Teeguarden

The Boy from the Vines

First edition

This book was professionally typeset on Reedsy
Find out more at reedsy.com

Contents

1. Chapter 1
2. Chapter 2
3. Chapter 3
4. Chapter 4
5. Chapter 5
6. Chapter 6
7. Chapter 7
8. Chapter 8
9. Chapter 9
10. Chapter 10
11. Chapter 11
12. Chapter 12
13. Chapter 13
14. Chapter 14
15. Chapter 15
16. Chapter 16
17. Chapter 17
18. Chapter 18
19. Chapter 19
20. Chapter 20
21. Chapter 21
22. Chapter 22
23. Chapter 23
24. Chapter 24
25. Chapter 25
26. Chapter 26
27. Chapter 27

28. Chapter 28
29. Chapter 29
30. Chapter 30
31. Chapter 31
32. Chapter 32
33. Chapter 33
34. Chapter 34
35. Chapter 35
36. Chapter 36
37. Chapter 37
38. Chapter 38
39. Chapter 39
40. Chapter 40
41. Chapter 41
42. Chapter 42
43. Chapter 43
44. Chapter 44
Epilogue

1

Chapter 1

The bell above the antique shop door chimed as Ruth stepped inside, the soft sound swallowed by the scent of dust and varnish. Afternoon light filtered through lace-curtained windows, glinting off silver frames and cracked porcelain. The air was cool, faintly perfumed with old paper and something metallic, like time itself had a smell.

She wandered between the narrow aisles, trailing her fingers along tables crowded with forgotten lives: letters bundled with ribbon, watches that no longer ticked, faded portraits staring from gilt frames. Every object seemed to hum with a story half-remembered. A student of history, she had no particular treasure in mind. She only wanted something that made her pause and whisper, wow.

A stack of yellowed maps caught her eye, inked with borders that no longer existed. She unfolded one, tracing the faint lines of Europe with her finger, then set it aside. It was the bottom drawer of an oak bureau that resisted her pull—sticking, then giving way with a sigh of wood and time. Inside, half-buried beneath a veil of dust, lay a small leather-bound book.

It was nothing remarkable at first glance. The cover was worn to softness, a thin cord tied loosely around it as if holding it together by habit. The page edges had browned to the color of tea.

Ruth lifted it gently, brushing away the dust until faint letters began to emerge on the cover: Joseph Durand.

Her breath caught.

The string snapped as she unwound it, brittle with age. Inside, the opening pages were written in a beautiful, careful hand, ink faded but elegant. Further in, the lines grew hurried, uneven. The handwriting shifted from artful to desperate, as though the writer had been racing against something unseen.

She frowned and pulled a notebook from her bag, sketching quick notes. A short translation gave ownership to a young man from northern France, living on a family vineyard. The entry mentioned Germany's advance into Denmark—April 1940, just before the Nazi blitz across Western Europe.

Her pulse quickened.

If the date was right, this book had survived the war.

Ruth carried it to the counter, setting it down with care. The shopkeeper peered over his spectacles, eyes soft with a kind of knowing sadness.

"Old stories," he murmured, almost to himself, before naming a modest price.

After paying, Ruth tucked the journal safely beneath her arm and stepped back into the street. Evening shadows stretched long across the cobblestones. She bought a baguette and a small wedge of cheese from a corner stall, hurrying toward her hotel as if afraid the words inside might fade before she could read them.

Paris glowed around her: the clink of glasses from café terraces, the distant roll of laughter, the warm spill of lamplight on rain-dark stone. She had been traveling across France for the past three weeks, a summer journey meant to give her more than classroom history could. She wanted to feel the places she'd studied, to understand the people and the reasons behind the choices they'd made. Yet this discovery felt different. Personal.

The cobblestones echoed beneath her steps as she crossed the bridge toward her rented apartment, the Seine moving slow and silver beneath her. Her flight home was only a few days away, but tonight, she had no plans beyond reading Joseph Durand's journal.

Later that evening, Ruth settled by the window. From her seat, she had a perfect view of Notre-Dame Cathedral, its newly restored spire rising proudly against the night sky. The soft wash of lights cast long shadows across the stonework, flickering like the ghosts of centuries past.

She lingered there for a moment, tracing the curve of the skyline with her eyes, then turned back to the journal resting in her lap.

April 5, 1940

David and I spent the day working on the northern slope. The vines are coming in nicely, heavy with promise. If the weather holds, we should have a fine harvest in a few months.

David worries about the Germans; news travels fast even this far from Paris, but his father insists we are safe here. He says the war will stay to the north, that France is strong enough to keep it there.

I want to believe him.

The fields are quiet tonight, the air still except for the hum of crickets and the faint rustle of wind through the vines. It's hard to imagine anything dark reaching this far into such peace. Still, the news is bad; they've taken Norway now. I don't know how our army stacks up against theirs, but I hope we never have to find out.

The first few entries were what one might expect to find in an old journal: ordinary reflections, written by someone who couldn't yet see the storm gathering on the horizon. Nothing except a location—northern France—and a name.

It wasn't particularly engaging at first, yet somewhere along the pages, the handwriting changed. The loops grew tighter, the ink pressed deeper into the paper. The words carried weight. Ruth found herself leaning closer to the lamplight, each page whispering louder than the one before.

May 10, 1940

The Germans are taking everything. Each day, the radio says France is holding the line, but every map shows more and more of Europe shaded gray.

David told me tonight about the ghettos in Germany, whole neighborhoods emptied. His uncle heard they're sending people east, but no one knows where.

At dinner, our families talked about building a cellar behind the vineyard house, a place for David's family if the Germans come this far south. Tomorrow we'll gather supplies while we still can. Father says prices are already climbing, and flour's nearly gone from town.

I can feel it now, the war is no longer something happening elsewhere. It's coming here.

Ruth lowered the book, her reflection trembling in the window glass. Notre-Dame's bells began to toll the hour, their echo rolling through the city like a memory too heavy to forget. She closed her eyes for a moment, trying to imagine the world Joseph had written from, a world on the edge of collapse yet still clinging to the rhythm of vines, dinners, and faith that tomorrow might remain ordinary.

Outside, the city shimmered, alive, unbroken. Inside, history waited, breathing between the fragile pages in her hands.

Her gaze drifted back to the text, tracing the ink stains that time had failed to erase. She could almost see him: this young man with dirt beneath his nails and fear behind his steady hand, writing by candlelight, unaware that his words would one day outlive him.

She turned the page.

Paris would fall within the month. France would fracture, its north and west swallowed by Nazi occupation, the south declared a "free zone" under Marshal Pétain's Vichy regime. The term free would soon become a cruel joke.

Deportations would not begin for two more years, but fear already had roots. If Joseph's family were Christians, then David's were surely Jewish, and Joseph's notes about helping them build a cellar now carried a weight Ruth could feel in her chest. Perhaps they had not understood what it would mean to be found hiding Jews in those days. Few did.

Out her window, she could almost see it—the invasion unfolding across the same streets now quiet beneath the Paris night. Red banners draped from balconies, boots striking cobblestone in perfect rhythm, orders barked in a language not their own. The occupation would last more than four years.

Ruth exhaled slowly and closed the journal, her fingers trembling against the worn leather. Outside, the bells of Notre-Dame faded into silence, and the ghosts of both wars—theirs and hers—seemed to whisper through the dark.

When she finally lay back on the narrow bed, sleep would not come. In the half-light behind her eyes, she still heard Joseph's voice, saw his family moving through the cellar's shadows, preparing for the inevitable—a storm that would crush belief, hope, and everything they'd once thought unshakable.

June, 1940

We all huddled in the dark last night, lights out, praying no one would sneeze or cough. It felt like the smallest sound might draw the tanks into the yard. We could hear the artillery pounding the town where the French battalions were staged.

When we finally stepped outside this morning, the earth around us was scorched. Smoke drifted low over the hills, and from the town came the cries of people trapped beneath the rubble.

Father brought the tractor, and Joseph and I worked the ropes and chains—pulling stones, tying beams, clearing what we could. Our hands bled; our backs gave out. We took turns driving the tractor just to catch our breath. Still, no one stopped.

Several people are missing. The town is quiet now, only the sound of weeping. No one complains about their torn hands anymore. We just look at one another, the same thought passing silently between us: what comes next?

What time was it? Ruth glanced toward the window, unsure whether the faint light belonged to morning or to the last of the night.

Joseph's voice still echoed in her mind, raw and unguarded, alive in a way words on a page shouldn't be. She could feel what he must have felt: the fear, the weight, the stubborn will to keep going. And now, somehow, she felt it too.

In that quiet half-light, she made a promise, not aloud, but certain all the same. She would find him. Joseph Durand. She knew he was long gone, but the man who had written those words deserved to be remembered. Who had he been? What town had he called home?

As a historian, she knew it wasn't a singular story. Countless others had lived the same terror, especially across the northern towns where France had braced itself for invasion. Yet this one felt different. Personal.

Ruth reached for her notebook to take notes—locations, names, dates, any detail that might lead her to Joseph. The northern slope of a vineyard, early June 1940. That put him in northern France, perhaps near the Belgian border, but that was still too broad.

She frowned, tapped her pen against the paper. The northern frontier stretched for hundreds of miles. There had to be something else, something in his words that would narrow the search.

She turned back to the journal, eyes scanning the brittle pages for any hint she might have missed.

2

Chapter 2

Ruth carefully turned back toward the front, scanning for any details—the town's name, a family name—that might shrink the area of her search. As she reached the beginning once again, the name and the writing already seemed different, like she had become a personal friend. Finally, it was two passages later, a piece that helped build the border of the puzzle, a small but significant detail.

June, 1940

I sat in the church today. The destruction mostly missed the abbey, only the outer walls scarred and the ground around the cemetery torn and blackened. The stone canopy above the old cardinal's tomb had split apart, one heavy slab toppling into a nearby headstone.

I stared at the carvings in the wall, the saints whose faces were half gone, hands chipped away by time and fire. Dust drifted through the light that cut down from the broken window above the altar. The air smelled of stone and smoke, of wax melted into the pews.

Father says we were lucky the abbey still stands at all. I wonder if that's true. It feels more like a ghost of what it was, a shell echoing with prayers no one dares to speak aloud anymore. A reflection of the feelings the Nazis have been leaving behind.

A light sparked in Ruth's mind. She couldn't remember the exact name, but she knew there was a church in Normandy that served as the burial place of two cardinals. She reached for her tablet, fingers flying before she could second-guess herself: cardinals, church, burial, Normandy, World War II.

The search returned a familiar name—Cathedral of Our Lady of Rouen.

She opened the first image. There it was: the towering Gothic nave, and along one wall, a monument depicting two kneeling cardinals, carved in white marble, hands folded in eternal prayer.

Her pulse quickened. For the first time, the journal had given her something tangible.

Ruth checked her watch, then her flight information. Forty-eight hours until she was supposed to leave France. Her room was already paid through then, nonrefundable, but that worked to her advantage. She could travel light, make the trip, and return before nightfall.

Over lunch, she spread maps across the small café table, tracing the rail lines toward Normandy. It was possible, a little tight, but possible. She could be in Rouen before afternoon.

Back in her room, Ruth packed a small backpack: a change of clothes, her passport, the journal, and her notes. Everything else she left behind.

She reached the station just as the train was boarding. The digital sign flickered: Rouen Rive Droite. A place she had read about a hundred times in history books—bombings, occupation, liberation—but this time, it wasn't about history. It was personal.

As the train pulled away from Paris, Ruth opened the journal again. The countryside slid past her reflection in the window—green fields, gray skies, a blur of villages that had seen too much and remembered everything. With every page, Joseph Durand's words carved deeper into her thoughts.

She wanted to know what happened to him. But she couldn't bring herself to skip ahead. The idea of discovering his fate felt too much like losing someone she already knew.

Sleep crept in at the edges of her vision. The words began to blur, shrinking down the tunnel of her exhaustion. She tried to keep reading, but the rhythm of the train lulled her under.

When she woke, the brakes hissed, and the jolt threw her forward. The overhead speaker crackled: "Rouen Rive Droite."

Heart pounding, she gathered her things and stepped off into the cool Normandy air. The faint salt in the breeze carried the memory of old wars—centuries of invasions, kings and queens trading crowns and vows, nations wounded by pride or insult. Here, history didn't rest; it lingered, layer upon layer, built into the stone.

She had little more than the church as her guide, but she went there first. The streets wound narrow and uneven beneath her shoes, the sound of bells echoing faintly through the old quarter.

When she reached the cathedral square, Ruth hesitated at the base of its Gothic façade, tracing the air as if she could touch the same stones Joseph once did.

Inside, the scent of candle wax and dust hung in the air. Light poured through fractured glass, scattering color across the pews. She wandered slowly down the nave until she found a quiet corner near the carved tombs, then sat and opened the journal again.

June 23, 1940

Today we had Mass. I sat through the service looking at the wall with the carvings. Sitting beside Father was a German officer; behind us, the pews were filled with soldiers.

Father Bernard gave the homily, the sacrament, everything he does every other Sunday, without a single hesitation. It was as if he didn't care who was watching. The church felt small, suffocating with their presence, but his voice never shook.

Afterward, I asked him how he could stand there and preach with them in the room. He didn't answer at first, just gave me that same calm, knowing look. Then he said quietly, "See you later, Joseph."

On our way out of town, the sound of boots echoed off the stone walls, sharp and hollow. Piles of rubble still littered the streets. A few soldiers leaned against what was left of the houses, boots propped on fallen stones that had once been someone's wall, someone's life. No one dared look at them too long. Stories are already spreading, people beaten, some even shot, for less than that.

David came by this afternoon. His father has been taken for questioning; no one knows where. We spoke quietly in the shadows near the garage, afraid even our echoes might betray us.

He asked if I could help them find a way west.

"It's rare to see someone sitting here like that—so still, as if the world's holding its breath," a man's voice said softly, pulling her out of the page.

Ruth looked up, startled. "Oh, Father. I didn't see you there."

The man smiled, lowering himself onto the pew beside her. "I didn't figure you did. I tried to find words that wouldn't make you jump." His eyes flicked toward the journal in her hands. "We get visitors, of course... tourists, mostly, during the week. But you don't look like one of them. Not the sort who wanders through snapping photos of statues or parroting bits of history they half-remember from a guidebook."

He studied her for a moment, expression shifting from amusement to something more thoughtful. "No," he said quietly, "you have the look of someone searching for something more than pretty decorations."

Ruth turned the journal in her hands so that the carved name on the cover faced him.

"I found this in a little shop near my hotel," she said. "Something about it just... felt meant for me. Like I was supposed to take it." She hesitated, then added, "After reading the first few passages, I realized the writer—Joseph—was here during the early days of the war. His family owned a vineyard somewhere north of here. I think he sat in this very church, maybe even in this spot, just days after the bombing."

She looked down at the worn leather, running her thumb along the frayed edge of the cover. "It sounds strange, I know. But it feels like his story found me."

Something in the priest's expression softened. Whatever she had expected—a polite nod, a distracted smile—it didn't come. Instead, he seemed to listen in a way that made her words feel safe, even sacred. For the first time since finding the journal, Ruth didn't feel alone in what she was discovering.

The two sat silent for a minute while the priest looked down in contemplation, as if he knew exactly how important the find was. What Ruth didn't know was whether it was because he had knowledge, or just the cosmic feeling of it all.

"Would you mind reading one of the passages to me?" he asked, in a voice that sounded as if he genuinely didn't know the answer. "I know it has to be incredibly intimate."

Ruth ran her hand across the cover, trying to summon the courage to read aloud to someone else. "Yes," she said at last. "I'll go to the passage after he was sitting here in the church. He ended the last entry with his friend David asking for help getting west."

June 24, 1940

The sun was about to go down last night. David and I were coming out of the vines when a car appeared on the road. It didn't need markings—the only ones riding in cars like that were German officers.

We dropped down between the rows, hearts pounding. The cracks between the leaves felt too wide, as if the vines themselves couldn't hide us.

They dragged Father out of the house. I could hear shouting, though not the words. Then it was clear enough. They forced everyone to their knees. David's mother and sister were bound and thrown into the car.

There was nothing anyone could do.

One of the officers had been at Mass earlier. Sat right next to Father Bernard, hands folded, head bowed. And now he was tearing a family apart.

David and I looked at each other. There was no longer a question; we had to get them west. I told him to keep calm, to not do anything that would ruin our chances... no heroics, no sudden moves. From what we're hearing, once the Nazis take someone for questioning, they rarely come back.

We spoke of the other families around town. David said he wouldn't leave them behind. If he couldn't save his own, he would try to carry others with him.

Ruth's voice faltered on the last line. She closed the journal gently, fingers lingering on the cover before resting it on her lap. For a moment, neither of them spoke. The stillness of the cathedral seemed to absorb the weight of Joseph's words.

"That was heavier than I expected," she said quietly.

The Father nodded, his tone reverent, almost like a benediction. "The power is in the acceptance of a divine call," he said. "Even if they didn't feel it directly, these two—this Joseph and his friend—were answering something greater. They stepped into purpose, not safety."

He paused, eyes drifting toward the stained glass above them, where colored light spilled across the stone floor. "His name... Joseph. It makes sense now, doesn't it?"

Ruth looked up at him, uncertain.

"Joseph," the priest continued softly, "was warned of the coming slaughter, and fled with Mary and the child to Egypt. He carried salvation away from destruction."

He turned back to her, voice gentle but certain. "Perhaps your Joseph was chosen to do the same."

Ruth drew a long breath, as if a heavy load had been set down across her shoulders. "Would you happen to know anything... maybe what family he came from, or which farm it could have been?"

The Father shook his head, his expression thoughtful. "Nothing comes to mind just yet. But perhaps we could look together, see what records still exist. There are a few archives we keep here, parish and local. Much was lost in the bombings, but not everything." He hesitated, then smiled. "It's still early. Would you be interested in seeing what we might find?"

Ruth wiped at the corner of her eye, steadying her voice. "Honestly, this is as far as I've gotten. I wouldn't even know which way to turn after walking out those doors."

He smiled again, rising from the pew. "Then let's begin there."

The Father led her through a narrow side corridor that smelled faintly of wax and cold stone. The echo of their footsteps followed close behind, swallowed and reshaped by the vaulted ceiling.

They passed through a small wooden door at the end of the hall. The hinges groaned as it opened, and a cool draft rose from below. A stairway curved downward into shadow.

"Records are kept beneath the old vestry," he said, taking a small flashlight from a hook near the door. "Some of these archives go back to the seventeenth century—baptisms, marriages, burials. The war years... those are harder."

Ruth followed him down, one hand brushing the rough wall as they descended. The air grew colder, denser, carrying the smell of dust and time. Each step sounded like it might wake something that had been asleep for decades.

At the bottom, the space opened into a vaulted chamber lit by two dim bulbs strung from the ceiling. Shelves lined the walls, all neatly labeled, some half-collapsed under the weight of centuries. Stacks of ledgers and brittle papers rested in uneven towers, their edges curled and yellow.

Ruth hesitated on the last step, the journal pressed against her chest.

"Feels different down here," she murmured.

The Father smiled faintly. "It always does. These rooms remember what the world forgets."

He set the flashlight on the nearest table and began pulling a few folders aside. "If your Joseph or his family were local, there might be a record: baptisms, property lists, even vineyard tithe documents. Many families offered a portion of their wine to the church."

Ruth nodded, stepping closer, her fingers hovering just above the fragile pages. "It's strange," she said quietly. "Reading his words up there felt like meeting a ghost. Down here, it feels like he's about to walk in."

3

Chapter 3

June 1940

We've gathered our things and are making preparations for our movement west toward the coast. We'll carry only two days' worth; we can restock in the next town.

David is convinced my papers will pass if I'm stopped. We've hidden a few packs and supplies beneath the barn. The vineyard is silent now; it feels so empty after the Germans took everyone away. I hope I'll come back someday, take over, and continue my family's legacy.

David has made contact with several families around town who need to be moved. One refuses to go. I don't want too many; the more we bring, the greater the risk of being seen. Yet I don't know if I can live with myself leaving anyone behind.

We leave before sunrise. We can slip out through the vines without passing through town. If someone is awake, I don't want them to see an exodus.

Descending into the dark, Ruth followed as the stone steps echoed beneath their feet. The air grew cooler with each turn of the staircase. There were no overhead lights, just small lamps plugged into wall sockets, their cords stapled into the concrete like veins running along the passage.

Dust drifted through the cones of yellow light, swirling each time the Father moved a folder or shifted a stack of ledgers.

The smell was unmistakable: old paper, candle wax, and the dry sweetness of time. It was the scent of history itself, of pages that had waited too long to be opened.

Surprisingly, the archives were more organized than she expected. Each shelf was labeled by year and purpose: Baptisms, Marriages, Burials,

Tithes. The war years, however, told a different story. Boxes blackened by fire. Ledgers half-eaten by mold. Pages missing corners or burned entirely through, like wounds that never healed.

Ruth ran her hand lightly over one spine. The leather cracked beneath her fingers.

"Here," said the Father, his voice low but steady. "Try these first, parish registries from 1930 through 1942. If your Joseph's family lived nearby, they would appear somewhere in these. Don't let that journal get swallowed up by everything else."

Hours passed, marked only by the rustle of paper and the quiet shifting of books onto desks. She read names—some joyful, others tragic—families joined in marriage, children baptized, lives marked and remembered long before war changed everything. These were stories of beginnings, of ordinary days before the storm.

Then, as her eyes swept another brittle page, she froze.

Durand.

Her pulse quickened.

Joseph Durand, baptized March of 1923.

The ink was faded, the edge of the page singed, but the name was there. Real. Solid. The boy who had written those desperate words had once been here, in this book, baptized by the same church whose stones now surrounded her.

Ruth turned from the table, excitement flashing in her eyes.

"I've found him," she said. "Joseph. Baptized in 1923."

The Father stepped closer, adjusting his glasses to see the page.

"That would make him one of the post-Great War children," he said with a quiet chuckle. "Families multiplied quickly after the last war. Hope always finds a way, I suppose."

Ruth nodded, her finger tracing the faded line of ink. "There's nothing else. The rest of the page is burned away."

He sighed, thoughtful but undeterred. "Still, that means we're on the right trail. The Durands were here; this was their parish."

The Father straightened, thinking. "If they lived nearby, there might be more than parish records. Many families tithed wine or grain to the church before the occupation. Sometimes we kept notes of their donations, especially the vineyard owners."

He crossed to another shelf where a stack of ledgers leaned precariously, their bindings swollen with age. Dust billowed as he pulled one free and set it on the table beside her. The cover read: Inventaire des Dons et Dîmes — 1938–1941.

Ruth leaned over as he opened it carefully, each page whispering against the next. Most of the entries were brief: dates, names, the weight or quantity of whatever had been offered. The ink had bled in places where water had touched the paper, smudging years into ghosts.

Then, halfway down a page dated Spring 1940, she saw it.

Maison Durand & Fils — Vin du Nord — trois fûts.

Three casks.

Next to it, in another hand, someone had scrawled a note:

Dernière livraison avant l'occupation. Famille non revue après juillet.

(Last delivery before occupation. Family not seen after July.)

Ruth's breath caught. "It's them," she whispered. "The vineyard. Joseph's family."

The Father nodded, eyes softening as he closed the ledger. "Then this is where their story goes silent."

Ruth traced the ink once more, the words trembling under her fingertips.

"Maybe silent here," she said softly, "but not finished."

He regarded her for a long moment, then smiled faintly.

"No," he agreed. "Not finished. But now we know which vineyard your Joseph was writing from. Let's shift our focus and see who owns it today. They may have something that could help."

Ruth looked up. "What would have happened to a vineyard if the family didn't make it through the war?"

The Father's eyes softened. "That depends. Many were seized by the Germans during the occupation—used to supply their own officers or requisitioned under new management. Some were left in ruins when the front moved through. Others..." He sighed. "Others were taken by collaborators, Frenchmen who found profit in loyalty to the wrong side."

She looked back down at the ledger. "And after the war?"

"Those who survived came back to find strangers living in their homes. Some reclaimed what they could, others left it behind. There were restitution programs, committees, tribunals. Most of it never reached the families who were gone."

Ruth closed her eyes for a moment, absorbing it. "So if no one from Joseph's family survived..."

"Then the vineyard could have been claimed by the state," he finished quietly. "Auctioned, merged, or left to decay. But if the land was productive, someone kept it alive. Vineyards don't like to be abandoned."

He reached for another book, a thick volume bound in cracked green leather, and slid it across the table. "Here. Postwar property transfers, Rouen region. It's not comprehensive, but we can try."

They worked in silence again, the soft scratch of paper filling the air. Ruth scanned lists of estates, her eyes blurring over endless names: Beaumont, Leclerc, Montrose, Dufresne...

"Aha, here it is," the Father said, pointing to a place halfway down a page stamped 1946.

Propriété: Domaine du Nord — anciennement Maison Durand & Fils.

Nouveau propriétaire: Philippe Marchand.

Her pulse jumped. "Domaine du Nord. That's the same name. The vineyard was transferred in 1946 to a Philippe Marchand."

The Father leaned closer, reading the line. "Marchand... that name's still known around here. There's a wine distributor by that name, third generation, I believe. Their estate is north of the city."

Ruth copied the entry into her notebook, underlining the name twice. "So that's where I go next."

The Father nodded, thoughtful. "If it's the same family, they might still have old records or letters. Many estates kept ledgers even through the war, sometimes hidden in the cellars."

Ruth smiled faintly, tucking Joseph's journal under her arm. "Then maybe it's time I visit one more vineyard."

He smiled back. "Just be careful. History has a way of remembering only what it's ready to reveal."

They moved back to the pew where they had first met, the fading light from the stained glass casting shifting color across the floor. Ruth opened the journal again, the worn spine creaking softly as if waking from a long sleep.

Now that she knew where Joseph's vineyard had been, the entries felt more vivid, less like history and more like memory. She could almost see it: the lines of vines bending beneath the wind, the hurried figures moving between them, fear hidden beneath purpose. She read on.

June 26, 1940

End of day one. We moved out before sunrise and quickly realized we'll make only a few miles each day. We can't cross open ground in daylight; it draws too many eyes.

Tonight we're deep in the Green Forest. The canopy swallows the stars, and the air is damp and cool.

Ten feet from where I sit, a mother nearly smothered her baby when it started to cry. The fear in this group is something you can feel in the air; it presses against your chest. Every sound is followed by the same thing: silence, then a long, trembling breath.

David and I agreed our best route is toward Cauville. The line between here and there runs through the least populated areas. I'll scout ahead tomorrow. We all rise around four, and I'll leave first, cutting a visible path for David to follow.

It's the best plan I can make. I'd rather be out front; if trouble comes, it'll find me first.

If we reach a town or see patrols, David will hold the group until I return. If the coast is clear, I'll double back. Maybe I can find a few supplies while I'm out. Food is already short.

God help us if the next town is occupied.

There was a small car-rental office just down the block. Father Laurent walked with her, hands folded behind his back, the last of the afternoon light glancing off the cathedral's stone. He would have given her a car himself if he'd had one.

Ruth smiled as they reached the narrow storefront. "Thank you, for everything," she said.

He nodded. "Go see what the land still remembers."

Inside, the rental clerk handed her a set of keys with little ceremony. She couldn't help but laugh quietly at the options—rows of tiny compacts that most Americans would have walked past shaking their heads. She chose the largest of them, a two-seater mini with just enough legroom to stretch.

Stepping outside, Ruth squinted up at the sky. It was late afternoon; the air had that heavy, golden quality that makes even modern cities feel older. She could almost picture Joseph's convoy threading through the forest, every sound an echo of fear, every mile another act of faith.

It was only five miles to the edge of the old vineyards, whatever that translated to in kilometers, and unlike Joseph's weary group, she would make the trip in minutes. Still, as she settled behind the wheel, a chill passed through her. She wasn't simply following history anymore; she was crossing into it.

With the journal open beside her and the Father's words still in her ears, Ruth turned the key. The little engine coughed to life. She eased onto the narrow road that wound north out of Rouen, toward Préaux and the shadows of the Green Forest.

4

Chapter 4

The road north from Rouen narrowed quickly, winding between fields and stands of poplar that leaned toward the morning light. Mist still clung to the low hills, veiling the land in soft gray. Ruth kept one hand on the wheel, the other resting on Joseph's journal in the seat beside her, as if it might slip away if she didn't hold it close.

She'd read enough of his words to know that this countryside was the same soil rolling past her window that had once been his world. Every turn of the road felt layered with his memory. She could almost see him walking here, leading frightened families through the early dawn, their footsteps pressed into mud now long dried and overgrown with wildflowers.

The rental car hummed softly, a faint mechanical contrast to the silence of the fields. Every so often, an old farmhouse appeared through the fog—stone walls dark with moss, rooflines sagging under the weight of years. Life had gone on here, but the scars of war still lingered if you knew where to look.

Ruth slowed as a sign appeared at the roadside: PRÉAUX — 2 KM.

Her pulse quickened. The Father's map had placed the old vineyard between here and the forest ridge beyond.

We leave before sunrise. We can slip out through the vines without passing through town...

Joseph's words ran through her mind like an echo carried on the mist. She pictured him—barely older than a boy—standing at the edge of the vines, the moonlight glinting off dew-soaked leaves, the shapes of frightened families moving quietly behind him. The silence of fear. The breath held before dawn.

The image was so vivid it pulled her back to the present. She spotted a weathered fence at the bend in the road, its posts tilting with age. One rail pointed inward toward a break in the tree line, the head of a faint path half swallowed by grass.

Ruth slowed the car, heart pounding, and pulled to the shoulder. The path looked ordinary enough, but something about it felt deliberate, like a marker left by time itself.

She stepped out of the car, gravel crunching beneath her shoes. The air was colder here, sharper, carrying the scent of damp earth and distant woodsmoke. She walked toward the fence, brushing her fingers along the rough grain of the post. Lichen clung to it like old scars.

Up close, the path became clearer. What looked like wild overgrowth from the road was actually a narrow track worn into the ground—too subtle for modern vehicles, too intentional to be accidental. Someone had walked this way often enough to leave a trace, long before concrete roads and satellite maps.

Ruth swallowed. She had seen these types of things before: wagon tracks, broken ground, bent trees. Things left by the Cherokee on the walk into the Territory. She studied the ground where she stood, then looked back at the journal on the passenger seat.

This could have been Joseph's escape route.

A breeze pushed through the trees, stirring the tall grass and making the path ripple like something alive. For a moment she hesitated, wondering if she was trespassing, not just on land, but on memory.

She took a step forward.

The world seemed to quiet around her. No passing cars. No humming engine. No tourists chattering in the distance. Just the soft hush of wind through branches and the steady thrum of her own heartbeat.

As the trees closed around her, the path curved slightly and then opened.

Just beyond the break in the brush, she saw the edge of cultivated rows. Neat, measured lines of vines stretched along the hillside, their winter-bare frames twisting like ink strokes against the pale sky.

Her breath caught.

This wasn't wild land.

This wasn't abandoned.

Someone was still tending this place.

She stepped fully out of the tree line, boots sinking slightly into the soft earth. A thin fog drifted low across the rows, the kind that clings to vineyards at dawn and dusk, turning every vine into a silhouette. Ruth stood still, listening—half expecting to hear voices, footsteps, the whispered urgency of people long gone.

But the only sound was the faint clatter of something metallic in the distance. A tool? A gate?

Her pulse quickened.

She walked a few more steps, brushing her fingers along the nearest vine. The wood was rough and alive beneath her touch, trimmed recently, the cut ends pale and clean. Someone had been here no more than a week ago.

And if someone maintained the vines...

Maybe someone remembered the name Durand.

Ruth followed the curve of the rows, stepping onto a narrow dirt lane that ran between them. It sloped gently upward, toward a rise she couldn't see over. The journal felt heavy in her hand, as though Joseph himself were urging her forward.

She climbed the small incline, breath held without meaning to, and at the crest of the hill the view opened wide.

A farmhouse stood below—stone walls the color of old parchment, shutters painted a deep blue, smoke curling from the chimney. Behind it stretched a cluster of outbuildings and what looked like a modern steel vat barn. The place was quiet but not deserted; the hum of machinery echoed faintly from somewhere deeper in the property.

Ruth exhaled, a mix of nerves and anticipation tightening her chest.

Someone lived here.

Someone owned this land.

Someone might know what happened to Joseph Durand.

She took one more steadying breath, then began the walk down the hill toward Domaine du Nord. The journal felt heavier in her bag, as if it were trying to anchor itself in the land it knew.

Ruth followed the fence line slowly, her hand skimming the weathered posts as she walked. The morning mist was lifting now, revealing more of the vineyard stretching out across the hill—a patchwork of rows running neat and disciplined toward the horizon.

She rounded a bend where the fence turned sharply, and there it was: a gravel drive, marked by a wooden sign that read DOMAINE DU NORD in elegant carved letters. Below it, a smaller metal plate read: Marchand Vins — Propriété Privée.

Ruth hesitated only a moment before pushing open the iron gate.

As she stepped inside, movement caught her eye. A woman in a dark green work jacket stood a few rows down, pruning shears in hand. Her dark hair was tied back, her posture confident and unhurried—the kind of ease that comes from belonging to land passed down through generations.

She turned at the sound of the gate and called out, "Bonjour ! Puis-je vous aider ?" Her voice was warm but curious.

Ruth cleared her throat. "Uh... yes, hello. I'm sorry, I didn't mean to intrude. I'm looking for someone from the Marchand family?"

The woman stepped closer, boots crunching over the gravel. "You've found one," she said with a smile. "Claire Marchand. My family has been here since the forties." Her gaze drifted to the journal clutched in Ruth's hands. "Are you... researching something?"

Ruth exhaled shakily. "Yes. And I think it might be connected to your vineyard."

Claire studied her face, not with suspicion, but with a kind of quiet, cautious interest—as if she'd seen this look before. As if she knew the weight of history better than she let on.

"Well," Claire said softly, gesturing toward the farmhouse, "it sounds like we should talk."

As Claire removed her gloves and walked to meet her on the path, Ruth tried to explain—how she'd found the journal in Paris, how the entries led her to Rouen, how the Durand name showed up in the church archives just yesterday. The words tumbled out too quickly, breathless with excitement and fear that she might somehow be wrong.

But halfway through Ruth's explanation, something shifted in Claire's expression.

A tightening of the jaw.

A subtle inhale.

A look that flickered between surprise and calculation.

Ruth noticed it instantly.

Claire stopped walking. "Durand?" she repeated carefully. "You're certain that's the name?"

"Yes," Ruth said. "Joseph Durand. His family owned this vineyard before the war. The records said it was transferred after they were gone."

For one fragile heartbeat, neither woman spoke.

And then Ruth saw it, the realization washing over Claire.

Not panic.

Not guilt.

But a sudden, uncomfortable awareness.

The kind a person gets when history, inheritance, and ownership collide in the same sentence.

As if she feared what might come next.

As if she thought Ruth might be here to claim something more than answers.

A vineyard.

A legacy.

Land that the Marchands had worked for three generations.

Claire swallowed, her voice quieter when she finally spoke. "Well... that does make this conversation a bit more complicated."

The words hung in the cool air, heavier than Ruth expected.

Ruth blinked. "Complicated? I—did I say something wrong?"

Claire didn't answer immediately. She just held Ruth's gaze for a long moment, studying her as though trying to decide what sort of person had just walked onto her land. Then she exhaled slowly, slipping her gloves into her jacket pocket.

"No," Claire said at last. "Not wrong. Just... unexpected."

She gestured toward the farmhouse again, her smile returning—smaller now, guarded around the edges. "Come. Let's talk inside."

Ruth followed her down the gentle slope, suddenly hyper-aware of each step she took. Her mind raced back through everything she'd said, replaying her own words:

His family owned this vineyard...

Before the war...

Transferred after they were gone...

Oh.

A tight, embarrassing heat bloomed in her chest.

She hadn't meant to sound like someone tracing ownership. Or accusing. Or implying anything at all beyond wanting answers. But maybe that's exactly how it had sounded to Claire, a stranger showing up with old documents and a name carved into leather, asking about who used to live here.

Ruth cleared her throat softly as they walked. "Just to be clear, I'm not here for... anything legal. Or to make claims or—" She waved a hand, flustered. "This isn't about property. I'm just trying to understand what happened to him."

Claire glanced over her shoulder. This time her smile reached her eyes a little more.

"I didn't think you were here for land," she said gently. "But when people show up with old names and older papers... well, you can imagine how it looks."

Ruth nodded, mortified and relieved at the same time. "I really am sorry. I didn't mean—"

"It's all right." Claire stepped up onto the cottage's stone threshold. "History gets tangled. It's not your fault."

She pushed open the worn wooden door and motioned Ruth inside.

They stepped in. Claire nodded toward a small wooden table before crossing into the kitchen. Ruth heard the soft click of the gas stove, the rush of flame catching, the whistle of the kettle beginning its slow ascent.

Ruth sat carefully, placing the journal on the table and opening it to the entry where Joseph's group had departed the vineyard. The inked words stared back at her, but something else hit her before she could read them.

A realization so sharp and sudden it almost knocked the breath from her lungs.

She was sitting in a room Joseph Durand had once lived in.

A kitchen he had walked through, maybe barefoot on these same clay tiles.

A table where he had eaten, prayed, worried, hoped.

The thought struck her hard, like a punch to the chest.

This wasn't a museum.

This wasn't a reconstruction.

This was his home.

Ruth's breath stilled. A dozen questions pressed in at once...

Where had he sat? Did he write here? Was this where he learned of families who needed help? Had he fled from this very doorway in the dark?

Her mind spun, caught somewhere between awe and grief.

5

Chapter 5

A sudden slap jolted her.

Claire brought two cups to the table, the ceramic clinking softly as she set them down. She added sugar to one, none to the other, her movements automatic. Only then did she glance at the open journal, her eyes flicking from the ink to Ruth's face.

"I brought something in," Claire said, her voice low, measured. "I thought you might... appreciate it."

She reached for the small wooden box she had set on the table and opened it carefully, almost reverently. Inside were several folded letters, a few black-and-white photographs, their edges curled and soft with age.

Claire lifted the top photograph and slid it closer to Ruth.

"This," she said quietly, tapping the image with her finger, "is the Durand family. We've kept these for as long as I can remember."

Ruth's breath caught in her throat.

Four people stood in front of the farmhouse she had just walked through: a lean man with rolled sleeves, a woman in a simple dress, a boy of maybe sixteen, and a younger child she couldn't quite make out from the faded print.

Ruth reached for the photo with trembling fingers, the weight of it almost overwhelming.

"That's Joseph," Claire added softly. "My grandfather kept anything he found when the property transferred. Nobody ever came asking. Until now."

Ruth swallowed hard, unable to speak.

The journal lay open beside her.

The photograph sat before her.

For the first time, Joseph Durand wasn't just handwriting on a page.

He had a face.

A family.

A life.

Claire folded her hands in front of her, bracing herself. "Tell me," she said, "what exactly did you find in that journal?"

Ruth explained—where she'd found it, how it had led her here, a summary of the entries so far. Then she began to read the next entry.

June 27, 1940

We've made it just outside Houppeville now—perhaps four or five miles. David and I realized quickly we'd only be able to cover a few miles each night. They need to stay hidden through the day, sleeping what little they can, and move only in the darkest hours, just before dawn.

David knows a couple of families here. I slipped into town and managed to locate one of them. Couldn't stay long. I left a note with a shopkeeper I trust—or hope I trust. It's impossible to know anymore who believes what or who listens to whom.

As evening crept in, another family appeared at the edge of the tree line. They pretended to be taking a simple stroll, but their eyes... fear gives people away. They were looking for us.

Our small band is now closer to twenty. Children of every age. Some who look like they were born yesterday, and others we have to watch closely so they don't run off trying to fight the enemy themselves. I don't know what we're walking into. Only that turning back is no longer an option.

We still agree Cauville is our target. Straight west tonight is best; it slips us between Rouen and Barentin. If we keep to the shadows and no one is betrayed, we might have a chance.

Ruth exhaled slowly as she finished reading, the weight of Joseph's words settling between them like another presence in the room.

"West," Claire murmured. "Toward Cauville..." She stood, walked to a shelf lined with old, dust-covered maps, and pulled one down. "If he meant the old road between Rouen and Barentin, that puts them here."

She traced a line with her finger—through forest, through valleys, through places Ruth recognized from the journal.

"They were threading a needle," Claire said quietly. "One wrong turn and they'd have walked straight into occupied patrols."

Ruth closed the journal gently, palms still pressed to the cover.

"He was just a kid," she whispered. "And he was leading twenty people."

Claire nodded, her expression tightening with something like admiration—and something like dread.

"Well," Claire said softly, "then you're going to want to see something else."

She reached for the small wooden box again—this time with a hesitation, as though deciding whether to cross a line of her own.

Claire lifted the lid and reached inside, her fingers brushing something thin and fragile. She pulled out a folded sheet of paper—brittle, yellowed, the edges feathered with age.

"Something my grandfather kept," she said quietly, placing it between them. "He found it in the cellar wall his first week here. He always believed it belonged to the last family who lived here... before the war."

Ruth's heart thudded as she unfolded the paper.

It wasn't a letter.

It was a list.

Names. Dates. All written in the same hurried, slanted handwriting she had been reading for days.

Étienne Durand

Born 1890 — Died 24 June 1940

Lisette Durand

Born 1895 — Died 24 June 1940

Then, lower on the page, the ink faintly smudged as if by a trembling hand—

Lucie Durand

Born 24 June 1931 — Died 24 June 1940

Her ninth birthday.

Ruth's breath hitched.

The list continued.

Millet Family — 1940?

No dates. No ages. Just a question mark.

As if the writer didn't know... or couldn't bear to write it.

Below the names, in a separate line, a small note—brief, blunt, carved into the page more than written:

Buried near the big oak northeast corner of the vineyard.

Ruth stared at the names, unable to lift her eyes from the page.

Étienne.

Lisette.

Lucie—dead on the day she turned nine.

The room felt suddenly cold. Her fingers tightened around the list as if it might dissolve if she let go. Joseph's handwriting—she could see it now, the panic in the slant, the grief in the pressure of each stroke. This wasn't history. This was loss, written by a hand that shook.

The journal beside her felt unbearably heavy.

Claire eased into the chair opposite her, her voice softer than before, as if even sound might disturb the memory laid out between them.

"My grandfather never knew who wrote it," she said. "Only that they weren't coming back."

She reached out, gently touching the edge of the list.

"He found it tucked into the cellar wall. Hidden. Protected. Like someone wanted these names remembered, even if everything else was taken."

Ruth swallowed, her throat burning.

Claire continued, her voice thin but steady. "The northeast corner—the old oak—that's our family cemetery now. My grandfather started it after the war. He wanted a place for the Durands, and for anyone else we found. Even if we didn't know the full truth."

Ruth looked up finally, vision blurred, her chest tight.

"Joseph buried them," she whispered. "His own family. He buried them himself."

Claire didn't look away. "It seems likely. Whoever wrote this... whoever carved these names into memory... loved them enough to make sure they weren't forgotten."

Ruth pressed the paper against her heart, tears gathering but refusing to fall.

He wasn't alone in this room anymore.

Not in these words.

Not in what he tried to leave behind.

Claire's voice gentled further. "There's more in the box. Letters. Photos. Little things we kept because someone had to. When you're ready... we'll go through them together."

Ruth nodded, unable to speak.

The list trembled in her hands.

Outside, wind whispered against the farmhouse walls, bending the vineyard rows as if bowing toward the old oak in the corner of the land, toward the names that still waited in the earth.

And Ruth knew:

This was no longer just research.

She was standing inside the story now.

They continued sifting through the box: old bottle labels with faded ink, small wooden trinkets carved by hands long gone, letters exchanged between Étienne and neighboring farmers. Nothing struck as deeply as the burial list, but each piece seemed to tug Joseph's memory closer, like someone slowly materializing out of fog. Every scrap she touched made him less like ink on paper and more like a boy who had laughed here, eaten here, prayed here.

Time slipped away unnoticed. The firelight had burned low, and the room was now washed in the orange haze of sunset. Ruth finally looked up, as if surfacing from somewhere far below. The journal and the fragile list lay open before her, two relics heavy with ghosts.

The smell of something warm drifted from the kitchen—a familiar scent of butter, garlic, the faint sweetness of wine. It coaxed her senses back to the present. Pots clinked, cupboards shut softly.

She rose without realizing it, her chair scraping faintly against the floorboards.

Claire returned with two plates, setting them gently on the table. "You're finished then," she asked, "or just taking a break?"

Ruth managed a tired smile. "I had almost lost my appetite before you came in here with that... but it all looks so delicious."

Claire poured another glass of deep red. "My family's been here since the war ended," she said. "What was left of the estate went up for auction after Liberation. My grandfather bid on it—what was left of it, anyway. He rebuilt from the ruins. Said the vines had earned another chance."

The line between reverence and regret hung in her tone.

Ruth looked at the stew steaming on her plate, then back to the journal beside her. "Do you have stories from that time? About your grandfather?"

"He didn't speak of it often," Claire said, wiping her hands on a linen towel. "He'd been too young to fight, but old enough to know fear. Later, he told me he'd shared photographs of this valley with the Allies, mapped positions, routes. I always wondered what he saw, and what he didn't say."

Outside, darkness had settled over the vineyard. The stars were so bright they painted the rows in silver. The air smelled of soil and something older.

Ruth touched the leather cover of the journal lightly, tracing its edges. The ache in her chest felt sharper now, a tension between distance and belonging.

She rose and crossed to the window. The vineyard stretched out before her in silent order, and above it, she could just make out the silhouette of the old oak against the night.

The wind brushed through the vines, creating a soft rhythm, like pages turning.

Tomorrow, she thought. Tomorrow, she'd go see it.

6

Chapter 6

Claire was already in the kitchen, the smell of coffee threading through the cottage as Ruth stepped out of her room. The soft clatter of cups and pans had become part of the house itself, a kind of morning heartbeat, and for a moment Ruth felt a sharp, unexpected jealousy of this rooted life. In a day, she would be back home, far from this table, this land, this history.

"Let's have some coffee and eggs before we head out—there's no need to walk on an empty stomach," Claire called as she heard Ruth approaching. "Besides, the sun won't be up for another forty-five minutes."

"How far of a walk is it again?" Ruth instinctively checked her watch. "I need to get back for my flight this afternoon."

"Don't worry," Claire said, pouring coffee into a mug and sliding it across the table. "I'll get you back in plenty of time." She nodded toward the window, in the direction of the oak. "It will only take ten minutes to get there. Plenty of time."

The room settled into a quiet made of small sounds: silverware tapping plates, coffee cups touching the counter. When they finally stepped out of the cottage, the sun was only beginning to hint at the edge of the sky. The smell of the vines hung heavy in the dewy morning air as they walked where Claire had pointed, gravel and dirt crunching under their feet. The grape clusters looked heavy on the rows, the kind of weight that spoke of a wet, generous summer.

As they crested a low rise, the tree appeared—the same sentry Ruth had pictured the night before, its dark branches spread wide against the paling sky. Beneath it, a man's silhouette leaned over the stones.

"That's strange," Claire murmured. "I don't usually see people out here."

They walked on in silence, a thin tension weaving between them. The figure beneath the oak stayed a shadow, the shifting branches making him seem to move like a puppet as they swayed, their slow creaking carrying faintly on the morning air.

A low voice called out as they drew closer. "Bonjour."

"Good morning," Claire replied, her tone warm but cautious, then added in English, "We don't usually see people out here this early."

His face was still lost to the backlight, but his movements were deliberate, unhurried. He stepped aside and gestured toward the gnarled roots of the oak, where the earth rose in rough, natural seats. "Such a pretty place, don't you think?" he asked, as if he were already part of their small circle. "I'm Ozias," he added as they approached.

Ruth moved nearer, enough that the angle shifted and his features came into view. For a breath, something in her chest tightened. Then she let her gaze drop to the stones at their feet.

"There's actually more here than I thought there would be," she murmured.

"Madame Claire's grandfather started all this after the war, didn't he?" the man said, glancing toward her. "My parents told me he wanted a place for the families who'd been here before... and the ones who came after."

Claire gave a small nod. "He did. We still bury our people here. A few of the neighboring farms as well."

"I come out now and then to tidy up," Ozias added with a faint, almost self-conscious smile. "I live in a village not far from here. My family runs a little bed-and-breakfast, so I'm often passing by. It feels wrong not to stop."

Ruth slipped a hand into her pocket and drew out the folded burial list. "Which ones are the Durands'?" she asked quietly.

Claire frowned in thought, then pointed toward the cluster of stones closest to the tree. "I think that's the start of them."

"Oui," Ozias said, stepping nearer and indicating one marker. "This one here is the oldest. I don't know all the family history, only that several were buried here at once."

"That would be right," Ruth began, then paused, the words catching. "I think there was a lot of heartbreak back then."

They fell silent, all three gazes moving over the stones. The vines whispered in long waves up and down the rows, the oak branches groaning softly as they swayed, sounds weaving into a low, aching hymn that matched the weight inside them.

Ruth found herself stealing glances at Ozias. There was something about the way he stood there—shoulders squared, hands loose at his sides—that made him seem as much a part of the place as the tree. There wasn't enough time to ask the questions she wanted, to learn the layers beneath his careful calm. The minutes crawled, and the silence between them thickened until it felt almost physical.

She rose and moved closer to the stones, tracing the simple yet deep carvings of the family names with her eyes. The chisel marks were uneven in places, as if whoever had carved them had been in a hurry, or too grief-stricken to steady their hand.

"They're more delicate than they look," Ozias said at last. His voice broke the quiet gently, but there was a note of defensiveness beneath it. "I try to clean them, but every time I do, it damages the letters. You can see where I chipped some of the edges."

Ruth reached toward one of the names, stopping just short of touching the stone. "If you hadn't tried, they'd be swallowed by moss by now," she said softly. "This way, at least, someone can still read them. Someone knows they were here."

A small line formed between his brows, something like relief easing his shoulders. "Maybe," he murmured. "I just don't want to erase what little they have left."

Claire rose, brushing her hands on her coat as if searching for the calmest way to say what came next. "We should probably start heading back," she said quietly.

Ozias drew in a breath, as if the words had pushed him a step backward. "I was just getting used to having someone to talk about this with," he admitted.

"I've run out of time, I'm afraid." Ruth stood, letting her fingers fall from the air above the stone. "It's time to get back to the land of the living, unfortunately."

For a moment, Ozias only looked at her. The grief of the place still clung to his features, but beneath it was something else, an ache that felt less like mourning and more like recognition. He couldn't tell if it was the weight of the graves or the way she listened that pulled him toward her; he only knew the thought of this ground without her in it felt suddenly, unexpectedly emptier.

"Ozias." Ruth said his name quietly, as if testing the way it felt in the air between the stones. For a heartbeat, she had the strange sense that he and this place were the same thing—rooted, weathered, holding more history than he would ever claim. "I wish I could stay," she managed, her throat tightening. "But life calls." She turned before the rest could spill out, blinking back tears as she walked back through the vines toward the cottage.

When she glanced over her shoulder, Ozias was still standing by the grave, the sun climbing higher until the light carved his features into sharper relief.

Claire drove Ruth to the station, and the car fell mostly silent, each of them keeping company with their own thoughts. On the platform, Ruth boarded the train that wound back toward Paris, the journal heavy in her bag, like an anchor trying to hold her in place.

Ruth leaned her shoulder against the train window and watched the countryside unspool in muted greens and browns. Fields blurred into villages, church spires into factory stacks, all of it sliding past in a steady, indifferent rhythm. A week ago, she would have been naming campaigns and treaties in her head, slotting each town into a neat margin note of history. Now, every roof and road felt like a place where someone might have once hidden in a cellar and waited for boots to pass by.

Her mind started revisiting her trip, replaying images of the places she had seen. In Brussels, she'd sat beside a stone fountain in a cobbled square, the water spilling over a basin worn smooth by centuries of hands. She'd eaten a paper cone of fries there, watching tourists pose and children splash, telling herself she was "feeling the layers" of the city. But all she'd really done was skim the surface.

Later, in a walled town straddling an old border, she'd walked along ramparts that had once divided one city-state from another. The guide had talked about sieges, about ladders set against stone and boiling oil poured from above. Ruth had trailed her fingers along the parapet and imagined neat lines of arrows, flags, the choreography of warfare. She hadn't thought much about the people pressed against each other in basements, listening to stone shake overhead.

There was a ruined castle, too, a gray husk crouched on a hill where Napoleon had passed and left it half broken. The informational plaque had given the dates, the campaign, the decisive maneuver that made the place fall. She'd taken a picture of ivy climbing over blackened stone and felt that quiet academic thrill at seeing a site she'd lectured about as a graduate assistant. Bombardment was an abstract word—until Rouen. Until the baptismal page in the parish register, its edges burned away like the castle walls, and the ledger note that simply said, Family not seen after July.

The train rocked and Ruth felt the journal shift, the small book she'd picked up while looking for something to hang on her wall. It was feeling more alive now. All those places had been fascinating; they'd left specific thoughts and images she would not forget easily. But those stories had been told. They'd marked their place in history. Joseph and his journal created history no one knew existed, except maybe those who had seen the graveyard.

She thought about the visit with Father Laurent, the dusty shelves they dug through together to find a hint of Joseph. The entry about Joseph sitting next to Nazis receiving communion. The walk through the vineyard to the gravesite, wondering where the two had sat and watched their world turn upside down.

Ruth was quiet the entire ride, looking out the window but seeing only Joseph and David leading a group of Jews to safety. Through the airport, she moved on autopilot—minimal pleasantries through security and the gate. She sat quietly as a couple filled the other two seats in her row. She didn't have to wonder what they did; they were sharing loud enough for the entire plane. After hearing about their three days in Paris, she looked at the screen where the plane was making slow progress back to the States.

Inside her, the sense of direction was reversed. Whatever path lay in front of her now, it no longer felt like she was simply going on with her life.

It felt like she was being slowly, steadily turned around to face the past.

7

Chapter 7

After what felt like an eighty-year flight, the wheels finally hit the runway in New York. Ruth shuffled through customs on tired feet, answered the standard questions, and let herself be carried along the familiar maze of signs and corridors toward her connecting gate to Tulsa.

At a kiosk near the terminal, she ordered a coffee. The exchange was as bland and scripted as every airport counter conversation—How was your trip? See anything good?—until the barista asked, "So, was it fun?"

Ruth hesitated, fingers tightening around the cardboard sleeve. "It was... life changing."

Something in her tone made the barista look up. For a moment, the easy rhythm broke. "That's a big word," the woman said, softer now, but there were other customers waiting, and the pause passed. Ruth took her cup, murmured thanks, and walked away, the words still echoing in her own ears.

At a nearby table, waiting for her connection, she turned the cup between her hands. Life changing. She almost laughed. That wasn't the kind of phrase you tossed at a stranger pulling shots.

I met a family that changed my outlook in a way I never expected, she thought, hearing the classroom cadence slip back into her mind. The places and sites everyone sees are beautiful, you can see the history. But when you truly feel the weight of that history, it doesn't really translate into small talk over coffee.

When she checked the departures board, her connecting flight to Tulsa was still an hour away. She drifted toward the gate and took an empty seat. The journal was still in her carry-on, exactly where she'd tucked it before leaving the vineyard. She hadn't been able to bring herself to put it in the overhead bin; even that small distance felt like abandoning him. The urge to see what came next pressed at her, an almost physical need to check in on him. She unzipped the bag and drew the leather book into her lap.

July 29

We have made it to a small farming village in the Pays de Caux. When I approached a man in the market for supplies, I told him I needed bread, something to feed a large family. He studied me for a moment, as if he recognized something—my voice, my face, I don't know. Then he told me to follow.

His farm sits close against the edge of the woods, the house and barn almost cut into the trees. The line of trunks and brush makes a kind of curtain, a natural cover for the group. He said the Nazis have come several times to take what they wanted. Chickens, mostly. But he would help us for a couple of days. He did not mention, at first, that he already had another family hiding there he hoped we could take with us.

David is excited. He and their daughter made a connection; they have hardly stopped talking since we arrived. It is hard to say anything. The farmer's daughter is striking, and I am not looking forward to putting distance between us.

Ruth closed the journal and unlocked her phone, typing in the village name. A map bloomed to life on the screen, and she began tracing a rough line between the northeast of Rouen and where Joseph said they were now, sketching in her mind the route they might have walked and where they might be heading next.

Something about the terrain stood out. The forest along that stretch was cut in a way that left a narrow corridor of cover, a path they could have followed most of the way inside the tree line. Still... how many were they up to now? She pictured the families she'd read about, counted quickly in her head. Ten, maybe twenty people if some families were large. That many bodies moving west, even under trees, would draw eyes if anyone happened to be looking.

She was deep in thought about the last passage, already mentally flagging it for later research, another clue to their movements, another line of inquiry to follow. The journal sat closed in her lap, worn leather and darkened page edges on display, Joseph Durand's name faint but unmistakable on the cover.

Ruth was still staring at the map on her phone when a rustle of bags and voices signaled new arrivals at the row. A couple about her age slid into the seats beside her, juggling duty-free bags and a boxed model of the Eiffel Tower.

"Oh, that's beautiful," the woman said after a moment, nodding toward the journal in Ruth's lap. "Is it one of those antique notebooks? I almost bought one in Paris, but I knew I'd never actually write in it."

Ruth glanced down at the worn leather, Joseph's name faint in the dim gate light. "Something like that," she said. "I found it in a little shop."

"Ugh, I loved those shops," the woman went on. "France is just... so pretty. We did Paris and a day trip to Versailles. I took, like, a thousand pictures."

Ruth managed a small smile. "It's definitely memorable," she said, the word feeling thin compared to the images in her mind of bomb-scarred stone, blackened ledgers, a burial list inked in a shaking hand. The woman had already turned back to her husband, debating which photos to post first.

Ruth let the conversation wash past her and placed her hand over the journal, thumb resting on the ghost of Joseph's name, as if to steady both of them.

She went back to her phone, staring at the map and jotting down the names of villages Joseph might pass through in the next few entries. She added a quick note about the farmer's daughter and the way Joseph had mentioned her, not because it mattered yet, but because it felt like the kind of detail that might matter later.

"Attention passengers. We will begin pre-boarding the flight to Tulsa in fifteen minutes."

Her phone buzzed almost on cue. A text from her mom lit the screen: So glad you're back, everyone is excited to see you and will be here tonight for dinner.

Ruth typed a brief reply. Can't wait. Boarding soon.—and set the phone face down. In her own notebook, she'd been making small notes and page numbers, a kind of rough index of moments she didn't want to lose.

A few minutes later, the man a seat down stood, juggling his bag and jacket as the first call for boarding sounded. As he stepped past, his carry-on brushed Ruth's knee. The journal slid from her lap, hit the floor with a soft thud, and fell open.

Ruth was faster. "It's okay," she blurted, scooping the book up with more force than she intended. Her heart thudded. The page it had fallen open to was muddied, the ink thinner and more blurred than the entries she'd read so far, as if whoever held the pen had been writing in the rain or with dirty hands.

The couple beside her glanced over at the commotion.

"Oh wow," the woman said, leaning in a little. "You really did find that in a shop? How lucky."

Up close, she could see it wasn't just "pretty" now. Her gaze caught on the darkened paper, the uneven lines, the way some words had bled into each other. Ruth's fingers tightened around the cover, angling it slightly away.

"Something like that," Ruth said quietly. "It's... very special." She began tucking her things away, wrapping the journal in a folded handkerchief as if covering a wound.

The boarding calls started a few minutes later. The Tulsa flight was a smaller plane, stuffed to the point no one could move without brushing a stranger's elbow. The hop felt longer than it was, a blur of recycled air and engine noise.

On the other side of the security glass, her mom was waiting, waving both arms as if Ruth were coming home from war. The moment Ruth stepped into the arrivals hall, she was swept into a hug that squeezed the breath from her lungs.

"Really, Mom..." Ruth glanced around, cheeks flushing. "It was just a trip. I'm happy to see you too. Where's Dad?"

"Oh, he's sitting in the car at the cell phone lot," she said with a dismissive wave. "Didn't want to pay for parking."

Ruth managed a laugh, the familiar complaint oddly comforting. The journal's weight in her bag thudded lightly against her hip with each step, a quiet reminder that part of her hadn't landed yet.

The blast of Oklahoma heat hit as soon as the sliding doors opened. Ruth followed her mom across the pickup lane to where her dad idled in their aging SUV, one hand on the wheel, the other lifting in a brief, sheepish wave. He popped the trunk, took her suitcase with a grunt, and they were back on the highway before she'd fully registered the familiar skyline.

"So," her mom said, twisting around in the passenger seat to look at her, "tell me everything. How was Paris? Did you see the tower at night?"

"And the food," her dad added. "You eat any of that fancy stuff? Snails?"

Ruth buckled in and watched the terminal recede in the side mirror. "Paris was... beautiful," she said. "Lights on the river, little cafés everywhere. I skipped the snails, but the bread alone was worth the flight."

Her mom laughed. "I knew it. And what was that place—Rouen? You sent a picture of some big church."

"The cathedral," Ruth said. Images flickered: stained glass, bomb scars, Father Laurent's quiet smile, Joseph's handwriting in the archives. "It was... different. Older. You can still see where the war hit it."

"Bet that was something," her dad said. "And the vineyard? You said you found some little village out there?"

"Yeah," Ruth replied, fingers brushing the side of her bag where it rested at her feet. "Northern France. It was quiet. Lots of vines, lots of fog. Nice people."

Her mom glanced at her more closely. "You sound tired, honey."

"Long day," Ruth said, forcing a small smile. She offered up one safe story about a mix-up with a train platform, another about a tourist who'd asked her for directions in rapid French. Her parents laughed in the right places, filling the car with familiar noise—questions about jet lag, the fall semester, whether she'd missed "real" coffee.

Through the windshield, the highway unspooled in straight gray lines, nothing like the winding roads north of Rouen. Ruth answered as best she could, but part of her was still walking between rows of vines, listening for distant footsteps in the dark.

Finally, the car took the turn everyone in the neighborhood knew—the last bend before home. Their house sat a few driveways down on the left. As her dad pulled in, Ruth saw that the curb was crowded with cars, the driveway leaving a single open space where he always insisted on parking. The street was lined with neighbors and family friends, gathered on the lawn and front walk to welcome the traveler home.

When she stepped out, the sun was beginning to slide toward the horizon, the light softening and the heat easing just enough to breathe. The front door stood open, and the noise spilled out, voices layered over clinking dishes, bursts of laughter. Inside, the smell was unmistakable:

her grandmother's pot roast. Somewhere beneath it lingered the sweet, buttery scent of an upside-down pineapple cake cooling on the counter. After weeks of baguettes and café fare, Ruth could almost feel the pounds returning just from the aroma.

8

Chapter 8

Ruth stepped into the living room and stopped. It felt like a holiday, every chair taken, cousins on the floor, neighbors crowded along the walls balancing paper plates and plastic cups. The hum of voices rose and fell in waves.

From the kitchen came the rich, familiar smell of pot roast and something sweet baking, and for the first time since she'd found Joseph's journal, her mind slipped away from vineyards and graveyards and back into the small orbit of home.

Questions came almost immediately, flung at her from every direction. Where did you go? What did you see? Was Paris as romantic as they say? Was there a guy? For the first thirty minutes, she answered on reflex, smiling, nodding, letting their curiosity wrap around her like another kind of jet lag.

Some guests had already started eating, drifting between the kitchen and living room with paper plates, but the closer friends and family were clearly waiting for her to sit before they treated it as a real meal. Her mom steered her toward the counter, where the pot roast sat keeping warm in the crock pot, surrounded by bowls of mashed potatoes and green beans laid out like an official family dinner.

The sudden hit to her senses—the steam, the salt, the familiar spices—pulled her sharply back into the house. For a moment, she wasn't standing in a graveyard or rattling down winding country roads or even walking cobblestones in Paris. She was home, in a kitchen she could navigate with her eyes closed.

As her mom handed her a plate, a familiar voice cut through the noise. "Make sure you get some of Grandma's potatoes before Uncle Mark eats them all."

Ruth turned to see Lena, her oldest friend, already in line with a plate balanced on one hand and a glass of iced tea in the other.

"You made it," Ruth said, the smile this time reaching her eyes.

"I'm not missing the triumphant return of Dr. Future-Historian," Lena said. "Now tell me which continent you're moving to permanently so I can start planning my vacation."

Ruth filled her plate and slipped into her usual seat at the table, just to the left of where her dad always sat and across from her mom. Lena claimed the chair beside her, their elbows nearly touching, and the two of them settled into a small bubble inside the larger crowd. Ruth gave her the highlight reel first: the fountains, the old city walls, the tiny shops you couldn't find at home, letting the familiar stories carry her voice while the heavier ones waited their turn.

"I left Brussels and went to Paris to spend my last few days. I had my time planned out for every site and museum," Ruth said, not yet conscious of where the story was about to turn. She described the river, the skyline, the way the tower glittered at night—then paused. "I was in a shop, just looking for something to hang on my office wall or bring back to school, when I opened a drawer and..."

Ruth broke off, sudden panic tightening her chest. Her hand flew to the back of her chair, then to the floor beside her. Her bag wasn't there.

"Has anyone seen my bag?"

"It's hanging on the hook inside the door," someone called from the living room.

Conversation dipped for a heartbeat, the room going oddly quiet as an uncle stepped over, lifted the strap, and set it beside her chair. Ruth exhaled only when the familiar weight bumped against her leg. The house seemed to exhale with her, the volume still muted as she stood and slipped into the entryway to pull the journal out, needing to feel the leather under her fingers before she could finish the story.

Ruth retrieved the journal from her bag and held it for a moment, thumb running along the softened spine before she carried it back to the table. Conversations had resumed, but not at full volume. A few nearby relatives watched her with open curiosity, eyes flicking from the worn leather to her face.

Whatever they were thinking—must be important, the way she reacted—stayed mostly in murmurs at the edges of the room. But Ruth could feel it: the shift in attention, the quiet expectation settling around her as she sat down again, the journal now resting by her plate. Everyone was waiting to hear this part of the story.

"Anyway," Ruth said, trying to gather herself, suddenly aware of how many eyes were on her. "I was in this little antique shop in Paris. I opened a drawer in an old armoire and saw this book, covered in dust, and this name," she tapped the faint letters on the cover—"was just barely visible through it."

She laid the journal flat on the table, careful and deliberate, as if setting down an artifact she'd just brushed free of sand. Around her, a few people leaned in, curious, but their questions stalled on their lips. The story they'd expected—a funny tour guide, lost luggage, a cute waiter—wasn't quite the story she was offering now, and the uncertainty showed in the puzzled glances that passed between them.

Ruth traced the name with her fingertip. "It turned out not to be a blank book," she went on. "It's a journal. A young man started it in 1940, on his family's vineyard in northern France, just before the Germans came."

Her dad lowered his fork. "Like... a real journal? From the war?"

Ruth nodded. "His name is Joseph Durand. At first he writes about normal things—weather, vines, dinners with their neighbors. And then the entries start changing. The handwriting gets tighter. He starts talking about bombings, about hiding people, about trying to get families out before it's too late."

Lena's voice was softer than usual. "So you're... reading his life."

"Pieces of it," Ruth said. "Enough to know he was the kind of person who didn't just sit and watch history happen. He moved people through it." She hesitated, feeling the room listening. "I went to the places he wrote about. The church. The vineyard. I met the family who owns it now."

For a moment, no one spoke. The TV in the other room murmured, a fork clinked against a plate, and the smells of pot roast and pineapple cake pressed around them. Ruth rested her palm lightly on the journal's cover. "It sounds dramatic when I say it out loud," she added, a faint, apologetic smile tugging at her mouth. "But it feels like I brought someone home with me."

Somewhere behind her, a chair scraped back and the television clicked off. The background noise of the house thinned as conversations faded, one cluster at a time, until most of the room had turned—subtly, but unmistakably—toward the table where Ruth sat. They might not yet grasp what the journal meant, but they understood this much: whatever story she was about to tell was not one to talk over.

Lena leaned a little closer and murmured, "For the record, when I asked about a guy, I meant one our age."

Ruth didn't laugh, but her shoulders loosened a fraction. "He was our age once," she said quietly. "When he started writing."

She drew in a breath, eyes dropping to the cover. "Joseph Durand lived on a vineyard in early 1940," she began. "His family owned and worked the land, and his best friend David's family lived nearby—either helping run it or working the vines with them. They were north of Rouen, almost directly inland from the cliffs where the Allies would land four years later."

She paused. Around the room, people who had been standing drifted closer, finding spots on armrests and the backs of chairs, settling in as if for a story their bodies understood would not be short.

"So," her dad said, leaning back with his hands folded over his stomach, "I'm guessing David's family is Jewish? Not many Davids out there in that region who aren't."

Ruth nodded. "Right. I forgot to say that. And to say it didn't bother Joseph is an understatement."

She smoothed a corner of the cover. "The journal starts in 1940, like I said. At first it's just his day-to-day—work on the vineyard, what he and David are up to, Mass at the cathedral in Rouen. For a working family, life seems... ordinary. Manageable."

Her voice caught on that last image. For a moment, she couldn't quite push the next sentence past the tightness in her throat. Lena's hand came to rest on her forearm, a quiet anchor.

"The next swing..." Ruth began, then had to start again. "Joseph and David were out in the vines when the Nazis came looking. They were hiding, watching. David's family was taken. Joseph's family was executed for harboring them."

Gasps broke around the room, sharp little intakes of breath that seemed to pull the air out of the house. Someone's fork clinked against a plate and stayed there, forgotten.

"He writes about burying them," Ruth said after a moment. "But it's almost… restrained. Just enough detail to know he and David did it, and where."

She reached for her bag again and slid a folded sheet from the side pocket, the paper already going soft at the creases. "This is what made it real," she added. "When I visited the vineyard, hunting him down through documents the church had, giving the vineyard's name. The current resident had this her grandfather found when he took over the property."

Ruth unfolded the page and laid it beside the journal. "It's his list," she said quietly. "Names of the people he buried and where, written in his hand."

Her dad slid his glasses up his nose and leaned in first. "Good grief," he murmured. "These are… all family?"

"Family and neighbors," Ruth said. "He notes if they were children, too."

He passed the paper to her grandmother, who held it carefully by the edges, as if it might crumble. "He wrote down where they lay," she whispered. "Like he knew someone might come looking someday."

"Is that where you went?" Lena asked. "That picture you sent with the big tree?"

Ruth nodded. "There's an oak at the edge of the vineyard. They think that's where he and David dug the graves." She touched a spot on the list. "When I visited, the woman who owns the vineyard now took me out there. A young man from a village about ten kilometers away—his family owns a bed-and-breakfast there—comes by weekly to clean and take care of the stones."

"Wait," Lena cut in. "A young man? That's a great attempt at not telling us about the strapping guy who just happens to own a bed-and-breakfast in a French village. Don't even try to just say 'the young man.'"

"I only really noticed him because of the way he cared for the family," Ruth said. "We exchanged information in case I had questions later, that's all."

Lena didn't argue, but the lift of one eyebrow made her skepticism clear.

"Anyway," Ruth said, steering back toward the journal, "the visit to the gravesite was the morning I came home. So I met Ozias for only a little bit, and that pretty much brings you up to date on Joseph."

The list was still making its way around the room. Her dad leaned back in his chair, staring at nothing in particular, clearly somewhere between the oak and the kitchen ceiling. Conversations rose again in pockets, soft exclamations, whispered what-ifs—as people processed the story even while they gathered dishes and said their goodbyes. The emotions seemed to leave with them, carried out onto the porch and into the darkening street.

When the door finally closed on the last guest, Lena leaned in until her shoulder pressed gently against Ruth's. "I'm staying over," she said. "You can tell me all about Ozias, was that his name?"

9

Chapter 9

Lena's overnight bag thumped onto the floor of Ruth's childhood bedroom with a familiarity that made the last three weeks feel like a strange dream. The walls still held the same framed maps and vintage travel posters Ruth had hung in high school, Europe flattened into tidy colors and borders. The journal on her desk made the whole room feel slightly off-center.

"Your grandma's gonna feed me till I explode," Lena said, toeing off her shoes. "If I slip into a pot roast coma, just roll me onto the air mattress."

Ruth smiled, sinking onto the edge of her bed. "You know she considers you one of her own. She can't help it."

Lena flopped down beside her, propping her head on one hand. "Okay," she said. "We survived the family history hour. Now I want the director's cut." Her gaze flicked to the journal. "Start with him."

"Joseph?"

"Nice try," Lena said. "The one with a pulse."

Ruth huffed a soft laugh and reached for the journal anyway, more out of habit than deflection. "There isn't a director's cut," she said. "Just... more context. Now there's grading. And rent. And all the normal things I still have to care about."

"Mm-hm." Lena sat up enough to lean over and tap the cover. "You flinched earlier like someone had knocked a baby off the table. That's not normal-things energy. That's this matters more than I want to admit energy."

Ruth turned the book in her hands, tracing the softened corners. "It's not just the book," she said quietly. "It's everything it's attached to now."

Lena waited. Years of friendship had taught her that silence, not rapid-fire questions, worked best when Ruth's voice took on that tone.

"I spent a lot of money on this trip," Ruth said after a moment. "I thought it would be... I don't know. Professional development. Add a little grit to my lectures. 'Here's a picture of the castle Napoleon razed, class. Here's a selfie at the Verdun memorial.'"

"And instead?"

"Instead, I ended up in a church basement reading a baptism record with the corner burned off," Ruth said. "Then in a vineyard, holding a list of people a twenty-something buried because their government and their neighbors decided they didn't matter. And the thing that keeps me up is that most of them don't exist anywhere else on paper. If I don't do something with this, it's like I put the journal back in the drawer and shut it again."

Lena was quiet for a beat. "So... you brought home a responsibility, not just a souvenir."

"Feels like it," Ruth admitted. "And that's before I factor in the living people."

"There it is," Lena said softly. "Ozias."

Ruth set the journal down on the comforter between them, as if that might make the conversation feel less direct. "His family runs a bed-and-breakfast," she said. "He looks after the vineyard's graves at the little cemetery. I think his grandfather helped the Marchands after the war, but I don't know the whole story yet. He treated Joseph like someone they owed a debt to, not like some stranger in an old book."

"And you liked that about him."

"I liked that he cared," Ruth said, sharper than she meant. She sighed. "I liked that he knew where every stone came from, who still visited, which names belonged to people no one had come back for. Most people go to France for wine tastings and Instagram. He spends his weekends cleaning moss off headstones and fixing fences so cows don't trample unmarked graves."

Lena's mouth tilted. "See, when you put it like that, he sounds a lot more interesting than 'a young man from ten kilometers away.'"

"It doesn't matter," Ruth said quickly. "I knew him for... what, two hours? He has a life. A business. A family who depends on him. I live halfway across the world and I'm about to be buried in grading and grad seminars. Whatever... static there was between us, it's not the point of any of this."

"Maybe not the point," Lena said. "But it's a point." She nudged the journal with a fingertip. "You're allowed to be drawn to someone who shares the weight you're carrying. It doesn't cheapen Joseph."

Ruth stared at the ceiling. The old glow-in-the-dark stars she'd never taken down were still faintly visible in the dim light. "When I was standing at the graves, I couldn't tell what I was reacting to," she said. "The oak, the list, Ozias. It all felt... tied together. Like the land and the stories and the living people had gotten knotted up."

"Welcome to being human," Lena said. "We're bad at compartmentalizing when everything hurts and matters at once."

Ruth snorted. "Put that on a mug."

"I will," Lena said. "Right after you publish your ground-breaking, career-launching work on Joseph Durand."

Ruth's eyes drifted back to the journal. "I don't even know if I'm allowed to publish it," she admitted. "Ethically. Legally. I have to ask Father Laurent about ownership, talk to the vineyard family, maybe even track down any Durands who might still be around. And even if I get permission... turning this into a project means every part of my life is going to revolve around someone else's trauma for the next however-many years."

"Your life already revolves around other people's trauma," Lena pointed out. "You literally study war for a living."

"This is different," Ruth said. "Textbooks are... buffered. This is a man describing his mother falling. His little sister. Writing their names and then going back into the vines to lead strangers to safety. It feels like opening a vein and calling it a primary source."

Lena's expression softened. "So what if you don't do anything?"

Ruth flinched at the thought. "Then he stays one more forgotten story in a drawer," she said. "And I go back to telling my students about 'civilian experiences of occupation' using generalized case studies and sanitized quotes. And I know there was, at least once, a specific vineyard, a specific church, a specific list. It would feel like a lie by omission."

"Okay," Lena said. "So you're not really deciding if you're going to do something with him. You're deciding how."

Ruth let out a shaky breath that wasn't quite a laugh. "I hate when you make things sound simple."

"That's why you keep me," Lena said. She slid off the bed and stretched. "So. Step one tomorrow: sleep in, drink coffee that does not come out of an airplane, and email your professor?"

"I should talk to Dr. Peters," Ruth admitted. "If I turn this into a thesis or article, I'll need his backing. And I should send a note to Father Laurent, let him know I got home and thank him. Maybe ask what he thinks about... all this."

Lena turned toward the door, then paused. "There's your structure, you know."

"For what?"

"For the next stretch of your life," Lena said. "Ruth in Tulsa, Ruth in archives, Ruth in France. Past and present. That's kind of your thing."

Ruth picked up the journal again, the leather warm now from her hands. "Maybe," she said. "If I can figure out how to live in both without losing my mind."

"That's what semesters and airline miles are for," Lena said. "Now come brush your teeth before your grandma decides we need a second dessert."

When the light was finally off and the house had settled into the creaks and sighs of night, Ruth lay awake for a while, the journal on the nightstand within easy reach. She could have opened it, could have followed Joseph another few miles west through the dark. Instead, she let her fingers rest on the cover and stared at the faint green ghosts of plastic stars on her ceiling.

Tomorrow would bring syllabi and emails and the first steps toward turning one man's desperate handwriting into something the world might see. Tonight, for a few more hours, she let herself simply hold the line between past and present, one hand on the book and the rest of her anchored in the house that had always meant safety.

10

Chapter 10

A couple of days later, life had begun to slide back toward normal—laundry baskets, half-read syllabi, and the meeting circled on her calendar with Dr. Peters. The email she'd sent him carried the one thing that didn't feel normal at all: a summary of Joseph Durand's journal and a request to talk about turning his story, and others like it, into a thesis on unknown heroes.

Over the next forty-eight hours, Ruth read deep into the later entries, after they left the farm where Joseph wrote about David and himself meeting girls there. He described the blue scarf Kate wore, blowing in the wind as they walked away, and the way the girl with David, her name smudged by time, covered her mouth when she laughed. They continued their travel west, moving from town to town. While most of the messages were simple notes on where they had arrived and what he saw of Nazi occupation forces, a couple stood out enough that she bookmarked them for study.

The first came a couple of days after they left the farm, when they arrived outside the canton of Saint-Romain-de-Colbosc. Joseph describes a meeting he had while looking for food and other supplies...

August 5th, 1940

I was in the market this afternoon and met a man; we fell into an easy conversation. Then he said he'd watched our group setting up outside the village. At first I was struck by fear, but he quickly lifted his hand slightly and said, "I'm with a group that may be able to help."

The way he said it, I think he was getting at, I'll help you if you help me. He said he would meet me in the morning just west of where the group is camped. He doesn't want the entire group to see him, but he could provide me with a place to move to and who to look for when we get there.

The August 5th passage caught Ruth off guard. She was aware of groups seeking safety as Nazis moved across France, the marches west, the hunger, the careful notes about patrols and uniforms. She'd always thought real networks didn't coalesce until a couple of years later, after the occupation settled in. The idea that someone could be working for a resistance group, or even for a British-backed contact, in that part of France in the summer of 1940 sent her into a fury of research, tabs multiplying across her screen as she chased down every mention of early cells. She even dug into OSS and SOE records, trying to pin down when Allied operatives first began slipping into France and how soon men like Joseph might have found themselves on their radar.

Half an hour later, her browser looked like a nervous breakdown—articles on early resistance in Normandy, timelines that started in 1941, a scattering of footnotes that leapt right over the summer Joseph was writing in. Each time she found a sentence that brushed against 1940, it was vague, cautious, hedged with words like scattered and sporadic. None of them said what his ink hinted at: someone was already passing messages and steering people, quietly, while the dust of invasion was still settling.

She sat back, rubbing her eyes. "You're either way ahead of the literature," she murmured to the journal on her desk, "or you're the piece it forgot to make room for."

Joseph and the group moved northwest with three more stops before reaching Cauville. There was no further detail about the man he'd met, only a trail of place names—villages where, just as he'd promised, Joseph found people willing to help them gather the supplies they needed. There was nothing official, but whenever he approached a shop or market, someone would catch his eye and say the phrase, "plenty of lamb."

The phrase lodged in Ruth's mind. On one tab, she had an article open about biblical imagery in resistance code words; on another, a dull paragraph in a monograph that reduced early Jewish flight to numbers on a chart. She jotted in the margin of her notebook: Plenty of lamb = Exodus / Passover? Covering doorways, covering people. Code as theology as logistics. Joseph continued taking notes about Nazi positions and how the occupiers were settling in, while David and the girl he'd met tried to keep courting in the margins of fear. The dual reality Joseph recorded between the grim lists of patrols and shortages alongside stolen moments of laughter and young love gave Ruth a sharper picture of what it meant to survive a war without ever being sure you'd live to see its end.

The next entry that sent Ruth into a tailspin was the arrival in Cauville.

August 9th, 1940

We have moved into the woods outside Cauville. We can smell the salt and hear the noises you would expect from a fishing village. There were so many places where we could see the fighting that had happened in the Nazi advance; Cauville appears to be relatively untouched so far.

We had been setting up camp for an hour, getting food distributed, when we heard someone approaching. Everyone was in a panic, but then I heard, "We have plenty of lamb." The others hadn't heard that before, but the mention of lamb put most of them at ease. David looked at me and told me the message was a call back to the Exodus. Even having not heard the exact statement before, the mention of having plenty meant they were covered.

The man who approached said they'd made contact with some British agents. Then he showed me to a spot where we could get down to the beach and said some fishing boats would be there. We will need to make the crossings over a couple of days. The boats they have can only carry twelve at a time, and we have almost thirty people wanting, or rather needing to get out.

Ruth lowered her forehead to the heel of her hand, staring past the words to a stretch of dark water she'd never seen. Thirty bodies, twelve at a time. In her mind, the neat math broke apart into questions: Who insisted others go first? Who stared at the receding boat and wondered if there would be room for them tomorrow? She pulled up a map of the Channel and traced the distance with her finger, imagining the sound of oars, engines, whispered prayers in at least two languages. This wasn't just a clever phrase in a textbook about escape lines. It was a boy at the tree line, counting heads and knowing some people would have to wait in the woods with their fear until the tide turned again.

Ruth was drafting a chapter that tried to introduce Joseph, the journal, and as much detail as possible without cramming everything in. The first attempt read more like a confession than a proposal. On the screen, a sentence blinked back at her: He was brave and selfless in a way that puts most of us to shame. She grimaced and struck a line through it in red. "That's not analysis," she muttered. "That's a fan letter."

She tried again: In the summer of 1940, one young man's journal suggests that improvised help for Jewish families in Normandy began earlier, and moved more deliberately, than existing narratives allow. Better. Still rough. But closer to something she could say in front of a committee without sounding like she'd fallen in love with a ghost.

An email dinged with the subject line, "I wanted to make sure you made it home." She smiled, assuming it was Claire checking in, then saw the address: oz@StPierreInn.com. Heat rushed into her cheeks, part embarrassment, part something else. Somewhere between the cemetery, the inn, and that careful subject line, Ozias had started checking boxes she hadn't even known she had.

Ruth stared at the subject line for a full thirty seconds before she actually opened the message.

Just wanted to make sure you made it home alright. – Ozias

Her fingers hovered over the keys longer than the email deserved. Part of her wanted to reply with something breezy and forgettable; another part wanted to tell him she still smelled damp earth and lichen whenever she closed her eyes. She typed, deleted, retyped, then finally settled on:

Hi Ozias,

I did, a little jet-lagged but in one piece. I really appreciate you checking in, and everything you did while I was there. I'm still thinking about the oak and the graves.

– Ruth

She clicked send before she could talk herself out of the last sentence, then pushed the laptop back and pulled her draft chapter up again. Her train of thought had left the station, so she began reading from the top, trying to get back on track. Everything early was covered well: an introduction to the journal and to Joseph, his family, and everything up to leaving to go west, trafficking refugees.

She lingered on the structure and decided to switch to an outline; she had the foundation, now she could start sketching out how to actually cover what was happening. Bullet points felt safer than paragraphs for the moment.

– Vineyard, cellar, bombing, decision to move west.

– First families, Green Forest, pace of march, fear.

– Contact at Saint-Romain-de-Colbosc ("group that may be able to help").

– Code phrase "plenty of lamb"—biblical resonance / local network?

– Cauville, boats, Channel crossings as early rescue operation.

She tapped the end of her pen against the page. Off to the side, almost as an afterthought, she wrote: Thesis? Unknown heroes who refused to be bystanders, before the world had language for what they were doing.

She hadn't read much beyond arriving at the coast and the initial plan to shuttle across the Channel. The temptation to skip ahead—to find out in three minutes what had taken Joseph weeks to live—itched at the back of her mind. She forced herself to resist, moving forward only as quickly as she could take decent notes. If she was going to argue for him in an office with framed degrees on the wall, she needed more than emotion. She needed a map of his choices.

The first sketch of her chapter left something to be desired; it sounded more like a fangirl tribute than an academic treatment of what Joseph was doing. She caught herself writing, He reads like a figure from legend dropped into the real war, and groaned. Delete. Replace: His entries complicate the presumed timeline of organized help in 1940, suggesting that at least one local network was already operating in the Pays de Caux. Still passionate, but anchored in a claim someone could test.

In the research she'd pulled, no one else seemed to have solid information about cells popping up this early. Accounts of Jewish families fleeing, yes—but British or French resistance operations in the summer of 1940 were a void on the page, blank spaces where Joseph's entries were suddenly loud. That contrast scared her almost as much as it thrilled her. If she was wrong, she'd look naïve. If she was right, she might have just stumbled onto the first clear trace of something the books had been smoothing over for decades.

The chime for calendar reminders went off, "Meeting with Dr. Peters: 10:00 a.m." When she looked at the clock, the realization hit that in less than an hour she would have to explain all of this without sounding like someone who had simply fallen in love with a story. She closed the laptop, slid Joseph's journal into her bag, and flipped her notebook to a clean page. At the top she wrote, in block letters:

Why this matters beyond me.

Underneath, she managed one sentence: Because if I leave him in the drawer, the gap in the story stays a gap. If I bring him into the room, we have to admit the gap was there.

She underlined it once, hard, then snapped the notebook shut. By the time she sat down in Dr. Peters's office, she told herself, she needed to sound less like a fangirl and more like the only person in the department holding a primary source from the summer of 1940 that refused to stay quiet.

11

Chapter 11

Ruth pulled into campus, the trees still lush and heavy with late-summer green, branches bowing under the weight of leaves. The wind never really stopped in northeastern Oklahoma; today it felt like a hair dryer held to her face, hot and relentless as it rushed between the brick buildings and across the parking lots. Students hadn't arrived yet, but faculty and facilities crews were already in motion, doing their final prep before the place was overrun by wide-eyed freshmen wandering in loose herds, and upperclassmen strolling with the easy swagger of people who already knew which shortcuts belonged to them.

The history department sat in the central building where the university had been founded, scaffolding and fresh paint marking a facelift that couldn't quite hide its age. The campus, woven into the heart of the Cherokee Nation capital, was small but carried a kind of quiet importance in the region. Tahlequah had been stretching outward for years now; with steady tribal revenue flowing into new projects and businesses, the town was thriving in a way that still felt almost improbable in such a rural corner of Oklahoma.

Sometimes, when she walked past the tribal courthouse on her way to class, Ruth felt the dissonance of it all, teaching forced marches and refugee columns from Europe in a place whose very streets existed because another people had been driven west at gunpoint. The fact that her students carried that history in their own families made Joseph's pages feel less like distant tragedy and more like a variation on a pattern the land already knew.

Dr. Peters's office was in a ground-floor corner, small and visibly old, standard for the departments sharing the building. The air conditioner sounded tired, pushing out air that felt only a few degrees cooler than outside. As Ruth approached, she heard his voice through the half-open door, grumbling to someone about trying to think in a hundred degrees and a wool tie. It was an ordinary complaint, but it landed in her chest like a warning; walking into a meeting with a sweating, overheated Dr. Peters felt like starting on the back foot.

"Come in," he called, before her knuckles finished the second knock. The greeting when she stepped through was warmer than she'd braced for. "Welcome back, Ruth. How was the trip?" he asked, gesturing to the chair opposite his desk.

"Great. I really enjoyed it," she said, hearing the automatic vacation tone in her own voice. She wasn't sure he was ready for the heavy parts yet, but she reached into her bag, pulled out the antique quill and inkwell set she'd found, and set the box gently on his desk.

His eyebrows lifted. "Wow. You didn't have to do that."

Ruth just smiled. The look on his face was worth the extra space it had taken in her carry-on. He'd spent years rhapsodizing in lecture about great statesmen hunched over desks, quills scratching by candlelight; now his gaze went distant for a moment, like he could see one of them in the wavering glow just beyond his office walls.

As he set the box back on his desk, he turned it slightly so the light caught the brass fittings, admiring the way it looked. "So—a new project," he said at last. "Tell me. I read your email, but I'm really excited to hear it from you." His attention snapped fully back to Ruth, and for a moment the heat seemed to bother him less.

Ruth launched into the same story she'd told her family, only trimmed and sharpened for a historian. She told him about Joseph, about the vineyard before the war, the cellar, the bombings, the choice to lead people west after the Nazis moved through. She brought him up to the coast—refugee routes mapped in the margins of a journal, coded phrases like "plenty of lamb," and the possibility that local cells and British contacts were already at work in that corner of France as early as the summer of 1940.

Ruth finished, realizing she'd been talking almost without a breath. Dr. Peters sat back, hands steepled, eyes on some point just past her shoulder.

"Alright," he said finally. "First things first: you have the journal with you?"

She nodded and slid it from her bag, the leather worn and dark against the edge of his desk.

He didn't touch it right away. "If even half of what you're describing is on those pages, this is not a term paper." He glanced up at her. "This is a thesis at minimum. Possibly a book."

Ruth felt her throat tighten. "That's what I was hoping. I just don't want it to sound like I'm in love with a story instead of doing the work."

"You are in love with the story," he said mildly. "That's why you'll do the work." He tapped the journal. "But you're right—admiration can't be the argument. The argument has to be: this changes what we think we know about early resistance activity and refugee movements in 1940."

She nodded, quicker than she meant to. "So... you think the early cells angle isn't crazy?"

"I think," he said, choosing his words, "that historians have called that summer a fog for a reason. We know families fled. We know organized networks and SOE circuits become visible later. What you're showing me is a primary source that suggests improvisational, semi-coordinated help was already there—just not in the record." He paused. "That's not crazy. That's promising."

Ruth exhaled, not realizing she'd been holding her breath. "I want to build the thesis around 'unknown heroes'—Joseph, the priest, the farmer, whoever these 'plenty of lamb' people were."

"Good frame," he said. "But this is too big for you to carry alone if you're also taking a full load of classes."

Her shoulders sank a little. "I figured."

He leaned forward, a different kind of energy in his face now. "What if you don't?"

"I don't...?"

"Carry it alone." He turned to his monitor, clicked open a tab. "You're enrolled in my 'World War II and Its Aftermath' seminar this fall, yes?"

"Yeah. Tuesday–Thursday."

"Then we adjust." He swiveled back. "I've been using a packet of translated letters and a couple of standard memoir excerpts. They're fine. They're also on every other syllabus in the country." He nodded toward the journal. "This is not."

Ruth blinked. "You'd put Joseph in the syllabus?"

"Carefully," he said. "You keep ownership of the project. The thesis is yours; any eventual book is yours. But as a teaching tool? Having twenty sharp students work through selected passages, compare them to official reports, hunt for corroborating details? That's invaluable—for them and for you."

She could already see it: the map on the whiteboard, pins marking village names, students arguing over whether "plenty of lamb" counted as resistance or just kindness. "You think they'd get into it?"

"Ruth," he said, almost offended, "it's a secret wartime journal from a vineyard in Normandy. Undergrads will line up to fight each other for that kind of primary source."

She laughed, the tension in her chest easing. "How would it work, exactly?"

"We limit the exposure," he said. "No scans floating around the internet, no copying the whole thing. You select a set of entries—early vineyard life, the cellar, the march west, the boats. I'll help you assemble a packet. Students read those in seminar, in this building, under our eyes."

"And then?"

"And then they do what students do best when pointed in the right direction." He ticked points off on his fingers. "They comb through French archives and digitized newspapers. They chase references to Saint-Romain-de-Colbosc and Cauville. They look up SOE timelines and early Free French broadcasts. They try to break that 'void' you found in the secondary literature."

Ruth felt a smile she couldn't quite suppress. "So my classmates become... research assistants?"

"Your classmates become co-learners," he corrected, but the corner of his mouth twitched. "You will still do the heavy lifting: framing the questions, building the argument, writing the thesis. But letting them help you test Joseph's account against the historical record? That's exactly what a seminar is for."

She traced the edge of the journal with one finger. "I like it. It feels... less like I'm trespassing alone."

"Good," he said. "Then here's what I propose. You and I draft a formal thesis prospectus over the next two weeks. In parallel, I rework the World War II syllabus to include a 'Durand dossier' unit starting mid-semester."

"Durand dossier," she repeated, tasting the phrase.

"That gives you time to finish reading the journal, to decide which entries you're willing to share, and to put together a brief context sheet for your classmates." He sat back. "By December, you'll have a mountain of notes and a roomful of students who feel personally insulted if anyone suggests Joseph wasn't real."

Ruth laughed again, the sound surprised and genuine. "He'll be very pleased to hear that."

Dr. Peters's gaze softened as it dropped to the journal. "Then let's make sure we do right by him," he said. "By the end of this year, I want you to be the person in this department who knows more about that summer in Normandy than anyone else in the building."

Ruth nodded, feeling the weight of the promise settle in beside the excitement. "Deal."

When she stepped back into the hallway, the blast of warm air from the corridor made the office feel like a sealed archive in comparison. She hugged the journal a little closer to her chest as she walked past the bulletin board—flyers for intramurals and tutoring services jostling beside a faded "Call for Papers" on wartime memory. In the margin of her notebook, just above her list of errands, she scribbled a single line: Entries to share? Vineyard, cellar, bombing, march, lamb, boats. By the time the first students found their way into Dr. Peters's classroom, she wanted to be ready to say Joseph's name out loud without her voice shaking.

12

Chapter 12

Two weeks later, classes started. Ruth had been given a small research space in the library—a glass-front room off the quiet floor that she "owned" for the semester, and longer if the project demanded it. Dr. Peters had secured it with talk of a potential book, a true story that read so much like fiction no one would believe it without the kind of documentation he promised she would dig up.

She had notes pinned all over the walls, a timeline stretched from one end of the room to the other as she tried to space out the entries without running out of space. Colored threads linked dates to place names—Rouen, Saint-Romain-de-Colbosc, Cauville, the unnamed strip of beach—while sticky notes marked questions for later. In the passages she'd reached, Joseph and David had put family after family onto the fishing boats, four full trips with no fixed schedule, only slipping people aboard when the gaps in Nazi patrols were wide enough to risk it.

David wanted to stay with Joseph, but the danger was too real. Others might slip through, but Jews stood out. Miriam, the girl David had met on the farm, made the idea of leaving Joseph only barely tolerable. They knew by now they would land on the English shore and be taken to a refugee camp where they could try to wait out the war.

August 16th, 1940

I watched as David and Miriam floated into the darkness on the last trip across the Channel. I almost had to force David to go, but I got Miriam to talk him into it. I just can't in good conscience let him stay here.

The man I met—codename Le Berger—asked me to scout some areas. Cover back the way I came, set up a central spot, and pass on information about movements and checkpoints. I told him I already knew a place. I didn't tell him yet, but I could use this to my advantage and stay near the farm where Kate lives.

I gave him the general area and said I could pass information through the church. I'll need to connect with the priest and get the drop arranged, but if it works, maybe the path we used won't close behind us.

Ruth practically had to peel herself away from the room for classes or for the basic necessities of eating and sleeping. The little office drew attention; no one could see clearly through the frosted glass, but they could see enough to know something unusual was happening inside. Rumors were running across campus—and even stronger within the history department—that Dr. Peters and one of his grad students were sitting on a source big enough to rewrite a piece of the war.

The first week of Dr. Peters's World War II seminar felt like any other—maps on the projector, dates on the board, the familiar arc from Poland to Dunkirk to the fall of France.

"When do we see actual resistance show up in the sources?" one of the seniors, Malik, asked, leaning back in his chair. "Like, organized networks, not just people hiding neighbors?"

Dr. Peters capped his marker. "Depends who you read. Most textbooks push meaningful, coordinated activity in France to '41, '42. Earlier than that, the record is... thin."

Ruth felt the weight of Joseph's journal in her bag. Thin was one word for it. Wrong might be another.

Another student, Jenna, frowned. "So if there were people doing things in 1940, they just don't show up?"

"Officially?" Dr. Peters said. "Mostly no. That's why we like diaries, letters, parish notes. They remember what the big reports can't." He glanced once, briefly, in Ruth's direction. "Later in the semester, we'll test that."

Weeks flew by in the pages of the journal. Joseph was running around the countryside, passing notes through the church that he could only hope someone was actually collecting. When he wasn't on the road, he stayed in a small apartment that overlooked the town square—an advantageous but dangerous place to be, close enough to watch the occupiers move and close enough for them to notice him watching.

The week before Dr. Peters planned to introduce the "Durand dossier" to the seminar, Ruth found it harder to concentrate in her library room.

Up to now, Joseph had been hers. People knew about him only through what she chose to share, summaries at her parents' table, a few passages for Dr. Peters, a line here or there to Lena. The idea of twenty undergrads passing his sentences around, underlining his fears in different colors, felt less like research and more like letting him go a little bit.

She stared at the stack of photocopied pages on her desk—the carefully chosen entries about the cellar, the march west, the boats, Le Berger. This was the right move. More eyes meant more questions, more chances to confirm what he'd seen. But it also meant Joseph's voice would no longer arrive in her head first.

Ruth clicked over to her email and scanned for the name she'd grown used to seeing near the top of her inbox. Nothing from Ozias yet. Her fingers were already on the keys before she'd fully decided what she wanted to say.

Hey Oz, she typed. Thought I'd beat you to it today. I'm feeling the stress of turning this journal into "real research" next week—letting a whole room full of people read pieces that have only ever lived in my head. Almost like opening my journal for everyone to read, suddenly this piece will be in the open.

She paused, then added, It feels a little like handing a friend to strangers. Did you ever feel that way, showing me the graves and the oak? Then she sat back, wondering if that was too much, and hovered over the delete key.

After a moment she sighed, highlighted the last lines, and erased them. She started again, lighter this time:

Hey Oz,

I thought I'd go first today and see how everything is going. I'll be starting the research into this journal next week and I'm really nervous about it. Anyway, hope to hear from you soon.

She read it once, decided it sounded like a normal person and not someone confessing to a diary, and hit send.

Father Laurent was next.

Father Laurent,

I just wanted to touch base and see if you've found anything on the questions I sent the other day, especially the names connected to the vineyard and any notes about refugees moving west in 1940.

I appreciate you doing this for me.

Ruth

Ruth was still only halfway through the journal, but by next week she would be able to frame Joseph's 1940 for the class. She could show them the primary source, lay out the pieces she already had—names, dates, villages—and then hand them the assignment to start chasing what lay beyond.

Dr. Peters stepped into the research room. At first he had come by every other day, especially after class, and they would walk to the library together. Now he paused just inside the doorway, taking in the walls: the timeline that, for the moment, stopped in early 1941, the small highlighted tags marking villages Joseph had visited, and the notes Ruth had added whenever an entry mentioned something unusual.

"You've done great work in here," he said at last, turning back to her. "This is genuinely exciting."

Ruth had paused when he walked in. "I think I'll start with a framing in the first class," she said, "then go into his pre-war life. Vineyard, family, the cellar—before I let them see the boats and Le Berger."

She gave a small, nervous chuckle. "Ease them in so it doesn't just sound like I fell for some guy's diary."

Dr. Peters smiled. "Good. Give them the world first, then the hero. Let them meet Joseph as a person before you ask them to treat him as evidence."

Ruth watched as Dr. Peters walked the timeline, shaking his head in disbelief as he traced Joseph's path from the middle of the journey to the coast and back again.

"He was what, seventeen? Eighteen?" he murmured. "Most of our students are older than he was when he was doing this."

He turned back to her. "Alright. Tomorrow we stop pretending this is just your project," he said. "Tomorrow Joseph Durand walks into that classroom. The journal excerpts stay on the course site, password-protected, no downloads, no sharing outside the room. We treat him like any other restricted archival source."

Ruth glanced at the stack of copies on her desk, at the threads on the wall, at the journal resting open beside her notebook. For the first time, the thought didn't feel like letting him go. It felt like opening a door.

"Tomorrow," she said.

13

Chapter 13

The classroom was a classic gallery, a wide, stepped room where twenty students were swallowed by the empty seats around them. The hum of a struggling air conditioner mixed with the faint smell of old wood and furniture polish. The chalkboard had finally been replaced with whiteboards over the summer; no one had complained. The midterm was behind them, and the students were loose and relaxed as Ruth walked in, a neat pile of stapled packets waiting on the front desk.

"Okay, I need someone to pass some things out," Ruth said, dropping her bag beside the lectern. "And before we start; anything you see or hear in this room stays in this room." She let her gaze move over the students clustered toward the middle rows, making sure the weight of it landed. "This is a restricted source, and I'm trusting you with it."

Students immediately started flipping through their packets, the rustle of paper and low voices swelling as they tried to make sense of what they were seeing. For a moment, the room sounded full, as if every seat were taken. No one noticed Dr. Peters slip in and take a spot by the wall until his voice cut through the murmur.

"I think Ruth already said it," he added, "but let me underline it: this material stays in this classroom and in the research room. No screenshots, no photos, no sharing outside the course site."

From the third row, Eric—the one who always had a comment—leaned back in his chair. "Wow. Enough with the setup," he said, though he'd already spread the packet out across three desks. A few students snorted; others looked up, suddenly more curious than annoyed, but no one actually knew yet what they were holding.

Just as the hushed voices edged toward open protest, Ruth reached into her bag and drew out the journal. The worn leather looked almost fragile against the fluorescent light. She held it up so they could all see the cracked spine and the faint name on the cover.

"This," she said, "is the original. You're holding translated excerpts." She let the silence stretch a heartbeat longer. "Over the next few weeks, you're going to come to know Joseph Durand, and a handful of others, operating earlier than most historians even imagine when they talk about resistance and refugee routes in 1940."

The response was a ripple of excitement and curiosity. "Can we see it?" someone called from the back. A couple of heads nodded in agreement before Ruth could answer.

She hesitated just long enough for Dr. Peters to step in. "Yes," he said. "We'll pass it around. Gently." He moved closer to the front. "Remember, this is an original journal that traveled through occupied French territory. We don't yet know how long, or exactly what happened to the man who wrote it. We are all taking this one step, one page at a time."

Ruth looked over at him, then stepped to the first row. She placed the journal in the waiting hands of the student there, her own grip lingering a fraction too long. The student glanced up, and for a moment they just looked at each other, understanding passing wordlessly between them: this wasn't just a source for Ruth, it was someone she wasn't entirely ready to share.

The journal moved from student to student, each of them reacting in their own quick way. "This handwriting is wild," someone murmured. "He was our age?" another said under their breath. When it reached Eric, he turned it carefully, thumb resting just shy of the ink.

"I can feel the energy on this thing," he said. "You obviously have a strong feeling about it, Ruth. Can you give us—"

Ruth cut in, lifting the translation packet instead. "If you look at the first page in front of you," she said, "you'll see a brief description of Joseph and the other recurring people in the journal, and another list of names I've already connected to real places and records. Those are your starting points for what you'll be looking up."

Eric had already moved to page two. "Are you sure you're reading this right? This reads like a made-up war movie."

Everyone chuckled, but all of them were engaged, ready to learn about Joseph. "Your syllabus for the rest of this semester has changed drastically. Let's talk about the education piece and how you'll be graded."

"Today, I don't want analysis yet," Ruth said. "I just want you to meet him." She tapped the packet. "Take a few minutes to skim the first two entries. Then we'll read one together out loud."

Chairs creaked, pages turned. The room went unusually quiet as twenty students dropped into 1940—cellar plans, radio reports, the slow realization that the war was coming to the vineyard. After a few minutes, Ruth nodded to Malik.

"Would you read the first entry for us?" she asked.

He cleared his throat and began, stumbling once over a French place name, then settling into the rhythm of Joseph's voice. When he finished, Ruth let the silence sit.

"Okay," she said. "Gut reactions. Don't overthink it. What kind of person are you hearing? And what, specifically, in the text gives you that impression?"

"He's a young farm boy helping his friend in the vines," one student said, then immediately winced as a ripple of laughter moved through the room.

Ruth waited for the noise to die down. "I would have read it the same way," she said. "Thank you. If you're laughing at her answer, why?" She let the question hang.

No one spoke at first. A few students shifted in their seats, suddenly more interested in the packets in front of them.

"I hope you're not trying to spare my feelings," Ruth went on, scanning the room. "When I picked this up in the shop, my first thought was exactly that, just a simple farm boy, his voice silenced a long time ago. But a 'simple' farm boy in 1940?" She tapped the packet. "That can be a very interesting place to start."

A hand in the back went up. "He sounds... normal," a student said slowly. "Like he doesn't know yet what's coming. The cellar plan feels almost casual."

Another voice cut in. "But he notices everything. The radio, the maps, the prices in town. He's not just helping with vines, he's paying attention."

Ruth nodded. "Good. So already we've got two Josephs, one quiet farm boy, one watcher on the edge of something bigger. Keep going. What else do you hear in his voice, and what, exactly, on the page makes you say that?"

A voice cut in from the side Ruth wasn't watching. "Just from the first couple of passages, Joseph is already getting anxious," the student said. "Every day brings more information, and he knows there's something big coming that he still can't see."

Ruth didn't make a show of it; the boy already looked pleased with himself. "Good," she said. "We're running out of time for today, so I want to leave you with this." She crossed back to the front desk, resting her hand on the stack of packets. "Consider these your syllabus for the rest of the semester. They stay in here or in the research room. Anything we hand out gets collected at the end of class."

A murmur rippled through the room, confusion and curiosity mixing.

Ruth raised a hand for quiet. "Joseph is our source," she said. "I don't want to go too deep yet, but you need to understand the questions raised in his journey don't just fill gaps. Some of his answers cut directly across what we currently believe about the early French timeline."

A hand shot up near the back. "Like... change-the-textbook kind of stuff?"

Ruth allowed herself a small, wry smile. "Potentially," she said. "Which is why we're going to move carefully, and together."

She turned to the board and uncapped a marker. "I'll be in the research room during these office hours." She wrote the times in a neat column. "If these don't work for what you need to complete a task, email me. We'll find a way through it."

The earlier laughter was gone now, replaced by something quieter and sharper—an almost overwhelming sense of buy-in. They weren't just doing an assignment anymore. They were stepping into live history with her.

Just as Ruth was capping the marker and turning to dismiss them, Dr. Peters stepped through the door. "I assume we have buy-in at this point?" he asked, though his tone suggested he already knew the answer.

The response was immediate, a chorus of "yes" and "absolutely," students talking over one another in their eagerness to be heard, to align themselves with whatever this was becoming.

"Good," Ruth said, cutting back in before the energy scattered. "For next class, I want one academic source from each of you—just one—on either Jewish refugee movement in 1940 or the earliest documented resistance cells. We'll put them on the board and see how they line up with Joseph's entries."

As the bell rang, they didn't bolt for the door. Instead, they formed a loose line at the front, waiting to talk to Ruth or Dr. Peters.

"Do we find out what happened to him?" one student asked, echoing the questions Ruth was still asking herself.

"We'll find out as we move through it," she said. "Page by page."

They finally spilled into the hallway with a strange mix of disappointment and anticipation, frustrated at having to wait, thrilled to know there was more to uncover.

"We have our research team," Dr. Peters said, watching them go. "They're as enthralled as you are, and as you were the day you first found him, I'm sure."

Ruth stood beside him, emotions knotted. Excitement, yes. But also a tight, protective unease. There were more eyes on Joseph now than ever before, and part of her still wasn't sure she was ready to share him.

She gathered the remaining packets into a neat stack. "I need to get back to the journal," she said quietly. "I'm only up to Joseph meeting Le Berger and the first outline of the plan. After that... I don't know where it goes."

Ruth pushed open the classroom door, the weight of the journal heavy in her bag. Dr. Peters fell into step behind her. "You know where to find me if you need anything," he said as he pulled the door closed.

The hallway air hit her like a wall. Oklahoma heat pressed through the glass doors at the end of the corridor, turning the walk between buildings into a small endurance test. Ruth shifted the stack of packets in her arms. "I need a wheelbarrow," she muttered as she crossed the courtyard.

By the time she reached the library, sweat prickled at the back of her neck. She shouldered the door open with her hip, grateful for the rush of air-conditioning, and threaded her way past the circulation desk toward the basement stairs.

A few minutes later she stepped into the research room, the familiar smell of old paper and dust wrapping around her like a welcome. She set the packets on the table, laid the journal in front of her, and exhaled.

"All right, Joseph," she whispered. "Let's see where you went next."

14

Chapter 14

Chapter 14

August 19th, 1940

The path back to Kate's farm was much easier without fifty people to quiet and stop for. I could move at night, slip between hedgerows, never worrying about small feet wandering off the path. Kate's father must have sensed me coming; even though I arrived walking into the barn under the moon, there was a blanket and note welcoming me back.

This morning Kate smiled as she saw me coming out of the barn. She calmly waved me to come to the house, which admittedly stung a little bit, because I was about to run into her arms. The feeling of a connection to another person now felt so far away.

The house was filled with the smell of breakfast, even coffee was boiling on the stove. It wasn't a lot of fare, but probably more than they would usually prepare. They must have seen me come in or noticed me somehow. Whichever it was, this feeling of home was overwhelming.

Ruth paused reading the passage; she didn't move. No immediate gasp, no scribbled note, just stillness. After a moment, she rose, crossed to the map, and pressed a red pin beside the yellow one at the farm outside Pays de Caux.

In her notebook she searched for the right words to capture yet another shift in Joseph. He was loosening his grip on anything like normal life, describing the food, the shelter, the sense of home, but not the company. The space between him and Kate was widening, and he seemed to know it.

She continued reading the August 19th entry...

After we ate, I stepped outside alone. The morning air was cool against my face, the sky still pale with the last of the mist. From here I could see the line of trees that hid the road, the same road I had taken the families along just days before.

Kate's father moved somewhere behind me in the yard, the scrape of a hoe against dry soil, the clink of metal on stone. Life going on. I should have gone to help him, or stayed in the kitchen to talk with Kate, but my feet wouldn't carry me toward either of them.

I watched the light creep across the fields instead, tracing routes in my head. How long to the next town if I cut across the pasture, how many places to hide if the Germans pushed farther west, how much food could be tucked into the space beneath the cart. My thoughts kept slipping back to paths and distances, not to faces.

Kate stepped out onto the stoop at one point, wiping her hands on her apron. For a heartbeat, I thought she might come stand beside me. Instead, she only lifted a hand in a small wave and went back inside. I felt the space between us like a cold draft.

I don't know anymore what anything means. A smile. A shared cup of coffee. A hand on my arm. After what we've seen in the forest, after burying my own, every small kindness feels too heavy to trust. Is it affection? Pity? Or just two people trying to remember they are still human?

For now, it is easier to think about routes and rations. Feelings can wait until after the war, if there is an "after" for any of us.

Ruth took another breath, looked around the room, trying to find the missing words to describe the shift. Not a route. A pivot. Begins to think like an agent. Pulls back from Kate. The words felt uncomfortably close to home. Lately, she had been doing the same, pushing students, colleagues, even friends to the edges while she poured herself into someone else's story.

Running her finger back over the date at the top of the page, August 19th, 1940, she thought of the barely three days between David and Miriam vanishing into the Channel and Joseph already being back in the barn, memorizing routes instead of faces.

She flipped back a page, scanning his neat, tight lines about Le Berger and the church drop, then forward again to the blanket on the hay and the coffee on the stove. The contrast made her throat tighten. He was standing in the middle of a life, the fields, family, Kate's half-smile and quietly stepping away from it.

In the margin beside the entry, she wrote, Not a route. A pivot.

She sat back, letting the pen rest against her lip. Up to this point, Joseph had been moving out of obligation and proximity: David needed help, the families needed a guide, the forest needed someone who knew how to read its shadows. Here, something shifted. He wasn't just reacting anymore. He was choosing a role.

Ruth reached for her notebook, turned to a fresh page, and drew a line down the middle. On the left she wrote, Helper, and under it, vines, cellar, first march, Green Forest. On the right she wrote, Courier/agent, then paused, listening to the word settle in.

Underneath, she added:

— Le Berger assignment

— routes, checkpoints, distances first

— emotional distance from Kate / "after the war" line

She capped the pen and pushed the chair back with a small scrape. The map on the wall pulled her like a magnet. Houppeville. The Green Forest. Pays de Caux. Cauville and the boats. She traced the pins with her fingertip, a rough arc from vineyard to coast.

"If this is the pivot," she murmured, "then everything after has to look different."

Joseph was beginning to think like an operative, putting routes before people, information before comfort. And she... she was doing something uncomfortably similar. Late nights in this room. Emails answered at odd hours. Students, colleagues, even Lena nudged to the outer edges while she rearranged pins and dates.

She forced herself to step away from the map and sat down again. The laptop screen glowed to life when she tapped the trackpad. Her inbox was a crowded mess of seminar questions, library notices, and one unread message from Ozias, subject line: Found something odd in the attic.

She hovered over it for a heartbeat, then dragged the cursor away. One thing at a time.

She opened a new document instead and titled it: Phase Two – Early Cells and Couriers, Summer 1940.

The first sentence came slowly, each word laid down like a tentative stepping-stone: By late August 1940, Joseph Durand no longer sounded like a vineyard son caught in the path of war; his entries read like the notes of a man learning how to move through occupied space without being seen.

She stopped, reread it, then added: This shift, from helper to courier, is marked not only by where he walks, but by what he is willing to set aside.

Her phone buzzed on the table. A text from Lena flashed across the screen: Movie night? I have popcorn and exactly zero interest in Nazis. Ruth smiled despite herself, then winced at the time. It was after nine.

Her gaze slid back to the journal, open to the page where Joseph stared at the light over the fields instead of walking toward Kate.

"I'll call you tomorrow," she whispered, more to the phone than to the book. She silenced the notification and slid the phone face down.

She read the August 19th paragraph one more time, letting his uncertainty about every small kindness soak into the room. The reluctance to trust a smile. The decision to focus on routes and rations because feelings could wait.

"That's our line," she said softly. "Right there."

She uncapped her pen and underlined the last sentence: For now, it is easier to think about routes and rations. Feelings can wait until after the war, if there is an "after" for any of us.

In the notebook she wrote:

Thesis angle – early couriers as emotionally self-protective as they were strategic. Survival of the work requires pulling back from normal life.

Then, below it, an almost reluctant addition:

Ruth doing the same?

A knock on the glass wall made her jump. One of her students, a kid named Malik, stood there, half-turned like he was ready to bolt if she waved him off. He lifted a hand instead.

"Do you have a minute?" he mouthed.

Ruth glanced at the clock. Office hours had ended half an hour ago. The journal sat in front of her, the map behind her, and between them, the fresh title on the screen: Phase Two.

She closed the cover of the journal gently, as if tucking Joseph in for the night.

"Yeah," she said, raising her voice enough for him to hear. "Come in."

As Malik pulled the door open, the weight of the day—of pins and dates and a farm girl named Kate—settled into something more solid. Act 2, whether she liked the term or not, had begun. Joseph was stepping into his new role on the page, and so was she.

15

Chapter 15

August 23rd, 1940

I left before the sun came up.

Kate's father was already in the yard when I stepped out of the barn, a shadow moving between the cart and the henhouse. He didn't call out, didn't ask where I was going. He just nodded once, the way men do when they've already had the conversation in their heads and don't need to waste words on it again.

"You know where the well is," he said quietly. "If you come back late."

"I'll come back," I told him.

The words felt strange in my mouth. I had no right to promise anything anymore. Not to him, not to Kate, not to anyone who set a plate in front of me and pretended the world wasn't on fire just beyond the trees.

The path into the woods was still marked by our passing. Bent grass. A scuffed patch of dirt where someone had stumbled under their pack. A strip of fabric caught on a thorn. It hadn't been that long since we'd gone through with the others, but already it felt like years. The forest took everything and folded it into itself.

I moved faster alone. No whispered reassurances, no shushing frightened children or steadying old men whose knees weren't made for marching through roots and mud. My pack rode light on my shoulders: water, hard bread, a little cheese Kate had tucked in without saying anything, and the folded paper I'd promised to deliver.

Le Berger had kept it simple. Notes on which roads the Germans were favoring now, which checkpoints had grown tighter. Questions about others. Can the eastern lane past Houppeville still be used? Is the bridge at Barentin guarded at night? Are there patrols between the Green Forest and the river?

I had my own answers to add. Places where the ground stayed soft even in August, good for muffling footsteps. A barn whose owner had slammed his door the moment he saw us. A field where we'd dropped flat and held our breath as a convoy rattled past.

Every tree seemed to carry an echo of the people who had walked beneath it. I could still see the mother who nearly smothered her baby trying to keep him quiet. The boy who kept looking over his shoulder as if he might sprint back toward home if he let himself.

Home. The word felt as far away as the horizon.

By mid-morning, the light had begun to push down through the canopy. I kept to the thicker patches of shade, listening. The forest had its own language. Birds frantic meant people where they shouldn't be. Silence meant something worse.

Near Houppeville I slowed, dropping to a crouch as the trees thinned. Through a gap in the branches, I caught sight of the road we'd skirted before. A cart rolled past, an old horse in the traces, the driver hunched against the day. Two soldiers walked behind, rifles slung, helmets catching the light.

I watched them until they disappeared around a bend, counting the cadence of their boots. Four steps between each clack where the road was broken. If I had to cut across here at night, I'd know how long I had between one pair passing and the next.

The town itself was quieter than the last time. Fewer people on the street, fewer shutters open. A sign that the rumors were true; more families had slipped away in the night, trusting the forest over the uniforms.

I pulled the cap low over my eyes and went in.

The shopkeeper I'd used before stood behind his counter, hands busy with nothing, just stacking and restacking the same three loaves of bread. He glanced up when the bell over the door chimed, eyes flicking once to my face, then to my hands, then to the street behind me.

"It's late for market," he said.

"I'm just passing through," I answered. "Heading west. I heard flour's still easier to find here."

His mouth tightened. "Nothing is easy," he said. But he reached for a sack all the same, weighing out what I could afford with the few francs I put down. His fingers brushed the paper I slid across with the coins, and for a moment I thought he might refuse it.

Instead he covered it with his palm, then with the corner of the cloth he was using to wipe the counter.

"Long road ahead?" he asked.

"Yes."

He didn't ask which one.

Outside, the church bell tolled the hour. I took the back lane to avoid the square, following the sound instead of the street. The chapel wasn't much to look at from the rear, just a stone wall with moss in the cracks and a door that had seen better years, but the saints over the front entrance were still mostly intact when I circled around. Their faces watched as I went in, eyes worn smooth from time and prayer.

Inside, the air was cool and dim. I kept my steps soft, counting the pews the way Father Bernard had taught us as altar boys. The confessional in the south corner still had the same crack in the wood at the base, just big enough for a folded scrap of paper.

I knelt, as if to pray, and slipped Le Berger's questions and my answers into the gap.

"Forgive me, Father," I whispered. "For the things I can't say out loud."

On the way out, I lit a candle and left it burning beneath a small statue of Saint Joseph. It was habit more than anything now, a way of asking for protection without presuming I deserved it.

The day stretched long and hot as I turned back toward the woods. Every farmhouse I passed, I catalogued. One with geraniums in the window and laundry still on the line. Another with shutters closed, no smoke from the chimney, a lock hanging crooked on the door like someone had left in a hurry.

Farther on, I saw the track where our group had waited the first night, the pressed-down grass in a hollow between the trees, the ghost of a fire ringed in stones. Someone had scattered the ashes, but a few blackened bits of wood still clung to shape.

I stood for a while, listening to the quiet. No crying babies now. No whispered questions about what waited on the coast. Just the wind.

Le Berger had asked me to think like him. To see movement the way he did. So I walked the paths again, not as a terrified guide with twenty souls behind him, but as a scout. Counting steps between cover. Marking which branches snapped under my boot and which bent. Noting where the forest floor dipped enough that a whole line of people could disappear if they dropped.

By the time the light began to slant gold, my legs ached and my throat felt scraped raw from breathing dust. But the farm's roofline finally rose up through the trees, a familiar silhouette against the sky.

Kate was on the porch when I stepped out of the woods.

She shaded her eyes with one hand, then let it fall when she recognized me. For a second I thought she might run down the path, skirts catching the dust, the way people in stories did. Instead she stayed where she was, fingers twisting in the edge of her apron.

"You're back," she said when I reached the gate.

"I said I would be."

She nodded, eyes searching my face for something I couldn't name.

"Did you find what you needed?"

"Enough to know which roads not to take," I answered. "And which ones might stay open a little longer."

Her mouth pressed into a line. "Come inside," she said. "There's soup. Papa kept some back."

Inside, the kitchen was warm and dim, the last of the day slanting through the small window over the sink. A pot bubbled on the stove. The smell of onions and lentils wrapped around me, a comfort so sharp it hurt.

We ate with our heads bowed, more from fatigue than from prayer. Kate's father asked a few questions, all practical—did I see any patrols on the eastern road, were there checkpoints closer to the river now, had anyone mentioned new restrictions near the markets.

I answered as best I could. Where the soldiers had been thick, where they had been thin. Which towns felt like they were holding their breath and which seemed already emptied out.

No one asked how I was. That felt right. I wouldn't have known how to answer.

Later, when the dishes were stacked and the house had gone quiet, I lay awake in the barn staring at the rafters. The blanket they'd left me the first night still smelled faintly of smoke and hay.

I thought of David and Miriam somewhere in England, if the boats had made it that far. Of the people who had walked behind me through the Green Forest, counting their breaths between each creak of the trees. Of the paper folded inside the confessional crack, waiting for a hand I would never see.

Le Berger wanted me to be his eyes and feet in this corner of France. To keep moving, keep watching, keep feeding information back so the path we'd carved didn't close behind us. It was work that needed doing. Work I could do.

But it meant standing at this threshold of Kate's farm—the circle of light from the kitchen window, the sound of her washing up—and choosing, over and over, not to step fully inside.

If I stayed too long in that circle, I might not be able to leave it again. And there were still too many people in the dark.

Ruth set her pen down and blew out a slow breath, the words of the entry humming under her skin like an aftershock. This was the longest entry yet, giving the clearest look so far into where Joseph was going, and what he was losing.

August 23rd, 1940. Five days after the pivot.

On the desk in front of her, the journal lay open, Joseph's tight lines steady and unbroken even as the life around him fractured. The research room was quiet except for the faint hum of the air conditioner and the ticking of the old clock on the wall—a tame, modern cousin to the church bells and artillery that marked his days.

She flipped back to the earlier entries, tracing the progression with the tip of her finger. Vineyard. Cellar. Green Forest. Houppeville. Cauville and the boats. Pays de Caux farm. Now this, the solo routes, deliberate drops, a farm treated as a hub rather than as a home.

On her laptop, the document titled Phase Two – Early Cells and Couriers, Summer 1940 still waited with its single paragraph. She woke the screen and added a new line beneath it:

August 23: First clear evidence of intentional courier work, scouting alone, revisiting prior routes without refugees, establishing information drops via church/shopkeepers. Safe house (Kate's farm) functioning as node, not refuge.

She hesitated, then typed another sentence: Emotional language continues to recede when he returns to the farm; practical questions dominate.

Her eyes slid to the map on the wall. The pins glinted dully in the fluorescent light. She rose, taking the journal with her, and stood close enough that the paper almost brushed the cork.

With her free hand, she traced the path Joseph had taken: from the farm out into the trees, down toward Houppeville, across toward the river, then back. It wasn't just a straight line; it was a loop, a pulse between danger and the illusion of safety.

"He's building a circuit," she murmured. "Not just running once."

The thought sent a small shiver through her. Circuits could be repeated. And repeated circuits could be discovered.

Behind her, the computer chimed softly. A new email notification blinked in the corner of the screen. Ozias Marchand – Re: Found something odd in the attic.

Ruth stayed where she was for a few seconds, one finger resting on the pin that marked the Pays de Caux farm.

She thought of Joseph lying awake in the barn, listening to the sounds of a house he wouldn't fully enter. Of the way he'd described the distance between himself and Kate as if it were a line drawn on the ground he couldn't cross.

Then she stepped back to the table and picked up her laptop.

The email preview showed the first line:

Hey Ruth, I was digging around in some old boxes above the stairs and came across a stack of papers with my grandfather's handwriting...

Her pulse kicked up.

She didn't open it. Not yet.

Instead, she clicked over to her seminar notes and created a new heading: Assignment 2 – Mapping Early Routes and Nodes.

Beneath it she wrote:

Using Joseph's entries from June–August 1940, identify at least two points where his movements shift from reactive (helping specific families) to structured (information gathering, repeated paths, drops). Support with one external source (map, troop movement, parish record, or eyewitness account).

She sat back, letting the assignment stare back at her for a moment. This was how it had to go. One foot in Joseph's world, one in her own. One in the past, one in the classroom.

Her phone buzzed again, a second text from Lena this time: You alive? Nazis or not, people need sleep.

Ruth smiled, the expression small but genuine, and typed back a quick reply: Alive. Buried in 1940. Rain check on the popcorn?

She hit send, then hovered the cursor over Ozias's email one more time.

"Routes first," she said under her breath, echoing a man who had walked through a different kind of darkness with different orders. "Feelings later."

With that, she turned back to the journal and the map, letting the unopened message sit in the corner of the screen like a small, bright question that could wait until morning.

16

Chapter 16

The next morning, Ruth's alarm went off before the sun had fully made up its mind.

She lay there for a moment, staring at the faint line of light seeping around the edge of the blinds. Her body wanted another hour. Her brain was already halfway back in 1940, circling the loop between the Pays de Caux farm, Houppeville, and the church with the cracked confessional.

By the time the coffee finished dripping in the kitchen, she'd checked the weather, skimmed a half-dozen emails from students asking if they could "clarify" the assignment she'd already explained twice, and mentally drafted an apology text to Lena for bailing on movie night. Again.

The research room key was cold in her hand when she let herself into the basement. The familiar smell hit her, the paper, dust, that faint tang of toner and old glue, something inside her eased. The little glass-walled box felt more like home every time she walked in.

She set her bag down, pulled the journal from its protective sleeve, and opened to the ribbon she'd left in place the night before. August 23rd, 1940 stared back at her, Joseph's entry about the confessional drop and the shopkeeper's careful hands so fresh it might as well have been written an hour ago.

She didn't reread the whole thing. Not yet. Instead she flipped forwards and backwards in a tight band, scanning the weeks around it. June in the Green Forest. July at the farm. The first mention of "we have plenty of lamb." The last trembling description of the boats rocking away into the dark.

A pattern was emerging. Routes tightened, then repeated. Stops went from desperate to deliberate. Words about fear didn't go away, but they slid into the spaces between notes about roads and patrols instead of filling the page on their own.

She reached for her notebook and added another bullet under *Courier/agent*: revisits routes not for escape, but for information

The cursor on her laptop pulsed on the last line of her Phase Two document. She woke the screen and reread what she'd written: *By late August 1940, Joseph Durand no longer sounded like a vineyard son caught in the path of war; his entries read like the notes of a man learning how to move through occupied space without being seen.*

She added:

His work shifts from moving bodies once to preparing the ground for multiple crossings. This is the earliest sustained pattern of courier behavior I've seen in a non-military, non-OSS source.

The word *earliest* made her pause.

She minimized the document before the imposter syndrome could start shouting about hubris and graduate students getting ahead of themselves. One thing at a time. Evidence first. Claims later.

Her inbox chimed as she clicked over to her email.

The subject line she'd been pretending not to see for two days sat near the top, stubbornly unread.

Found something odd in the attic.

She stared at it, thumb hovering over the trackpad as if it were a live wire.

"Just open it," she muttered.

The email unfolded on the screen, longer than she'd expected.

Hey Ruth,

I hope it's okay that I'm writing about this instead of just sending the polite 'hope the research is going well' message. I was up in the attic yesterday, the space above the stairs you almost hit your head on twice, trying to clear out some boxes my mother has been after me about since June.

Most of it was exactly what you'd expect: old linens, a box of chipped plates no one can quite throw away, a very ugly lamp I promise has never been in a guest room. But at the back, behind everything, I found a wooden crate with my grandfather's name burned into the lid. I don't remember ever seeing it before.

Inside were papers. A lot of papers. Some hotel records from just after the war, some receipts I couldn't read because the ink has nearly surrendered, and a stack

of loose pages in his handwriting. The dates on top made me think of you: summer 1940.

Most of it is pretty mundane—lists of supplies, notes about repairs, a page where he was clearly trying to figure out how to spell "peeling paint" in English and giving up. But there are a few lines that don't fit with the rest. I'll copy one of them here exactly as he wrote it (sorry for the accent marks, I'm typing fast):

"The boy from the vines passed through again last night. He does not stay, but the forest opens for him. The old path to the cove is not empty."

He doesn't give a name anywhere on that page. Just "the boy from the vines" and a note in the margin that says "Green Wood" with a question mark. It made me think of your journal, and the way you talked about the vineyard and the forest, and I wondered if it might mean something to you or be nothing at all and just a tired man being poetic about a stranger.

If you'd like, I can scan those pages and send them. The ink is faded but still readable with a little effort. My mother says my grandfather kept "stories from the bad years" tucked away, but I didn't realize they were this literal.

I hope the semester has started well and that your students appreciate what you've stumbled into. There are not many people I'd trust with words that old.

Take care,

Oz

Ruth read it once straight through, heartbeat picking up as the lines blurred from content to handwriting and back again. Then she read it again, slower.

The boy from the vines passed through again last night.

Her fingers tightened on the edge of the desk.

She looked up at the map.

Vineyard. Green Forest. Old path to the cove.

Her brain tried to pull them together too fast. She tapped the spacebar and forced herself to breathe.

"Okay," she said under her breath. "Slow down."

It could be coincidence. There were other vineyards. Other boys. Other forests. People borrowed phrases without realizing it all the time. But the dates—the "summer 1940" on Oz's pages all lined up with her pins a little too neatly to ignore.

She clicked into her Phase Two notes and typed:

Possible independent mention of "boy from the vines" + forest route in coastal region, from Ozias's grandfather's notes (summer 1940). No name given. Need scans before drawing any connection.

Even as she wrote *possible* and *need* and *before drawing any connection*, her mind had already started sketching it in.

If the boy in Oz's attic pages was Joseph, that meant somewhere in the Marchand family history there was a firsthand account of his route from the perspective of the people waiting at the edge of it. Not just refugees moving west, but hosts. Innkeepers. Witnesses.

Her throat went a little dry.

She went back to the email and reread the closing lines: *There are not many people I'd trust with words that old.*

That part did something to her that had nothing to do with maps.

Trust was a finite resource in 1940. It didn't grow on hedgerows now either.

She snapped the journal shut before she could get sentimental about a man who'd been dead for decades and his grandson who ran an inn on a cliff.

"Work first," she told herself. "Then feelings. That's the deal."

She hit reply.

Hey Oz,

You absolutely picked the right person to send that to. "The boy from the vines" and a forest route in summer 1940 is not nothing—that description overlaps a lot with what I've been reading. I don't want to jump ahead of myself, but it could be an important local perspective on the same movements I see in the journal.

If you're willing to scan those pages (or even just take clear photos in good light), I would be very grateful. Even the "mundane" bits can help—supplies, repairs, what the inn was doing during those months. All of it builds the backdrop.

Semester has begun. I've just introduced Joseph to a room full of students and told them they're responsible for helping me figure out where he fits in the bigger story. No pressure, right?

I hope the autumn bookings aren't too overwhelming and that the ugly lamp has found a home where it can do the least damage.

Thank you again for thinking of me when you opened that crate. It means more than I can fit in an email.

She hovered over the last sentence, debating whether to cut it. It sounded dangerously close to stepping over a line she wasn't sure she'd drawn yet.

She left it.

Her cursor drifted up to his line about there not being many people he'd trust with words that old. The echo of the tour he'd given her—stories under the oak, the graves, the careful way he'd spoken about the ones who hadn't come back—sat with it.

She hit send before she could talk herself into being less honest.

On the desk, her phone buzzed.

We still on for lunch or did your French boyfriend steal you? – Lena

Ruth let out a startled laugh, the sound ricocheting off the glass like something foreign.

Her fingers flew over the screen.

Not my boyfriend. And yes, lunch. But it might have to be late. I'm buried under "Phase Two" and a stack of maps.

A bubble appeared almost immediately.

You keep saying "Phase Two" like you're planning a heist. Save me a seat in the cafeteria. I'll text when I'm walking over.

Ruth set the phone down, the smile lingering even as she turned back to the work.

On her desk calendar, she scribbled *Oz scans?* in the margin next to next Thursday's date. It was a small act of faith, assuming he'd send anything at all, but she didn't erase it.

She spent the next hour building out the next seminar block.

On the whiteboard in her mind, she saw it clearly: a timeline running from April to August 1940, with Joseph's entries pinned at intervals. Underneath, a second line for external evidence. Maps. Parish records. Military reports. And, if she could verify them, a set of innkeeper notes from a cliffside village looking out over the Channel.

She opened a blank document and titled it *Assignment 2 – Mapping Early Routes and Nodes.*

The outline came quickly.

Using Joseph's entries from June–August 1940, identify at least two points where his movements shift from reactive (helping specific families) to structured (information gathering, repeated paths, drops). For each point, provide:

1) Quoted lines from the journal that show the shift.

2) One external source that either supports or complicates that reading (map, troop movement, parish record, eyewitness account, etc.).

3) A short reflection (150–200 words) on what might have motivated that change in behavior.

She sat back, imagining how the room would take it.

Eric would probably grumble about how she was "overcomplicating a guy just trying not to die." Malik would dig into troop movements like he'd been waiting his whole life for an excuse. Someone quietly diligent in the second row would find a parish bulletin that mentioned "unusual traffic" on a road Joseph had used three times.

The thought steadied her.

Lena's text had come in fifteen minutes ago. *Heading your way. Don't let the dead guy keep you from fries.*

Ruth glanced at the journal, open to August in the middle of the desk. The dead guy was, in fairness, very much alive on the page.

"I'll be back," she told him, as if he were a person she was leaving at a café table.

She slid the protective cover over the journal, locked the research room, and headed upstairs into the light.

Campus was warm but not unbearable, the late-September sun slanting through the trees. Students moved in loose clusters, laughing, gesturing with coffee cups and phone screens, living in a present Joseph could never have imagined.

Lena spotted her by the fountain and raised both arms as if she were greeting someone returning from war.

"You survived your morning with the ghosts," she said as they fell into step. "How's the boy from the vines?"

Ruth blinked. "What?"

Lena shrugged. "You said something about a vineyard kid in your text last week. I'm picturing him with tragic eyes and dirt under his fingernails."

Ruth huffed out a breath that might have been a laugh. "That's... not entirely inaccurate."

"And the innkeeper?" Lena nudged her with an elbow. "The one with the oak tree and the very intense email subjects."

“He found some old papers,” Ruth said carefully. “His grandfather’s. There might be something in them that lines up with Joseph’s route.”

Lena’s eyebrows rose. “So he’s useful and probably cute. I approve.”

Ruth shook her head, but she didn’t deny it. “Right now he’s a potential source,” she said. “I’m trying not to make him anything else until I see what’s actually in those pages.”

“Spoken like a true historian,” Lena said. “People first, feelings later.”

Ruth almost corrected her, *routes first*, but stopped herself in time.

Back in the research room an hour later, grease from the cafeteria fries still faintly on her fingers, she sat down to the same arrangement: journal, map, laptop, phone. The box of her world.

A new email from Oz winked in her inbox: *Uploading scans tonight. The lamp has been banished to the storage closet. Victory for all guests.*

She let herself smile, just for a second, then clicked back to her Phase Two document.

There would be time to open the attachments when they arrived. To line his grandfather’s words up with Joseph’s. To see where the lines overlapped and where they broke apart.

For now, she set her hands on the journal and pulled it a little closer.

“All right, Joseph,” she whispered. “Let’s see what you walked into next.”

The clock ticked on, steady as footsteps on a forest path.

17

Chapter 17

September 3, 1940

I am no longer certain which place I should call home.

The farm is a bed when there is a space in the barn. The woods are a roof when there is nothing else. The road is a spine that connects all of it, Kate's fields, the hedgerows, the creek that smells of iron, and now the winery where German boots sleep on Durand stone.

The house at our vineyard is occupied.

I saw it with my own eyes tonight.

I camped in the line of trees east of the old north slope, just inside the Green Forest where the ground drops and you can look through the birches and see the roof. The air was damp, the kind that makes wool grow heavy on your shoulders and the pages of a notebook curl. From there I watched the place that used to be ours.

I left a note for Father Bernard.

Do not send anyone openly down the main drive. If a family must come from town, they need to leave the road before the last bend and follow the hedgerow behind the orchard wall. There is a gap in the stones where the plum tree roots have pushed them apart. It is still there. I used it tonight.

Father, if you find this:

"Home" means Kate's farm.

"Barn" means the loft on the west side, above the broken ladder rung.

"Creek" is the narrow stream behind the Renaud fields, the one that runs rusty in summer.

"Green Forest" is the stretch of woods between there and Praux, where the canopy swallows the stars.

"Oak" is the last safe meeting point before the coast road.

I will leave one page like this with you when I can. The rest I will carry.

Tonight I sleep in the ditch between the orchard and the road, wrapped in a blanket that still smells of Kate's barn. My back is against the roots of the plum tree that pushed our wall apart. I can hear their voices through the stones.

Ruth crossed to the wall and added a new card to the timeline under September 1940. German unit now at vineyard house. Note left with Father Bernard. She circled the word occupied twice, then stepped back and studied the line of pins that showed Joseph's movements.

Did Claire know anything about Nazis living in the house, or was that another piece lost between generations?

Questions crowded her as she wrote fast in the margin of her notebook, arrows tying Joseph's coded list to her own labels for Kate's farm, the Renaud fields, the Green Forest. When the notes stopped feeling like work and started feeling like a weight, she forced herself into the chair again and pulled a regional map closer.

The paper was already crowded with pencil lines that traced possible routes and meeting places. Looking at the spread of them, she realized how far he had gone on foot, how much ground one boy had covered while pretending he still had a home to go back to.

Her eyes burned. She pushed away from the table for a moment, then turned to the computer and clicked open the folder of attachments Oz had sent, searching for anything that might mention German officers at the house.

Ruth clicked open the first attachment in Oz's latest email, a scan of a narrow, yellowed notebook page. Handwriting looped across it in neat French, a different voice than Joseph's but living in the same years.

The caption he had typed above the image was pure Oz.

Found this in a crate of "unsellable trash" in the cellar. Great-grandfather's log. He mentions "a boy from the vines" twice in June 1940 and something about "forest paths" and "families who walked at night." Thought it might belong to your wall more than to my storeroom.

Under that, a second line:

Also, before you accuse me of procrastinating, I promise I only opened the crate because a guest asked if we had any "authentic wartime clutter." You are having a bad influence.

She felt the corners of her mouth tug up.

The page itself was mostly mundane. Deliveries in liters. Notes on repairs to shutters and roof tiles. A list of guests who had stayed "longer than expected" that summer.

Halfway down, a small entry:

June 27, 1940. The boy from the vineyards came again, late, with eyes like he hadn't slept for days. Said the forest kept more people alive than the town that week. Left before dawn. Paid in thanks, not in francs.

Ruth whispered the line once under her breath. The boy from the vineyards. Forest kept more people alive.

Her throat went a little dry.

She scrolled to the bottom of Oz's message.

I can send more pages if these help at all. Or if you just like excuses to email me. Both are acceptable scholarly motives.

She snorted, then hated that it made her cheeks warm.

Her reply came quicker than she intended.

You are wildly overestimating my free time, you know. But yes, those lines help. They echo exactly the period I'm tracing from Joseph's side, right down to the "forest keeping people alive." I owe your great-grandfather more gratitude than any historian is supposed to feel for a stranger with a roof to fix.

If you keep "finding" crates like this, I may start to suspect you're doing it on purpose just so I'll write back.

She paused, re-read the last sentence, and left it. It was honest enough and vague enough to pretend she had meant it as a joke.

At the bottom she added:

P.S. One day I want you to walk me around that cellar again and tell me which boxes you're secretly afraid of. Purely for research, of course.

Send.

The whoosh sounded louder than usual in the quiet apartment.

She pushed away from the desk and rubbed her eyes. When she looked up, the wall of maps and index cards stared back, dates and red thread crossing like a web. Joseph's September 3 entry sat near the center now, pinned beside a new index card she'd labeled Oz logbook, June 27. Two boys from the vines, separated by a lifetime.

On the desk, her phone buzzed.

She ignored it, pulled her laptop closer, and opened her course management page instead. There was still a stack of discussion posts to grade, and tomorrow's seminar needed a cleaner structure than what was scribbled in her notebook.

Her cursor hovered over the roster.

Office hours, she thought.

She created a new calendar block for the next afternoon and labeled it: Archival work session – Joseph packets.

There was a knock at her office door the next day before she had even finished taping the new printout of Joseph's entry to the corkboard behind her desk.

"Come in," she called, juggling a stapler and a stack of handouts.

The door opened just far enough for a head to appear. Dark hair, earnest eyes, the usual half-skeptical squint she was starting to recognize from the back row.

"Hi, Ms. Ward? Do you have a minute?"

Eric.

Of course.

He stepped inside without waiting for a full invitation, backpack slung over one shoulder, a notebook already in his hand. He looked more nervous than his in-class sarcasm ever suggested.

"I saw the sign-up sheet for the research session," he said. "It was full. I wondered if... I mean, if you had room for one more person who doesn't like group work but also doesn't like being wrong."

Ruth blinked.

"Being wrong about what?" she asked.

He shrugged, tried for casual.

"About your guy," he said. "Durand. I still think parts of the journal read like someone edited them after the fact, but my roommate is sick of hearing about it, and the library database hates me. I figured if I'm going to keep poking holes in it, I should at least know what I'm talking about."

There it was. The annoyance and the unexpected sincerity tangled together.

Ruth gestured to the chair across from her.

"Sit," she said. "You can have the unofficial extra spot, as long as you understand that 'poking holes' comes with a reading list."

He dropped into the chair, setting his notebook on his knee.

"You say that like it's a threat," he said. "I like reading lists. I just don't like romances disguised as archives."

It landed sharper than he probably intended. Ruth felt a small, guilty flicker at the word. Romance. Oz's email. The line she hadn't deleted.

She reached for the stack of packets on the desk and slid one toward him.

"This is not a romance," she said, a little more firmly than necessary. "It's a primary source. A boy on the move in occupied France, writing tight because he doesn't have the luxury of pages."

Eric studied her for a beat, then took the packet.

"Fine," he said. "Prove it."

She almost smiled.

On the computer screen behind him, the corner of her email window still showed the top of Oz's message. Both are acceptable scholarly motives.

She clicked the window closed.

For the next hour, the only lines that mattered were Joseph's.

18

Chapter 18

The classroom was buzzing as chatter between students rose about what they had found, who researched what, and what they thought about Joseph. Real or not real. Or at least maybe real but embellishing.

Phrases floated up out of the blur of voices.

"He sounds too cinematic."

"No, look at the dates, that line-up is weirdly specific."

"If he made it up, he did better research than I did for my midterm."

Ruth let the noise run a moment longer. The energy meant they cared. Then she capped her pen and stepped back from the whiteboard.

Two parallel timelines ran across it now, black marker for 1940, blue for the work they were doing in the room. Arrows connected dates to place names, to question marks, to the word routes she had underlined twice.

"So," she said, turning back to the semicircle of desks, "someone tell me what changes for Joseph between June and September. Short answers. Instincts first, citations second."

Hands went up.

"Troop movements," Malik said without waiting to be called on. "The Germans are pushing farther west. His routes get longer and more complicated."

"Good," Ruth said. "Where do you see that in the text?"

"In the August entries," Malik said, flipping pages. "He stops talking about one family at a time and starts talking about the forest, the roads, checkpoints. He is watching patterns."

"Write that down," she said. "Patterns."

Casey lifted her hand.

"He also stops using some names," she said. "Early on he says David's name every other sentence. By September, it is 'families' and 'groups' and 'someone's mother' instead of individuals."

Ruth nodded, adding another arrow between the two timelines.

"So, shift in language. Fewer names, more roles," she said. "Good. What else."

Eric sat with his packet open, thumb marking a page, eyes narrowed. When the room fell quiet, he cleared his throat.

"I think he gets professional," he said. "Less feelings, more logistics. The September entry reads like he is writing for someone else's eyes. Not just his. Like he knows Father Bernard or whoever is going to use it."

A couple of students nodded, surprised to find themselves agreeing with him.

Ruth nodded slowly.

"Professional is an interesting word for a man sleeping in a ditch," she said. "But yes, the tone shifts. Anyone else see that, or see something that contradicts it."

A few heads bobbed. Pens scratched.

In the second row, Jenna squinted at her packet.

"I think he is still feeling a lot," she said. "He just hides it under route notes. When he says he is 'no longer sure where to call home,' that is huge. He just moves on from it in like one line."

"Good catch," Ruth said. "A feeling with no follow-up can be as loud as a paragraph sometimes. Make sure you mark those when you see them."

Eric glanced from the board to her, then back down at his notes.

"I mean, that is kind of what I was getting at in office hours yesterday, Ruth," he added. "The way you talk about him, it is like he is your colleague, not some kid with a pencil who got lucky and survived long enough to be found in an antique shop."

There was a little ripple of laughter at the back of the room. Someone whispered, "He said lucky, uh oh," under their breath.

Ruth felt the faintest heat in her cheeks, but her voice stayed even.

"Two things," she said. "First, I am fine with disagreement, but not with you sandpapering language until it sounds like cynicism. He was not lucky. He was deliberate. Your own argument about his 'professional' tone backs that up."

She saw his ears go pink.

"Second," she added, "I liked it when you called me Ms. Ward. Let's stick with that, shall we."

He blinked, caught off guard, then gave a half smile.

"Sorry," he said. "Habit. Every historian on my dad's bookshelf is a doctor."

"Every historian in this room is a student," she said. "Including me."

A few more pens moved. Someone at the window muttered, "That's going in my notes," just loud enough for the row around them to laugh again.

The tension eased. Ruth turned to the board again and drew a small box around September 3, 1940.

"Back to Eric's point," she said. "Professional or not, we can track this change. September is where Joseph starts writing like a guide instead of just a witness. Your task this week is to prove or disprove that claim with evidence."

She picked up the remote and let the assignment instructions slide onto the projector. The light washed over the room, turning faces pale as they bent over their packets. The rustle of paper filled the air.

"Assignment two," she read. "Using Joseph's entries from June through September 1940, identify at least two points where his movements shift from reactive to structured. That means from 'I am helping who is in front of me' to 'I am running a pattern.' For each point, you will need a quoted line from the journal, one outside source, and a short reflection on what might have pushed that change."

Groans and scribbles, the usual chorus.

From the front row, a quiet student named Theo raised his hand halfway.

"Outside source like what," he asked. "Newspaper, church record, that kind of thing."

"Exactly," Ruth said. "Anything real you can put up against Joseph. Troop reports, refugee statistics, local histories, even family stories if you can find something concrete behind them. I want you to see when he lines up with the record and when he jumps ahead of it."

Eric tapped his pen against the desk.

"So we are basically trying to prove you wrong or right about your own thesis," he said.

"You are trying to test the source," Ruth corrected. "If that ends up testing me a little too, I can live with it."

He grinned at that, and a couple of students leaned in over their packets like they had just been given permission to argue.

Somewhere in the back of Ruth's mind, a different line hummed. Both are acceptable scholarly motives. Oz's teasing email about excuses to write back. The way he had called her the right person to trust with "words that old."

She pushed it aside and tapped the date on the board.

"Start here," she said. "The boy from the vineyards is on the move. Let's see if you can keep up."

Chairs creaked as they settled in. For a few minutes, the room went quiet, paper and highlighters and the faint ticking of the clock blending into a steady background.

Ruth moved slowly through the rows while they worked, glancing down at margins filled with half sentences and question marks.

On Malik's page, she saw:

Pivot? Helper to courier. Routes > people.

On Jenna's:

Less David. More "we." Is he protecting them or himself.

On Eric's, the handwriting was tighter than she expected.

If this is embellished, why keep the boring logistics. Boring is what makes it feel real.

She did not comment, just let her hand rest on the back of his chair for a heartbeat before moving on.

When the last few hands lowered and the rustle of pages died down, she went back to the front.

"Alright," she said. "We are almost out of time. Before you go, I want one sentence from each of you. No speeches. One sentence that begins, 'By September, Joseph sounds like...' and then you tell me who you hear."

Groans again, but this time they came with a current of interest.

They went around the room.

"By September, Joseph sounds like a scout."

"By September, Joseph sounds like someone who has decided not to get attached."

"By September, Joseph sounds like he expects not to come back."

That one sat heavy for a moment.

Eric glanced at his notes, then met her eyes.

"By September, Joseph sounds like a guy who has already lost his home and is pretending he hasn't noticed yet," he said.

Ruth did not trust herself to say much.

"Good," she managed. "Write those down on your packets. You will need them when you start drafting."

The clock over the door clicked over to the hour.

"Remember," she added as they began to gather their things, "these packets do not leave this building. You can use the research room if you need more time with them. My office hours are posted on the course site. Email me if you are stuck."

They filed out in small clusters, still arguing in low voices about whether a farm boy could really have memorized that many routes, about whether fear sounded different in 1940 than it did now.

At the doorway, Malik paused.

"Ms. Ward," he said. "I found a parish bulletin from Rouen that mentions 'unusual nighttime traffic' near one of the roads you marked on the map. Can I bring it by your research room later."

Ruth felt her fatigue lift just a little.

"Yes," she said. "Absolutely. Bring it and we will see where it fits."

Eric was one of the last to leave. He hovered near the front with his backpack half on.

"Ms. Ward," he said, catching himself, "sorry about earlier. The thing about luck. My grandfather uses that word for everything and I forget it hits wrong for some people."

"It is fine," she said. "Just remember that 'lucky' can erase a lot of work. Joseph did not trip and fall into helping people. He walked into it on purpose."

He gave a short nod.

"Yeah," he said. "I am starting to see that."

Then he was gone, swallowed by the hallway noise.

Ruth gathered the extra packets into a neat stack and slid them back into her bag. The whiteboard still held the twin timelines, black and blue lines running side by side.

She did not erase them.

By the time she crossed the courtyard to the library, the Oklahoma heat had settled like a hand on the back of her neck. Her mind kept jumping tracks, from Joseph in the ditch by the plum tree to Oz in his cliffside inn, to Eric calling him "your guy" in front of a room full of students.

In the cool, dim light of the research room, the world shrank again.

She set her bag down, pulled Joseph's journal out, and laid it on the table. The wall of maps faced her, pins in Rouen and Saint-Romain, in the Green Forest and by the unnamed strip of coast.

On the desk, her laptop blinked with a new notification.

Subject line: Attic crate, part two.

Oz.

Ruth stared at it for a long second, then clicked it open.

Found another page I thought you'd like, the first line read. Great-grandfather writes that "the boy from the vines" came back in September and left a note at the church. He says the priest said, "Paper remembers longer than a tired mind."

She felt her chest tighten. Joseph's phrase. Her own phrasing in last night's notes. The echo across years.

Beneath that, Oz had added:

Also, for the record, I am firmly on the "real and not embellishing" side of your mysterious vineyard boy. If that helps your students at all, you can quote me as "anonymous coastal innkeeper with excellent instincts."

Ruth let out a quiet breath that might have been a laugh.

She typed back, fingers moving before she could second-guess herself.

My students will be thrilled to know the anonymous coastal innkeeper is on their side. Thank you for the line about the priest. That gives me another pin for the wall.

She hesitated, then added:

They heard about "the boy from the vineyards" today. I am trying very hard to keep this a class and not a story I am secretly in love with. Some days I am more successful than others.

She deleted the last sentence, then, after a moment, retyped a softer version.

Some days I remember to keep my historian hat on. Some days I just want to stand under that oak again and let the story be what it is.

Send.

The whoosh sounded small in the quiet room.

Ruth turned back to the journal and opened to the September entry she had just had her students dissect. The ink had thinned in places, the paper worn at the edges where someone had turned it too many times.

"Alright, Joseph," she said softly. "They are trying to keep up. So am I."

Outside the frosted glass, footsteps passed and faded. Inside, the only sound was the slow turn of a page, a pencil tapping once against a notebook, and the low hum of the air vent over her head.

The boy from the vineyards was on the move.

So was she.

19

Chapter 19

The pot roast was the same as always, but the table felt different.

It was supposed to be their weekly dinner, the standing date that had slowly become whenever they could all manage it. Tonight the usual crowd had squeezed in around the leafed-out table: her parents, Grandma at the head, Uncle Mark already on his second helping, Lena anchored at Ruth's side like another daughter.

Ruth was moving the food around her plate more than actually eating.

"Ruth, what's wrong? You're in your own world." Her mom's question cut through the overlapping conversations and brought everything to an uneven pause.

Forks stilled. A cousin's laugh died halfway out of his mouth.

Ruth blinked and looked up.

"Sorry," she said. "I'm here. Just... kind of stuck between here and 1940."

Her dad huffed a small laugh.

"Well, bring a little of 1940 to the table then," he said. "Some of us haven't had the latest chapter."

Lena nudged her elbow.

"Yeah," she said. "Last we got, Joseph had just turned into a part-time ferry service in Cauville and pushed his best friend onto a boat. What's happening now?"

Ruth set her fork down for real this time.

"He made it back to the farm," she said. "To Kate's place. A couple of days after David and Miriam crossed."

"Alive?" Grandma asked, as if that were still in doubt.

"Alive," Ruth said. "But not really home. That's kind of the point."

She glanced around the table, measuring how much to give them.

"So," she began, "after the last boat goes out, this man Le Berger pulls Joseph aside. Basically tells him, you're useful. You know the roads, the woods, the churches. Go back, scout, send information through the priest. Turn what you did once into something repeatable."

Her dad whistled low.

"Recruitment," he said. "They saw what he was doing."

"Exactly," Ruth said. "So Joseph goes back the way he came. No fifty people this time, just him and a pack. He walks the same paths, but now he's counting steps, timing patrols, marking which barns are safe and which doors slam."

She picked up her glass, then set it back down again.

"He stops at Houppeville," she went on. "Leaves a paper for the shopkeeper to pass along. Hides a note in a cracked confessional. Stays at Kate's farm, but only half-stays. Eats their soup, answers her father's questions about roads and checkpoints, then sleeps in the barn and lies there staring at the rafters instead of letting himself belong."

"Why?" one of her cousins asked. "If he's safe there, why not just stay?"

"Because staying would make it harder to leave again," Ruth said quietly. "And he knows he'll have to. He writes about standing right outside the house, smelling coffee, hearing Kate move around in the kitchen, and choosing the fields instead. He keeps saying it's easier to think about routes and rations than feelings."

Lena shot her a sideways look at that, but stayed quiet.

"And the vineyard?" her mom asked. "Have you gotten to that part yet?"

Ruth nodded once.

"He goes back," she said. "Just long enough to see the German unit has taken over the house. Officers in the kitchen. Trucks in the yard. Guards in my grandparents' bedroom window."

She caught herself, corrected.

"In his parents' window," she said. "He watches from the orchard and realizes he doesn't have a home anymore, just paths. Leaves a coded note with Father Bernard spelling out what 'home,' 'barn,' 'creek,' 'Green Forest,' and 'oak' really mean if someone finds his pages later."

Uncle Mark shook his head.

"That's a lot for a kid," he said. "How old were you again when you were complaining about freshman roommates?"

"Not walking supply lines under occupation," her dad added.

Across from Ruth, Grandma was staring at her plate, lips pressed thin.

"So he kept going," Grandma said. "After burying his people. After getting his friend out. After losing his house. He still kept going."

Ruth swallowed.

"Yeah," she said. "He kept going."

Silence settled for a moment, heavy but not unfriendly. The only sounds were the faint hum of the fridge and the clink of someone shifting their knife.

Lena cleared her throat.

"And in the present tense?" she asked softly. "What's going on with you in all this? Besides turning your students into research assistants."

A couple of chuckles broke the tension.

Ruth rolled her napkin between her fingers.

"Class is intense," she said. "They're starting to push back, in a good way. One of them called Joseph 'too professional' yesterday, like he didn't buy that a vineyard kid could think like that that early. I made him re-read the September entry out loud."

Her dad grinned.

"Poor kid," he said. "Did he survive?"

"He did," Ruth said. "He even came to office hours to argue some more. I think we're going to make a historian out of him whether he likes it or not."

"And France?" her mom asked, not quite casually. "Any news from the innkeeper?"

Lena's head snapped around.

"Thank you," she said. "Someone had to ask."

Ruth felt heat rise in her face.

"He emailed," she admitted. "He found some of his grandfather's pages from 1940. There's a line about 'the boy from the vines' and a forest path to the cove. I'm waiting on scans."

"So he might have seen Joseph," Grandma said quietly. "Or someone like him."

"Maybe," Ruth said. "I'm trying not to jump ahead. But if it lines up, it would mean Joseph isn't just talking into the void. There were people on the other end, noticing."

Her mom watched her for a long moment, eyes soft.

"And you?" she said. "Are you still noticing the rest of your life? Or do we need to put a limit on how many nights a week you're allowed to live in 1940?"

A few smiles sparked around the table.

Ruth looked down at her plate, then back up.

"I'm trying," she said. "Days in the research room. Evenings in Oklahoma. Weekly pot roast as reality check."

Lena bumped her shoulder.

"And popcorn," she said. "Do not erase popcorn from the schedule."

"Right," Ruth said. "Research, family dinners, popcorn, and the occasional email from a French innkeeper. That's the balance I'm aiming for."

Her dad lifted his glass.

"To Joseph," he said. "And to the girl stubborn enough to follow him this far without forgetting to come home for dinner."

Glasses and water cups lifted in a loose, uneven echo.

"To Joseph," they murmured. "And to Ruth."

She took a sip, throat tight, and let the warmth of the room settle around her. For a few minutes, the journal stayed zipped in her bag by the door, close enough to feel present, far enough away to let her be a daughter and a friend again.

Outside, Oklahoma night gathered at the windows.

Later, when the dishes were done and most of the family had drifted out to the porch, Ruth and Lena ended up alone at the table, the pot roast pan covered in foil, only two dessert plates left between them.

Lena pushed a crumb around with her fork.

"You know what keeps hitting me?" she said. "How much you and Joseph are accidentally in the same mess."

Ruth frowned.

"I'm not exactly dodging patrols in the Green Forest," she said.

"You know what I mean," Lena said. "He's standing outside Kate's kitchen window, smelling coffee, hearing normal life, and choosing the road because he thinks duty has to come first. You're in a different decade, but you're doing a softer version of the same thing."

Ruth stared at the grain of the table.

"He thought if he stepped all the way into that life, he wouldn't be able to leave again," she said. "And he needed to leave. People were depending on him."

"Right," Lena said. "And you think if you step too far into anything that smells like an actual life here, or over there... you'll mess up the work. Or you'll owe someone a version of yourself you can't give yet."

Ruth let out a breath.

"Oz keeps sending these pieces from his grandfather," she said quietly. "Little lines that line up so closely it feels like someone planned it. The 'boy from the vines,' the priest talking about paper remembering longer than a tired mind. And all I can think is, I don't get to have feelings about the innkeeper while I'm still figuring out how to carry Joseph."

Lena's voice softened.

"Maybe it's not about 'getting to' have them," she said. "Maybe it's just about naming that you're in the same kind of in-between. Joseph knew he couldn't start a life with Kate while the world was on fire. You know you can't build something solid with a man on a French cliff while you're half-living in archives."

Ruth rubbed a thumb over a water ring on the table.

"So nothing starts until the work is done," she said. "That's a depressing thought."

"I don't think that's it," Lena said. "I think it's that the work is part of who you are. Same as it was for him once he said yes to Le Berger. The trick is not letting that swallow every other part. Kate deserved more than a door Joseph never walked through. You deserve more than a lifetime of research rooms and almost-emails."

Ruth was quiet for a long moment.

"Tonight Grandma asked me to start from the beginning again," she said. "Joseph on the vineyard, David's family, the cellar, the march west. The words felt... easier. Like a path I know now."

Lena's mouth tilted.

"A well-worn path you know you're going to keep walking," she said.

Ruth nodded.

"Yeah," she said. "I think I am."

"Then maybe that's the point," Lena replied. "You keep walking it. You keep doing the duty part. And when the ground stops burning quite so much, you see who's still there at the kitchen window or under the oak."

Ruth huffed a small laugh.

"Under the oak," she echoed. "You really are going to make a mug with that."

"Absolutely," Lena said, standing and grabbing the plates. "Front side: 'Duty first.' Back side: 'But not duty only.'"

Ruth watched her carry the dishes to the sink, the sounds of her family's voices floating in from the porch. For the first time that day, the pull between past and present felt a little less like a tear and a little more like a bridge she might be able to walk without falling.

20

Chapter 20

The next class time was creeping closer, the little clock in the research room ticking louder than usual.

Ruth stood in front of the wall, marker in hand, updating the line that had become Joseph's world. New arrows, fresh dates, a couple of sharp question marks where her students had poked holes and she needed better answers ready.

Behind her, the journal sat open on the table, just a few feet away, waiting. The ribbon marked the start of the next entry. She could see the first line from here if she let herself look.

For the last hour she had been doing everything but that.

New color for "civilian witnesses." A sticky note about Oz's grandfather's phrase. A margin list titled Eric's challenges, with possible counter-arguments scribbled beside it. Anything to keep from reading the page that would pull her under again.

Her family's voices from the night before still tugged at the edges of her mind. Her mom's worry about how much of her life was disappearing into 1940. Lena's quiet comparison between Joseph standing outside Kate's window and Ruth hovering over an inbox from a French inn.

Losing yourself, they hadn't quite said.

But it was close.

She capped the marker and let her hand fall to her side.

"You don't get to teach him if you're afraid to read him," she muttered.

The room was silent enough that her own voice sounded like someone else's. She crossed back to the table and lowered herself into the chair. For a moment she just rested her fingers on the paper, feeling the faint texture of ink and age.

Then she began to read.

October 2, 1940

They are hanging men on the mairie wall now.

I came into town by the back lane, behind the mill. From there you can see the square, the church, and the town hall all at once.

The red flag was on the balcony. Below it, where they used to post market notices and festival days, four bodies hung by the neck. Their feet almost touched the cobblestones.

Each had a board tied around the chest.

Saboteur.

Enemy of order.

Friend of Jews.

German on top, bad French underneath. The paint was still shiny in places.

They put them between the mairie door and the little shrine of the Sacred Heart. The plaster Jesus looks down with open hands. No one was looking up.

People walked past with their eyes on the ground. A woman I knew from Mass held her daughter's hand so tight the girl whimpered. She did not stop.

Two German soldiers smoked on the church steps. Their rifles leaned on the rail where old women used to rest after services. One laughed. Ash fell on the stone.

There was a paper nailed under their feet. It said any act against the occupiers would be answered "like this." It said the town was responsible for its own peace. It used the word justice.

I had to look away at that.

Inside the church it smelled of wax and damp stone. Someone had lit candles at the side altars. Through the walls I could still feel the wrongness outside, like a bruise.

Father Bernard stood near the front, hands on the back of a pew. When he came and sat beside me, he did not look at me first. He looked at the crucifix.

"I saw you by the tree," he said.

I nodded.

"They call this justice," I said. "You tell us not to hate. They hang men in front of the church and say hate is obedience. What are we supposed to do with that?"

For a while he said nothing.

Then, very quietly, "We keep walking the roads that do not end at that wall."

He does not know about the notes, the paths, the people in the Green Forest. But it felt like he did.

On my way out I looked one more time. The ropes creaked in the wind. Someone had left a few wildflowers near the mairie steps, close enough to see, far enough that they did not touch the soldiers' boots.

None of the signs used the word Christian. Only their words for traitor and order.

I went back to the farm through the fields. From there, if you did not turn your head toward town, the sky and the vines could almost trick you into believing it was still April.

It is not.

They are putting death on the walls and asking us to learn from it.

I will.

Just not what they want.

Ruth let the last line sit on the page for a long moment.

They are putting death on the walls and asking us to learn from it. I will. Just not what they want.

Her eyes drifted back up to the middle, to the part her students would circle without really knowing why.

Justice.

Order.

Friend of Jews.

Words shed grown up hearing in one context twisted inside out in another. A cross three meters away from a rope. A priest telling a boy to keep walking roads that did not end at a wall while the occupiers nailed their own commandments into the stone.

She picked up her pen and wrote in the margin, beside the date:

Loss of language = loss of humanity. "Justice" used for terror. Church meant for mercy, wall used for fear. Joseph still hearing Father Bernard, not the signs.

On her yellow pad, under the heading *For class*, she added:

- Ask them what it means when the same street holds baptism, Mass, and public hanging
- Contrast Nazi "order" with Gospel mercy
- Joseph's resistance is not just moving bodies, it is refusing the lesson the wall is teaching

She checked the time. Ten minutes to get upstairs.

Closing the journal, she rested her palm on the cover for a heartbeat.

"Okay," she said softly. "You saw what happens when power kills and calls it holy. Let's see if they can."

Ruth's pen hovered over the margin.

Loss of language = loss of humanity, she had written, then underlined *justice* three times before it started to look like something else entirely.

The room was so quiet she could hear the tick of the clock over the door and the faint hum of the vent. Outside the frosted glass, footsteps came and went, blurred shapes moving past like another timeline she was only half part of.

Her family's words from the night before pressed in at the edges.

Duty first. But not duty only.

Roads that do not end at that wall.

Roads that do not end in this room.

She closed the journal, letting her hand rest on the cover until her breathing slowed.

"You are not the only one split," she said under her breath, hardly aware she'd spoken. "Church and wall. France and Oklahoma. Joseph and..."

Her phone buzzed in her bag.

The screen lit with a preview she didn't open: *Ozias St. Pierre – Re: Attic crate, part three.*

Her chest gave a small, treacherous twist.

She turned the phone face down and pushed her chair back, telling herself she could not walk into the classroom thinking about an inn on a cliff and a boy from the vines hanging on a wall at the same time.

Her hand was on the journal when the doorknob rattled.

"Yeah," she said. "Come in."

He slipped through the door, the smirk he usually wore hanging on his face.

"Still in the journal then?" Eric asked. "Well, I found something I wanted to show you."

Ruth was stuck between being annoyed and curious.

He held out a printout from an academic search engine. The header showed an article from a town near Rouen, not Joseph's but close enough. The grainy photograph mirrored what Joseph had described around the church: bodies on the mairie wall, a notice tacked under their feet, the steeple in the background.

"I wonder if Joseph is a real person or someone who was writing about World War Two and finding information like this to build the story," Eric said.

His eyes flicked toward the timeline on the wall and she could see, in the small tightening of his mouth, that he realized how on the nose his find was.

Ruth's first instinct was to snap back. Instead she grabbed a pen, taking quick notes in the margin of the printout, copying the date, the town name, the phrasing of the notice.

As she drew breath to give a curt response, Eric cut in.

"How close to this episode is the entry you have on the wall?" he asked.

For a heartbeat, the room felt too small. The October circle on her timeline. Joseph's line about learning the wrong lesson. The article's date, hovering just a few days away.

"I am curious about whether you think this supports or goes against your claim," she said, keeping her voice even. "But right now we need to get to class."

She purposely did not answer his question. Mostly because she was wondering the same thing herself, whether the piece he had brought was proof of Joseph's truth or proof that someone could have built a very convincing lie from stories like it.

Ruth folded the printout, slid it beside the journal, and stood.

"Bring it with you," she added. "If you are going to set my room on fire five minutes before class, you can at least help me explain the smoke."

Eric snorted, but he picked up the paper.

They stepped into the hallway together, the path to the classroom suddenly feeling longer than the stairs back from 1940.

The walk to the classroom was quiet.

They crossed the courtyard side by side, shoes scuffing the concrete, neither one quite matching the other's pace. The crisp fall air slipped between the buildings, carrying the dry sound of leaves rustling in the trees overhead.

Ruth clutched her bag strap a little tighter, feeling the weight of the journal and Eric's printout against her hip. She could sense him just off her shoulder, full of questions he had not decided how to ask yet.

The empty space between them felt tight and tense, filled with everything they were both thinking and not saying, until the classroom door finally came into view and gave them somewhere else to put it.

21

Chapter 21

The class was tense.

They were past the novelty of discovery and not yet close enough to an ending to feel secure. Somewhere near the halfway mark of the semester, the project that had once felt expansive now felt brittle—like it might fracture under the weight of its own unanswered questions.

Eric led the charge.

He always did.

"What we're really doing," he said, pacing just enough to irritate her, "is treating Joseph as a fixed point when the evidence suggests he's anything but. At best, he's a composite. At worst, he's a narrative convenience."

A few students nodded. Others stayed quiet, watching Ruth more than they watched him.

"And that's not an accusation," Eric continued. "It's just... academically irresponsible to keep framing his actions as singular when there are multiple plausible alternatives. Someone else could have written this. Someone else could have acted. Someone else could have—"

"Enough," Ruth said.

Her voice cut sharper than she intended.

Eric stopped, but he didn't sit. He never sat when he thought he had momentum.

"You're asking us to accept Joseph as real," he said, calmer now, almost reasonable. "But every time we press on attribution, you pivot to moral weight instead of historical certainty. That's not scholarship. That's belief."

The word landed harder than the others.

Ruth dismissed the class early.

No discussion. No closing remarks. Just the scrape of chairs and the quiet satisfaction of a challenge unanswered.

Dr. Peters was waiting in the hallway.

He fell into step beside her without asking, hands tucked into his coat pockets, matching her pace as they moved toward the library offices.

"If you disappear into belief and play deaf to other views," he said gently, "your thesis won't hold up to scrutiny."

Ruth didn't respond.

She could still hear Eric's voice. Narrative convenience. Composite.

"You're frustrated," Peters continued, "because right now you can't defend the position cleanly. And that's uncomfortable. But Eric and his crew are doing you a favor. They're red-teaming your work as you go."

They reached the office door.

Ruth stopped, hand on the handle, jaw tight.

"I'm not asking them to believe," she said. "I'm asking them to read."

"And they are," Peters said. "They're just reading against you."

She didn't answer.

Inside the office, Ruth dropped her bag onto the desk harder than necessary. Papers slid. A book thudded against the edge. She paced once, twice, then turned back, already mentally rewriting the next lecture.

That was when she noticed the envelope.

It lay on the floor near the desk leg, half-hidden beneath the chair. Cream-colored. Thick. Out of place.

She picked it up.

It was heavier than she expected, the paper stiff, formal. The return address was printed, not written, but whoever had chosen the font had tried—unsuccessfully—to mimic a hand. No logo. No postage stamp advertising urgency or charity.

Just a faint embossed crest, barely visible unless the light struck it at an angle.

European.

Ruth sat.

She opened it carefully.

Inside were two items: a letter and a folded photocopy.

The letterhead read:

Diocese of Saint-Martin-sur-Loire

Office of Ecclesiastical Records

The letter itself was brief. Precise. Almost cold.

Madame Ruth,

In response to your inquiry, we confirm the existence of a sacramental record within the parish archives of Saint-Étienne-des-Champs.

Baptism Record — 14 June 1944

Parish: Saint-Étienne-des-Champs

Officiant: Bishop Henri Delacroix

The individuals named were verified against contemporaneous parish and civil documentation.

The record reflects acknowledgment of union and residence. No additional commentary is preserved.

Respectfully,

Office of Ecclesiastical Records

Ruth exhaled slowly.

She unfolded the photocopy.

It was a register entry—aged, narrow, its margins stained with time. The handwriting was careful, deliberate. Two names were entered in block script.

She recognized the mother immediately.

The girl from the farm.

But the father's line remained blank. Just the name of her father as godfather, and the baby's name.

Below their names was the date. The parish. The bishop's mark.

Joseph's name was nowhere on it.

No witness line bearing his name.

No indication he had ever been there at all.

Ruth felt the first stirrings of something like panic.

This was real. Verifiable. Archived.

The document did not confirm him. It did not deny him either.

It simply recorded the outcome, and nothing about the passage that made it possible.

Ruth sat there for a long time, the paper resting on the desk between her hands.

This did not solve anything. If anything, it sharpened the fracture.

The journal had always claimed restraint. Absence. Stepping aside.

But this—this could be something solid to move the narrative her way or Eric's way.

Frantically, Ruth picked up the journal, skimming entries moving forward. More and more entries about movements and Nazi actions, heartbreaking scenes of the absence of humanity. For more than a year, Joseph reported similar actions to what he had described up through early 1941.

Late 1941 started moving toward something more. More connections to English OSS, leading a cell collecting and passing information to the Allies. It was fascinating, but now she was on her own mission.

Eric had challenged his existence; the letter from the bishop had made it more ambiguous. But it provided an opportunity to test the story one way or another. Fear was driving her movements now, not excitement to learn.

Finally—

June 1942

It was time we did it. We could not just hide it anymore; we didn't want to. But if we had done anything in public, it would have brought the attention of the Nazis, and I don't want their attention on this. If they ever caught me, they would know she was connected to me.

The bishop held a secret marriage between us with only her mother and father in attendance. Her father was not all smiles, like her mother. He liked me, but didn't like the thought of his daughter being tied to the resistance.

When I started staying at the farm between trips, I wanted to maintain the separation from what the farm offered. But I could never maintain enough distance from her that would have helped our hearts, connecting the way they did. Never hid how her hair blew in the breeze while she brought food or other things from the house to the barn. How her eyes melted the walls I had up against the world.

I would have never thought I would be married to such a woman, but I really didn't even acknowledge it could happen at all when I saw my family fall.

Ruth lowered the journal slowly.

She did not reread the entry. She didn't need to. The shape of it had already settled into place.

June 1942.

A private marriage.

No registry. No witnesses beyond family.

Deliberately unrecorded.

June 1944.

A baptism.

Documented. Archived. Verified.

A child brought into the Church under a name that could survive scrutiny.

Between the two was a gap Joseph had never tried to close.

She pulled the photocopy back toward her and studied it again, this time not as evidence, but as structure.

The absence of a father's name was not unusual. Nor was the presence of the grandfather as godfather. In rural parishes during the occupation, such arrangements were common enough to avoid suspicion and rare enough to pass without comment.

Nothing about the document contradicted the journal.

Nothing in it confirmed Joseph either.

That was the problem.

Joseph's account described a life lived deliberately outside the record. The baptism confirmed a life that had crossed into it.

Together, they formed a sequence that could be argued in two directions.

If Joseph were real, this was the cost of his restraint. If he were not, then the journal had anticipated history with unsettling precision.

Either way, the center could not hold.

Ruth leaned back in her chair and closed her eyes.

Eric was right about one thing.

She could not prove Joseph.

Not without breaking the very logic Joseph claimed to live by. Not without demanding that a man who survived by leaving no trace suddenly account for himself on paper.

That kind of proof would not be historical.

It would be coercive.

And yet—she opened her eyes again—Eric was also wrong.

Because the journal did not ask to be authenticated.

It asked to be read alongside what remained.

A private marriage that could not be written down.

A public baptism that could.

A man who removed himself at precisely the moment history would begin taking notes.

That was not narrative convenience.

That was the pattern.

Ruth gathered the journal and the photocopy together and stacked them neatly, aligning the corners as if order might make the conclusion cleaner.

It didn't.

But it clarified something else.

This chapter of the work could no longer be about whether Joseph existed.

The evidence would not allow it.

The question had shifted—quietly, irrevocably—to something far more difficult:

If Joseph was real, then he chose a form of action that scholarship could never fully recover.

And if he was not, then someone had understood the shape of sacrifice well enough to invent him convincingly.

Either way, the argument was no longer Eric's alone.

Ruth looked at the clock, then at the door.

The semester was moving faster now.

And whatever Joseph had been, he had reached the point in the record where neutrality was no longer possible.

She closed the journal.

22

Chapter 22

Here's Chapter 22 with the two small additions woven in: a concrete external record and a brief seminar ripple via Malik. I've marked the new bits with [ADD] so you can see them easily.

Chapter 22

Something in the last few entries Ruth had read refused to settle.

It wasn't what Joseph said—it was what he stopped saying.

She went back, this time not reading forward but scanning for a change in cadence. The journal had always been spare, but around mid-1942, the entries shifted. Fewer references to paths and nights. More dates. More repetition. Less danger in the language.

Just after the marriage entries, she found it.

July 1942

I was assigned a truck with bed rails. It passes easily as a delivery vehicle. For the last several weeks, I have been moving supplies between towns along the same routes.

It has eased concerns at the farm. With a visible occupation, I am less of a liability.

I have become familiar with several checkpoint crews.

There are those who inspect my papers each time, even after weeks of seeing me.

Those who stop me only long enough to take an apple from the back.

And those who barely look up at all.

I note the difference.

I pass what I can along—small observations, delays, changes. Messages are placed where they belong, in crates destined for abbeys and other locations known to receive them.

I do not stay with anyone long enough to be remembered.

Ruth sat back.

This wasn't a pivot into heroics. It was the opposite. Joseph was narrowing his footprint, not expanding it.

A delivery driver moved often and belonged nowhere. He was expected to pass through, not to linger. His papers changed. His cargo rotated. His presence explained itself.

She flipped ahead.

The entries followed the same pattern for months. Routes repeated. Weather noted. Delays logged. Nothing dramatic. Nothing declarative.

The extraordinary had been buried inside the ordinary.

Ruth closed the journal and glanced at her phone on the desk. The unread email from Oz sat at the top of her inbox, its subject line truncated.

She ignored it.

For now, this was enough.

Joseph hadn't vanished from the record.

He had blended into it.

She didn't realize how long she'd been staring at the screen until the office lights dimmed automatically.

The journal lay closed beside her laptop now, the delivery entries having done their quiet work. She had moved on to external records—scanned testimonies, postwar summaries, transportation logs compiled years after the fact. The language was flat. Administrative. Men reduced to roles and outcomes.

Courier.

Driver.

Status unknown.

[ADD] One line in a transport ledger from 1945 stopped her cold: Driver missing on route, presumed dead. No name. No age. Just a function erased mid-sentence. It was exactly the kind of gap Joseph seemed to be writing toward, and away from.

Her inbox refreshed.

She hadn't meant to open it immediately.

Oz's message sat there, timestamped earlier that afternoon.

What struck me isn't that Joseph disappears.

It's that he becomes ordinary.

That's usually where people stop looking.

Ruth read it twice.

Then once more, slower.

She hadn't told him about the delivery entries yet—not directly. She'd sent scans, page numbers, a few clipped notes. He'd found the shape of it on his own.

Her reply window opened before she could talk herself out of it.

I missed it at first.

I kept expecting escalation.

But this is where he survives.

She paused, fingers hovering.

Then added:

And it scares me more than the woods ever did.

She sent it.

Too fast.

Ruth leaned back in her chair and rubbed her eyes. The office smelled faintly of coffee gone cold and old paper. She reached for her mug, found it empty, and stood to refill it.

Her phone buzzed.

A text from Lena.

Lena: I hope you got some rest. You looked like you hadn't slept in a week. Did you talk to Oz yet?

Ruth snorted and typed back.

Ruth: You always want me to talk to the guy.

Almost immediately, the reply came.

Lena: Because it's always true when I do. □

Lena: You were working all weekend. And yes, please tell me he kept you up. At least this one emails you back.

Ruth: It's Monday. I have too much to do to keep this up.

Lena: That's not a defense. ☺

Ruth left her on read.

An email notification flashed in the corner of her screen—Malik, subject line: Ordinary men. She clicked it open.

I was walking home and watched our UPS guy make three stops on my block, he'd written. I see him every week and couldn't tell you his name. If someone like him started running messages, I don't think any of us would notice until he was gone.

Ruth stared at it for a moment, then flagged it for later. They were starting to see it too.

Thirty minutes passed.

Another buzz.

Lena: You're different.

Ruth stiffened and typed.

Ruth: Different how?

Lena: Quieter.

Lena: And you keep checking your email like it might explode.

Ruth: I'm waiting on correspondence.

Lena: Uh-huh.

Lena: Is it the archive guy?

Ruth: Yes.

A pause.

Lena: You're lying.

Ruth: I AM NOT.

Lena responded with a single wink.

Lena: You get defensive when it's personal.

Lena: And you don't usually let your work get personal.

Ruth exhaled and set the phone down.

It's not like that, she typed—then deleted it.

Another chime from her laptop.

Oz again.

Exactly.

Ordinariness is camouflage.

Drivers don't get remembered. They get replaced.

Ruth stared at the line.

Then she picked up her phone and typed.

Ruth: You're impossible.

The reply came slower this time.

Lena: And you're lonely.

Lena: And tired.

Lena: And carrying something you don't want to carry alone.

Ruth didn't respond.

She didn't need to.

She turned back to the laptop and typed one final reply.

If this is camouflage, then the question isn't how he survived.

It's how long men like this are allowed to.
She shut the laptop before the answer could arrive.

23

Chapter 23

The room was too bright for the subject matter.

Ruth noticed it immediately—the way fluorescent light flattened everything it touched, turning faces pale and papers lifeless. The seminar room was full, more than usual. Faculty along the back wall. Graduate students clustered near the windows. Someone had brought coffee that smelled burned.

She hadn't been warned.

The agenda slide at the front of the room read:

ARCHIVAL ATTRIBUTION & NARRATIVE AUTHENTICITY

Case Study Discussion

Her case study.

Ruth took her seat without comment, notebook closed, pen resting untouched on top. She scanned the room out of habit, noting who avoided her eyes and who didn't bother pretending.

Eric sat two rows ahead, leaning back, one ankle hooked over his knee. He wasn't smiling. That was new.

The moderator cleared his throat. "Thank you all for coming. This won't take long."

It already had.

"The purpose of today's discussion," he continued, "is to address questions that have arisen regarding the Joseph journals and their representational framing."

Representational.

Ruth felt the word settle like grit.

"As you know," he went on, "the materials have generated significant interest. That also brings scrutiny. Particularly around attribution, authorship, and—"

"Replaceability," Eric said, cutting in.

A few heads turned.

The moderator hesitated, then nodded. "Yes. Replaceability."

Ruth didn't move.

Eric leaned forward now, hands clasped loosely. "What we're circling," he said, "isn't whether the events occurred. We've largely accepted that similar actions took place across multiple resistance cells. Supply movement. Message passing. Route monitoring."

He glanced back at Ruth briefly, then returned his attention to the room.

"The issue is whether Joseph represents a singular actor or a narrative consolidation."

There it was.

"If the function is shared," Eric continued, "and the behavior aligns with documented roles—couriers, drivers, intermediaries—then insisting on Joseph as the actor becomes... problematic."

Problematic.

Ruth's jaw tightened.

A faculty member near the window spoke up. "Are you suggesting fabrication?"

"No," Eric said quickly. "I'm suggesting emphasis. Editorial emphasis."

He shrugged slightly, the gesture almost apologetic.

"The journal may be authentic. But authenticity doesn't guarantee exclusivity. In fact, what makes the account compelling may also make it... representative."

Ruth felt the room shift.

Representative meant interchangeable.

She raised her hand.

The moderator nodded. "Dr. Peters."

Ruth stood.

She hadn't planned what to say. That, too, was new.

"You're arguing," she said evenly, "that because Joseph's actions align with known resistance patterns, he matters less."

Eric opened his mouth, but she didn't stop.

"That because others did similar work, his voice is redundant. Replaceable."

She let the word hang.

"That's not a historical argument," she said. "It's a moral one disguised as methodology."

A ripple moved through the room.

Eric frowned. "That's not fair."

"No," Ruth said. "It's precise."

She gestured toward the screen. "The reason Joseph reads as ordinary is because he chose to be. Because survival required it. Because visibility was a liability."

She paused, aware of how fast her heart was beating.

"If you strip him of authorship because he succeeded at erasing himself, you're not correcting the record," she said. "You're completing the work of the regime that hunted him."

Silence.

The moderator cleared his throat again. "Let's—"

"Joseph doesn't disappear because he didn't exist," Ruth said. "He disappears because people like him were not meant to be remembered."

Eric stood now, expression tight. "You're projecting."

"No," Ruth said. "I'm reading."

The room felt suddenly smaller.

The moderator stepped in, voice calm. "We appreciate your perspective, Dr. Peters. But the question remains—without corroboration, how do we responsibly frame this material?"

Responsibly.

Ruth sat. She didn't answer. Because for the first time, she understood the real danger.

It wasn't that Joseph would be disproven.

It was that he would be accepted and diminished.

The meeting dissolved soon after, conversation breaking into smaller knots. Ruth gathered her things slowly, letting others pass. No one spoke to her directly. In the hallway, she leaned against the wall and closed her eyes.

Courier. Driver. Status unknown.

She pulled out her phone.

Oz's last message was still there, unread since the meeting began.

She didn't open it. Not yet. Instead, she opened her notes app and typed a single line:

If he was ordinary, then history will not protect him.

She stared at it. Then added:

And neither will I, if I'm not careful.

She locked the screen and pushed off the wall. Whatever came next, it would not stay academic.

Ruth didn't go back to her office.

She walked instead, down the long corridor that connected the faculty wing to the older stacks, where the ceilings lowered and the walls absorbed sound. It was quieter there. Less performative. She needed the quiet to settle the static still buzzing behind her eyes.

Her phone vibrated in her hand. Oz. She hesitated, thumb hovering. Then answered, "Hi," surprised by how steady her voice sounded.

"I saw the calendar entry," Oz said. "I figured something happened."

Of course he had.

She exhaled slowly. "They turned it into a case study."

There was a pause. Not the awkward kind. The listening kind.

"About Joseph?" he asked.

"About whether he mattered."

Another pause. Longer this time.

"That's not the same question," Oz said finally.

"No," Ruth said. "But it's the one they asked."

She leaned against the wall, feeling the cool of the stone through her jacket. Students passed at the far end of the corridor, voices low, lives uninterrupted.

"They weren't hostile," she continued. "That would've been easier. They were... tidy about it. Careful. As if they were doing him a favor by reducing him."

Oz made a quiet sound she couldn't quite place. Not disagreement. Recognition.

"They called him representative," she said. "Replaceable. As if that settles it."

"It settles something," Oz said. "Just not what they think."

Ruth closed her eyes. For a moment, neither of them spoke.

Then Oz said, "You know what struck me today?"

She waited.

"They're right about one thing," he said. "If Joseph did what others did, then proving him doesn't elevate him. It contextualizes him."

"That's what they said."

"But they missed the consequence," Oz replied. "Context doesn't dilute responsibility. It multiplies it."

Ruth swallowed. "They don't want responsibility," she said. "They want containment. A clean narrative."

"And you won't give it to them."

It wasn't a question.

"No," Ruth said. "I can't. Not anymore."

She hadn't realized that was true until she said it.

Oz didn't rush to respond. When he did, his voice was quieter. "Ruth," he said, "if Joseph exists the way you think he does... then the danger isn't that he disappears."

She waited, heart thudding now.

"The danger," Oz continued, "is that he survives long enough to be erased properly."

Her grip tightened on the phone.

"That's what this is," she said. "Isn't it?"

"Yes."

She laughed softly, without humor. "I spent months trying to prove he was real."

"And now?"

"Now I'm trying to figure out how to keep him intact."

Another silence.

This one felt different.

"He won't let you," Oz said.

"Who?"

"History," he said. "Institutions. Even good ones. They polish things down until they don't cut anymore."

Ruth stared at the floor.

"I don't want him polished," she said. "I want him seen."

Oz didn't answer right away.

When he did, there was no hesitation in his voice.

"Then you're going to have to stop defending him," he said. "And start telling the truth about what happens to men like him."

Ruth closed her eyes.

She could see Joseph now, not in the woods, not running, not hiding. Just driving. Passing through. Being waved on.

"How do I do that," she asked, "without turning him into a warning?"

"You don't," Oz said gently. "You let him be the cost."

The words settled heavily between them. Ruth felt it then—the shift she'd been resisting. This wasn't about winning an argument. It was about choosing what kind of ending Joseph deserved.

"I don't know how this ends," she said.

"I do," Oz replied. "I just don't know when you'll be ready to read it."

She opened her eyes.

"That's not fair."

"No," he said. "But it's honest."

They sat with that.

"I should go," Ruth said finally. "There's... work."

"I know," Oz said. "I'll be here."

After the call ended, Ruth didn't move. She stood there, in the quiet corridor, feeling the weight of what she'd stepped into. Joseph wasn't a mystery anymore; he was a responsibility. And for the first time, she understood that Oz wasn't standing outside the story, reading along. He was already inside it.

24

Chapter 24

March 1944

I was dropping crates when a boy from the abbey slipped a folded note into my hand. There was a pilot hiding near Canteleu. They needed him moved toward the south, to find a road that would carry him, step by step, toward Spain.

The message said only, Take him if you can. Lose him if you must.

Not far from town I reached the crossroads. The road west, toward the coast, was thick with hard checkpoints, the kind where they count every crate and ask where your father was baptized. The road south had posts that barely looked up, or only paused long enough to take an apple from the back.

I turned south.

Outside Canteleu they had him waiting in a ditch, wrapped in a farmer's coat. Under the tarp, surrounded by crates, he was just another shadow. We hardly spoke. Names are a luxury now; the fewer we know, the less we can give away if someone is taken.

He told me to call him Chuck. I doubt that was his real name. His French was broken, but his smile was not.

We hid him in the loft at the farm for two nights. Kate's mother brought extra bread without asking why I suddenly needed a third plate. Her father did not look up at the rafters.

On the third night I took him as far south as I dared, to a narrow lane where another guide was meant to meet us. At the edge of the ditch he gripped my hand once.

"If we make it," he said in rough French, "I'll owe you a drink."

I told him to make it first. Then we would see.

The entry was still on the screen when Ruth walked into the classroom.

Another day of debate, she thought.

She set her bag down where she could either take the board or retreat to the desk, depending on which way the room tilted.

"Ah, Ruth, have a seat. We have something here that might surprise you. It did me," Dr. Peters said, gesturing toward the front. His tone was neutral, but his eyes weren't. Something was already in motion.

Students filtered in with their usual shuffle of backpacks and whispered side conversations. When everyone had settled and the door clicked shut, Peters nodded to Eric.

"I think we have something here that might push our argument one way or the other," Eric began. He walked to the board and tapped the projected page. "This entry, I came across in my last visit to the library office."

Ruth's stomach tightened. She had read past March in a blur after the last fight with Eric, but she hadn't sat with this passage. Seeing it enlarged, "Chuck" highlighted in the middle of Joseph's careful handwriting, she felt a flash of anger at herself for not having prepared an answer.

Just as she shifted in her chair, ready to stand and defend Joseph, Eric slid the next screen into place.

An official after-action report header filled the board: 357th Fighter Group.

"When I read this entry," Eric said, "I thought I'd finally found the piece that proves Joseph is an allegory."

Ruth's pulse spiked.

"If you haven't thought of who 'Chuck' could be," he went on, "let me remind you of Chuck Yeager."

A few students exhaled sharply. Others broke into a low buzz of whispers. Even the ones who couldn't remember the details knew the name: shot down over France, rescued by the resistance, later famous for other reasons.

"To claim he was helping Chuck Yeager felt too cinematic," Eric said. "I was ready to say it all but proved I was right."

He let the sentence hang there, the but turning in the air.

"Then I found this."

He stepped aside and pointed to a paragraph in the report, already underlined.

"I was near Rouen when I was smuggled to a farm for a few days, and then south," he read aloud. "The driver named Joseph fed me and hid me. The family was him, his wife, and her parents."

The room went very still.

For a long second, Ruth didn't move. Joseph's words and the report's words sat side by side in her mind: the ditch, the loft, the road south, Kate's parents, the nameless pilot with broken French and a promise of a drink.

Her throat felt dry. Whatever she said next would tilt the whole conversation.

"Alright," Ruth said at last, forcing her voice to stay level. "So our options just got more complicated. Either someone built a very convincing fiction out of this report, or Joseph and this pilot actually crossed paths."

She looked from the after-action sheet back to the journal on the screen.

"In either case," she went on, "we don't get to use 'Chuck' as a cheap cameo. We treat both accounts as witnesses. We ask where they overlap, where they don't, and what that does to our neat little categories."

A few heads nodded slowly. The initial buzz in the room shifted into something more thoughtful.

"And for the record," she added, glancing at Eric, "thank you for bringing the report instead of just the punchline."

It wasn't smug. It was honest. The corner of his mouth twitched.

After class, the students drifted out in small knots, still arguing quietly. Eric stayed behind, hovering near the front row until the last backpack disappeared through the door.

"I really thought this would sink him," he admitted, tapping the 357th header with a knuckle. "Make him look like a fanfic. Instead..."

"Instead you rescued him," Ruth said before she could stop herself.

Eric blinked. "Rescued who?"

"Joseph," she said. "From sounding too cinematic." She shrugged once. "And you rescued me from sounding like I'd fallen for a story with no anchor."

He looked down at the paper again, something wary but genuine in his face. "I never wanted to kill Joseph," he said. "I really wanted to make sure we did our due diligence before putting him out into a world that would want to play gotcha."

Ruth stood in silence for a beat, letting the moment stretch.

"I'm not sure I can let my guard down yet," she said, "but I definitely feel a little lighter."

"For what it's worth," he said, "I still think we have to keep pushing on attribution. But I'm... less sure he's just a composite. Or that you're just believing because you want to."

The admission landed heavier than she expected.

"Then we're both doing our jobs," she said quietly. "You keep pressing. I'll keep refusing to let the wall have the last word."

He gave a short, almost respectful nod.

"Fair enough," he said, and left her alone with the journal and the report between them.

In the research room a few minutes later, Ruth dropped both documents on the table: Joseph's "Chuck" entry and the 357th paragraph side by side.

He thought he was going to gut you, she told the journal silently. Instead he pulled you out of the ditch. This Eric is harder to dislike.

Her laptop chimed. At the top of her inbox, Oz's name waited with a new subject line.

Ruth stared at the screen a moment longer, Oz's lines about the attic and "your vineyard boy" blurring with the 357th report still open on her desk. Her chest felt crowded—relief, validation, and something else she didn't want to name yet.

She typed You won't believe what my student found today and deleted it, unsure whether she wanted him in the middle of her Eric-shaped gratitude.

She picked up her phone instead and typed:

I need a debrief.

Joseph might have met someone famous. Eric finally stopped trying to kill him. And I think I'm in more trouble than I thought with a certain French innkeeper.

The typing dots appeared almost immediately. Ruth watched them bounce and thought, Oz is so far away, it would never work, the thought the main thing she was willing to name while she tried to push Lena off their connection.

Popcorn and triage tonight? Lena replied.

I'll bring the snacks. You bring the emotional crisis.

Ruth exhaled, half laugh, half sigh.

Deal, she wrote back.

For once, she left the journal sleeping on the table and walked out with only her keys and phone. Tonight, the roads she needed to walk were between her and Lena, not between Rouen and Spain.

25

Chapter 25

Later that night, Ruth sat on Lena's sagging couch with a bowl of popcorn between them, a movie flickering on mute more for light than for attention. Lena had one leg tucked under her, but her focus was clearly on Ruth, not the screen.

"So," Lena said, stretching the word out, "you are officially in trouble with three different men, one of them technically being dead."

Ruth snorted. "They're not—"

"Joseph, Oz, Eric," Lena counted off on her fingers. "Ghost boy in the vines whose journal you smuggled home, cemetery caretaker with cheekbones and generational trauma, and seminar nemesis who just discovered humility and Google Drive comments. Tell me I'm wrong."

Ruth sank deeper into the cushion, staring at a kernel she'd been rolling between her fingers as if it might offer an escape route.

"I don't know if 'in trouble' is the right phrase," she muttered.

Lena arched an eyebrow. "You texted me 'EMOTIONAL CRISIS' in all caps from the airport. Start with the dead guy. Then we'll get to the breathing complications."

Ruth blew out a breath. "Dead guy," she echoed. "Right. I should probably clarify that before you start planning ghost-therapy sessions or smudging my apartment."

Lena's mouth curved. "Clarify away."

"He's not—" Ruth stopped, pinching the bridge of her nose. "It's not like I'm in love with a spirit guide. Joseph is... homework that grew a conscience. I bought his journal like it was a quirky souvenir, shoved it in my carry-on, and now he's living rent-free in my head."

“So: emotional support dead Frenchman,” Lena summarized. “Got it. Continue.”

“The journal feels like a responsibility,” Ruth said, her voice dropping. “If I turn it into a project, my whole life gets carved into ‘before I opened that drawer’ and ‘after I followed him to Rouen and the vineyard.’ If I don’t, it’s like I shoved him back into the dark and pretended I never saw his family’s burial list.”

Lena let the joke fall away, studying her. “Okay,” she said quietly. “That’s one.”

Ruth closed her eyes. “Oz is... different.”

“The cemetery caretaker with cheekbones and a tragic backstory,” Lena supplied. “The one who tends your dead guy’s family graves and runs a bed-and-breakfast ten kilometers away. Proceed.”

“He’s not tragic,” Ruth protested. “He just—he treats that oak like a relative. He knows which families still visit, which names never get flowers, which stones chip when he tries to clean them. Standing there with him felt... I don’t know. Like the land had witnesses, and I accidentally became one of them.”

“And you maybe wanted to climb him like the oak,” Lena muttered.

Ruth choked on a laugh. “Lena.”

“What?” Lena shrugged. “You stood next to a guy who understands why grave dirt matters and why unmarked burials still count. In your world, that’s basically foreplay.”

Ruth let her head fall back against the cushion. “He lives an ocean away.” She ticked it off like a list. “He has a business, a family, roots. I have a one-bedroom, a syllabus, and a return ticket that already brought me back to Oklahoma. Whatever... spark there was is real, but it’s not the point. Joseph is the point. His journal. His family. The people he led west.”

“Joseph is a point,” Lena said. “Ozias is another. You’re allowed to plot more than one data set at a time, Professor.”

Ruth winced. “Which brings us to complication number three.”

“Ah, yes,” Lena said, tone sharpening with interest. “Monsieur Humility. Tell me about Eric suddenly discovering self-awareness and footnotes.”

Ruth stared at the mute TV, watching light shift across the ceiling. “He emailed before I got on the plane,” she said. “Long apology. He said he’d read my conference paper, that he’d been a jerk in seminar, that he didn’t realize how much he'd been parroting other people's work and steamrolling mine."

"And?" Lena prompted.

"And then he offered to help," Ruth said. "Funding leads, archive contacts, feedback if I want to write on Joseph. He attached actual line-by-line notes on my draft like he'd listened to my argument instead of waiting for his turn to talk. Very collegial. Very supportive. Very confusing."

Lena narrowed her eyes. "What did you feel when you read it?"

"Suspicious," Ruth said immediately. "Then irritated. Then... weirdly seen. He flagged a source I'd been second-guessing and suggested an angle I'd only scribbled in the margin. That's new."

"So now your options are," Lena ticked them off, "one, devote your life to a dead man whose journal might become your thesis, your book, or your midlife crisis; two, pine politely over a French caretaker you may never see again but who knows where every Durand is buried; three, possibly collaborate with, befriend, or make out with a reformed academic rival who suddenly wants to boost your career."

Ruth groaned into her hands. "When you say it like that, I sound unhinged."

"You sound like a woman standing at three different runways," Lena corrected. "Ghost, vineyard, seminar room. All of them pointing backward into history and forward into your future at the same time."

Ruth let that settle, the only sound the faint crackle from the TV and the soft rustle of popcorn as Lena shifted.

"I don't know how to pick," Ruth admitted. "Or if I'm supposed to pick. It feels like if I lean into one, I betray the others."

"Maybe you don't pick yet," Lena said. "Maybe you start smaller."

Ruth glanced over. "Smaller how?"

"Pilot project first," Lena said. "You don't have to map your entire life tonight. You just have to take the first non-dramatic steps."

Ruth squinted at her. "Examples, please, before my brain turns this into a dissertation proposal."

"Administrative Ruth first," Lena said, counting on her fingers. "Email Father Laurent, thank him, and ask what he knows about legal and ethical ownership of war-era journals. Email Claire, send her a proper thank-you and maybe a scan or copy of that burial list and baptism record, so she knows you see her family's side of this too. Then write down what you actually want from Joseph: is this a thesis, an article, a book, a public history project, or just a promise not to forget him?"

Ruth swallowed. "And Oz?"

"Reply to his last message like a normal human being," Lena said. "Tell him you got home and survived your family pot roast gauntlet. Ask how the vines and the graves are. If it fizzles, it fizzles. If it doesn't, you can deal with that version of complicated when it actually exists, not just in your head."

Ruth considered that, tension easing a fraction from her shoulders. "And Eric?" she asked.

Lena popped a kernel into her mouth, eyes glinting. "Make him prove it. Let him send you those funding leads, connect you with that archive in Rouen, read the next draft. If he's serious about not being a jerk, he'll stick around whether you ever touch his hair or not. Your job is to treat him like a colleague until he earns an upgrade."

Ruth laughed, helpless and a little hoarse. "You skipped right to touching his hair?"

"I've sat through enough of his monologues to know that's where you'd go if he ever shut up long enough," Lena said. "Besides, you're the historian. I'm just here to document the era in which Ruth finally lets more than one person matter at once—the dead, the distant, and the irritatingly helpful."

Ruth leaned her head against Lena's shoulder. "I hate that you're good at this."

"You love that I'm good at this," Lena corrected softly. "You're not in trouble with three men. You're just standing at the part of the story where the threads start crossing—Joseph's past, Oz's vineyard, Eric's emails, all tugging on the same part of you."

"Feels like turbulence," Ruth murmured.

"Good thing," Lena said, nudging the bowl toward her, "you've already proven you're fine with long flights."

26

Chapter 26

The next day, Ruth noticed the calendar reminder blinking at her from the corner of the screen.

DEPARTMENT MEETING – PROJECT REVIEW

3:00–3:45 p.m.

Location: Chair's Office

She blinked, then checked the time. 2:53.

Of course.

The journal lay closed beside her keyboard, the weight of it familiar now, an extra limb or a borrowed organ. On the monitor, her gradebook stared back at her, rows of names and half-filled columns waiting for the last participation notes and assignment scores. Mid-November already. A few more weeks, and she'd owe the registrar a neat set of numbers for a semester that had been anything but neat.

She closed the gradebook tab and reached automatically for the journal, then stopped herself halfway. No. Not this time. She slid it gently into her bag instead, the leather thudding softly against the bottom.

When she stepped into the hallway, the light had shifted to that late-afternoon gray that made the building feel more like a waiting room than a place of learning. Students moved in clumps toward the exit, voices low, backpacks slung over one shoulder. One or two nodded when they saw her, the uneasy half-smiles of people who had spent weeks discussing a dead Frenchman and weren't yet sure how normal to act about it.

On the second floor, the door to the department chair's office stood half open.

Inside, the air felt overheated, as if the vents had mistaken Oklahoma fall for January. Dr. Peters sat in the chair closest to the window, jacket folded over his lap like a shield. Beside him, the associate dean of arts and sciences—Dr. Malik today, not the dean himself—scrolled through something on a tablet. The department chair, Dr. Singh, glanced up from a printed agenda as Ruth stepped in.

"Ruth. Thank you for coming," Singh said. "Come, have a seat."

That tone, Ruth thought. The one they used when telling undergraduates they weren't in trouble, exactly, but there were concerns.

She sat in the empty chair opposite the desk, bag resting at her feet. She could feel the journal through the canvas, like a pulse.

"We'll keep this brief," Singh began. "I know it's the end of the day, and we're all juggling too many balls at once."

Ruth folded her hands in her lap. "Sure."

Peters offered a small, encouraging nod. His eyes were softer than they had been in the seminar showdown. Witness, not prosecutor.

Malik set the tablet down, steepling his fingers. "I've been hearing interesting things about your seminar, Dr. Peters," he said. "Both of you, actually. Quite the... experiment."

Ruth's mouth went dry. Experiment was not her favorite word in the context of students and a wartime journal.

Singh clicked her pen. "The seminar has been a success in many ways," she said quickly. "High engagement, strong work from the students, very positive course chatter. But it's also raised some questions. And as we look toward the close of the semester, we need a clearer sense of what this project is, institutionally speaking."

There it was.

Ruth tried to keep her voice even. "You mean beyond the course itself."

"Exactly," Malik said. "There are two concerns, really. One, we need to be sure we can fairly assess student outcomes before the term ends. Two, the university's research committee has expressed interest in supporting your work on the Durand materials, but they'll need a more formal proposal."

Ruth's heart ticked faster. Interest, she thought. That was new. Terrifying, but new.

"I thought this was just going to be a pilot," she said. "A special topics seminar while I figured out what, if anything, I could responsibly build from the journal."

"It can remain that," Peters said mildly. "But pilots either land or reroute. They don't circle forever."

Singh slid a single sheet across the desk. At the top, Ruth recognized the university's internal grant letterhead. Her name was highlighted in yellow.

"The committee's seen the summary Dr. Peters forwarded about your find," Singh said. "The journal, the Rouen archives, the vineyard, the corroborating documents. They think there's something here—possibly a monograph, possibly a collaborative digital project with the library. But they need to know what you want this to be. And we, as your department, need to know how you're framing it when you put our name on it."

Ruth stared at the page. The words swam for a moment: early-career support, emerging research, narrative authenticity, risk assessment.

"So what are you asking me for, exactly?" she said.

Peters leaned forward slightly, elbows on his knees. "A project statement," he said. "Nothing enormous. Two pages, maybe three. How you plan to treat the journal in your scholarship. How you've framed it for the seminar. What claims you're prepared to make, and how you intend to support them."

"And," Malik added, "what level of evidentiary caution you're committing to. Remember, the more central Joseph becomes as a singular actor, the more the institution has to be comfortable putting its weight behind him."

There was that word again. Singular.

"You've already seen the tension," Peters said quietly. "In the case-study discussion. Between treating him as representative and treating him as... specific."

"Replaceable versus responsible," Ruth said before she could stop herself.

Peters's mouth twitched. His eyes met hers, acknowledging the line she'd thrown in that day, and its staying power.

"We can't answer that question for you," he said. "But we need to know which way you're leaning."

Ruth felt suddenly aware of Oz's last email waiting unread at the top of her inbox, of Eric's after-action report printout still folded between pages of her notes. The room's fluorescent light seemed to flatten everything the way it had in the seminar: faces pale, papers lifeless.

"And what about the students?" she asked. "They signed up for a seminar on wartime testimonies. They didn't consent to being co-opted into a political fight over one journal."

"No one's asking them to," Singh said. "But how you write the course up in your end-of-semester report needs to match the way you describe the project to the committee. If you sell this as a neutral exploration of narrative, but your assignments implicitly treat Joseph as proven singular hero, that's going to be a mismatch."

Ruth bristled. "I have never called him a hero in class."

"No," Peters said. "You've been very careful. But you and I both know that caution has limits. Your last session walked right up to them." He glanced at Malik. "That's why we thought now was the right time to ask you to articulate your stance."

Malik spread his hands, palms up. "Think of this as protecting you," he said. "And the work. If we send an application upstairs that says, in effect, 'We have discovered a previously unknown singular resistance figure and will now center him in our research,' we'd better have a strong justificatory framework. If, instead, we say, 'We're using a journal, likely representative, to explore anonymity, ordinary courage, and memory,' that's a different risk profile."

And a different outcome, Ruth thought. One where Joseph was not a man but a motif.

She swallowed. "What are the parameters?" she asked. "What do you need to see in this statement?"

Singh ticked them off on her fingers.

"One, a clear description of the material—journal provenance, corroborating documents, gaps.

"Two, your framing of authorship and attribution. Is he a composite? A likely individual? Something in between?

"Three, your ethical approach. Families, ownership, trauma, representation. We don't want to be blindsided by a letter from a Durand descendant or the Marchands, or a complaint that we've appropriated someone's grandfather for tenure points.

"And four," Malik added, "your pedagogical stance. How you've presented all this to your students. Because the committee will ask, and we'll need to stand behind whatever you've already done once they read the syllabus."

Ruth's hand drifted unconsciously toward her bag, fingers brushing the canvas above the journal.

"And the timeline?" she said.

A shadow of apology crossed Singh's face. "End of next week," she said. "The committee meets the following Monday. If we get it in their hands by then, you're eligible for spring and summer support. Travel, a course release, maybe even a graduate assistant."

Course release. A graduate assistant. Concrete help where badly wanted abstraction had been living for months.

"You're also at the point in the semester where you have to finalize your grading schema for this course," Malik said. "If your project statement says, 'We treat Joseph as X,' but your rubric implicitly treats him as Y, students will sense that disconnect. And the administration might, too."

"So I have a week to decide whether I flatten him," Ruth said. Her voice came out flatter than she intended.

"You have a week to decide how you will talk about him," Peters said gently. "Which is not the same thing. But yes. The window is narrow."

Silence settled for a moment. The hum of the vent, the tick of the small analog clock on Singh's bookshelf, the faint echo of a copier down the hall all pressed around them.

"We're not trying to trap you, Ruth," Malik said. "The fact that we're even having this conversation is a sign of trust. Most early-career faculty would kill for a committee reaching out like this."

"I know," Ruth said. "And I do appreciate the support. It's just..." Her throat tightened. "Most people don't have to choose how much to endanger a dead man when they fill out a grant form."

Peters's gaze sharpened, then softened. "The choice isn't whether to endanger him," he said quietly. "It's whether to let the institution participate in the erasure you've already named."

Ruth looked at him. "That's not making this easier."

"It's not meant to," he said.

Singh slid the letter a little closer to her.

"Can you do it?" she asked. "Two or three pages. By Friday?"

Ruth thought of Lena's voice: pilot project first. Start smaller. Then of Oz's: If Joseph exists the way you think he does, the danger isn't that he disappears. It's that he survives long enough to be erased properly. Then

Eric's hesitant admission: I never wanted to kill Joseph. I just wanted to do due diligence before the world tried to play gotcha.

"Yes," Ruth said slowly. "I can do it."

"Good," Malik said. "And, off the record, I'll say this—I've sat through a lot of proposals. Most of them don't have half the spine yours will, whichever way you go."

Ruth managed the ghost of a smile. "That's both comforting and terrifying."

"Welcome to research," Singh said wryly. "We'll look for your statement by end of day Friday. Send it to me and Dr. Peters; we'll get it in shape for the committee."

They rose together. Papers rustled, the meeting's spell breaking as everyone reached for their next obligations.

At the door, Peters touched her elbow lightly. "If you'd like to talk through options," he said, "I'm free tomorrow afternoon. We can take a walk or hide in the seminar room. Whatever feels less like being put under a microscope."

Ruth nodded, throat thick. "I might take you up on that."

He gave a short nod. "Then you know where I'll be."

In the hallway again, the building felt cooler, though the thermostat hadn't budged. Students' voices floated from a nearby classroom—something about extra credit, about whether a quiz was cumulative. Ordinary concerns. Replaceable worries.

Ruth walked back to her office, closed the door and leaned against it, letting her bag slip to the floor. The journal thumped softly against the carpet.

She sank into her chair and pulled the grant letter toward her. End of next week. Framing. Attribution. Ethics. Pedagogy.

Her notebook lay open where she'd left it, a line from the case-study day underlined twice: If he was ordinary, then history will not protect him. And neither will I, if I'm not careful.

She uncapped her pen and, beneath that sentence, wrote a single new line.

Decide who I'm willing to lose.

Then, below that, three words stacked like a list she didn't yet want to admit was real.

Oz.

Eric.

Joseph.

She set the pen down, heart pounding. For the first time, the question wasn't just who Joseph would be on paper.

It was who she would be when she signed her name under his.

27

Chapter 27

Shortly after getting back to her office, Ruth opened her computer to the familiar ding.

From: Ozias Marchand

Subject: You asked about my grandfather

Ruth's fingers stilled on the trackpad.

She'd written "Decide who I'm willing to lose" in her notebook not ten minutes earlier, her own list of names staring back at her. Oz. Eric. Joseph.

Perfect timing, she thought, hearing Lena's voice.

She clicked.

Ruth,

I've been thinking about our last conversation. You were discussing the challenge with proving Joseph to be a real singular person. I might be able to help a little more directly, or at least point to someone.

My aunt, my mom's cousin, and her daughter came to visit last year after her father died. She brought his ashes and some personal items. We buried them at the cemetery under one of the stones.

Not one of the Durands. The one next to them, the one you touched without knowing, the day you stood under the oak and asked why the letters were so worn.

Her father was David. David met her mother because of the escape, the march through the forest, the drive toward the coast while the Nazis were looking the other way.

They made it to England first, then on to America after the war was over. He didn't talk about it much, from what she says. But when he did, he always came back to the same two points:

There was a boy from a vineyard who refused to leave them behind.

That boy's name was Joseph Durand.

My aunt told me this at the graveside. I think she was surprised I didn't already know. She said, "You keep this place tidy, you should know whose shadow you're sweeping." Then she put the urn down and said, "If that French boy hadn't come back for my father, I wouldn't be here to bury him."

You can probably imagine what that did to my sense of "representative courier."

I got her permission to pass her contact information to you. She lives in the States now. She said, "If your historian friend wants to hear it from someone who was raised on the story, she can call me. I won't have dates and ranks for her, but I'll have the parts my father couldn't stop seeing when he closed his eyes."

I know this isn't the kind of corroboration that lets you write 'archival confirmation' in your margins. It's another voice, another memory. But this time, the voice belongs to someone whose whole life was built on the fact that a specific boy from a specific vineyard took a risk.

Whatever you decide to call Joseph in your work—composite, singular, something in between—remember that for one family in America and one branch of mine here, he already has a name, a face, and a grave they chose on purpose.

Her email and permission are below. Use them if and how you see fit.

No pressure, of course. Just an innkeeper adding one more weight to your scale.

Oz.

Ruth rubbed at the bridge of her nose, the words tilting the room a few degrees.

Her father was David. If that French boy hadn't come back for my father, I wouldn't be here.

Oz had just casually handed her exactly what the department kept asking for and what she'd been telling herself might not exist: a living, reachable person whose family narrative lined up almost perfectly with the journal's bones.

Another ding. A text.

Lena: You okay, or did the meeting eat you?

Ruth typed with her thumbs before she could talk herself out of it.

Ruth: Dept wants a proposal that defines what kind of "thing" Joseph is. Oz just sent me the contact for David's daughter. "If that French boy hadn't come back for my father, I wouldn't be here." Direct quote.

There was a pause. Then:

Lena: Oh.

Lena: So the universe is not being subtle.

Ruth huffed out a breath that wasn't quite a laugh.

Ruth: Apparently not.

Lena: File under "reasons representative sounds like a lie now."

Ruth looked back at the email, at the promise of a voice on the other end of a phone line in America who had grown up with "Joseph Durand" as a fact, not a footnote.

Safe, she thought, was getting narrower by the minute.

Ruth stared at her own words, a fresh flush of embarrassment creeping up her neck.

Ruth: I can't believe this is only coming out now. I never actually said "Joseph and David" to him in the same sentence. I gave him vibes and vines, not the index.

Lena: Historian fails to share names, news at eleven.

Lena: Beating yourself up is pointless data. Use it instead. Give him the whole list next time.

Ruth winced, because she was right. She'd treated Oz as a witness at the edge of the story, not as someone whose family might already be standing in the middle of it.

She opened a new message before she could talk herself out of it.

From: Ruth Peters

To: Ozias Marchand

Subject: Re: You asked about my grandfather

Oz,

I don't have the right words yet, but thank you—for trusting me enough to pass her name, and for telling me what that stone actually is for your family.

I'm also kicking myself. Until now, I've talked to you about "a boy from the vines" and "families" and "routes," but I never gave you the full set of names on my side. I'm realizing how much I've expected you to help me carry this without handing you the whole weight.

When I catch my breath, I'd like to send you a clearer outline of what's in the journal—who's on the page with Joseph and David, where they are when. If nothing else, it will make sure we're not missing any connections your aunt or your mother might recognize.

For now, please tell her I'm grateful, and that I'll be in touch if she still means it about talking.

Ruth

She hit send before she could soften any of it, then pushed the chair back and reached for the bag on the floor. The journal slid into her hands with the familiar weight of something that no longer felt like an object at all.

If David had a daughter in America who grew up with "Joseph Durand" as a fixed point, then there had to be something in these early pages she'd skimmed past, looking for routes instead of roots.

She flipped to the front, fingers finding the early entries by muscle memory.

April 5, 1940.

David and I spent the day working on the northern slope. The vines are coming in nicely, heavy with promise. If the weather holds, we should have a fine harvest in a few months.

Her pencil paused over the margin. Before, she'd underlined "northern slope," "promise," "fine harvest." Geography, agricultural detail, the calm before the storm.

Now her eye snagged on the way Joseph had written their names together, without explanation, as if anyone reading would obviously know who David was.

David and I.

She turned a few pages.

May 10, 1940.

David told me tonight about the ghettos in Germany... His uncle heard they're sending people east, but no one knows where.

David told me. His uncle. Not mine. The little pronoun had been a clue all along—two families, two worlds, sharing a table while the radio hissed out maps shaded gray.

Ruth flipped again, farther into the section she'd rushed through on the plane.

July 29.

We have made it to a small farming village in the Pays de Caux. When I approached a man in the market for supplies, I told him I needed bread, something to feed a large family. He studied me for a moment, as if he recognized something, my voice, my face... David stayed back with the others near the cart. He doesn't like to be seen in the open anymore. I don't blame him.

She'd circled "Pays de Caux" the first time, pinned it on the map, moved on. Now she underlined "doesn't like to be seen in the open anymore," the tight little sentence that sounded like someone who had already been marked once and had no intention of offering a second clean shot.

At the bottom of the page, in Joseph's cramped hand:

If we make it to the coast, it will be because David keeps their spirits up when I have nothing left to say.

Ruth sat back, the pencil resting against her lip.

A boy from a vineyard who refused to leave them behind.

That boy's name was Joseph Durand.

It wasn't just that the facts lined up. It was the tone. The way Joseph talked about David—like a twin axis, not a side character. Routes and morale. Driving and singing. One without the other wouldn't have been enough.

Her mind slid, unbidden, to Oz's line about his mother and aunt choosing that particular stone because "if he has a grave anywhere, it's here." To the way he moved under the oak, as if the ground there ran through his calves as much as the vineyard soil did.

Maybe, she thought, he was closer to Joseph than even he realized—woven into both lines without being told what that meant. One branch from the cellar, one from the vines, sharing a tree that had become their common language.

She turned back one more page, to the very first mention.

David and I.

In the margin, she wrote, very small:

David = the beginning of Oz.

It was not a genealogical conclusion. It was a narrative one. But as she looked at the neat, deliberate ink of Joseph's hand and thought of the urn in Oz's story, the distance between her research room in Oklahoma and that unmarked stone under the oak felt narrower than it ever had.

28

Chapter 28

Ruth sat with the information spread in front of her, the connections swimming in her head as she thought about the EMOTIONAL CRISIS text she'd sent to Lena what felt like a month ago. Joseph's world was everywhere—Oz's email still glowing in her inbox, David's daughter's name scribbled in the margin, early entries open to "David and I" as if they'd always been waiting for her to notice.

On the left side of the table, she'd laid out the people:

Joseph – vineyard, journal, routes.

David – cellar, march, coast, father of the woman in America.

Oz – innkeeper, graves, grandson of that escape.

"David's daughter" – now a real email address instead of a hypothetical.

On the right, the paper:

The grant letter, with its talk of "risk profile" and "representational framing."

Her notebook, the fresh page where she'd written "Project Statement – Sharp Version" and immediately wanted to throw up.

She pushed back from the table and paced once across the room, then back again. The office was too small for this much past.

"Composite," she muttered. "Representative." The words tasted worse each time. Calling Joseph representative had always bothered her. Now, with a living woman whose entire existence hinged on a specific boy from a specific vineyard, it felt like lying in a language the committee found comfortable.

Her gaze landed on the journal, still open to an early entry.

David and I spent the day working on the northern slope...

"How did I miss you for this long?" she whispered. "How did we miss you?"

The clock on the wall ticked louder than usual. Outside, someone laughed in the hallway, the sound thin through the door. Her phone buzzed once—an email auto-notification from the learning management system—and she ignored it.

She thought of Lena's last text:

File under "reasons representative sounds like a lie now."

And Oz's line:

No pressure, of course. Just an innkeeper adding one more weight to your scale.

"This is a terrible scale," she told the empty room.

A knock on the doorjamb made her jump.

"Ruth?"

She turned. Eric stood in the doorway, one hand braced against the frame, the other holding a folder to his chest. He looked like he'd started the day trying to be professional and then lost a fight with his own tie somewhere around noon.

"Hey," she said. Her voice came out hoarse.

"Can I...?" He nodded toward the inside of the office.

She gestured to the chair across from her. "Come in before the paper avalanche gets you."

He stepped over a stray stack and sat, eyes flicking over the table. "Wow," he said softly. "You've built yourself a command center."

"Feels more like a crash site," she said.

He gave a quick, acknowledging huff of air. "Peters told me about the committee," he said. "The proposal, the deadline."

"Of course he did." She sank back into her own chair. "So you're here as the advance scout for the inquisition?"

He winced. "I probably deserve that," he said. "But no. I'm here because you look like you're about to either solve a major problem or set the building on fire, and I wanted to know which before it happens."

Despite herself, the corner of her mouth twitched. "You have a talent for encouragement."

He nodded toward the nearest page. "New documents?"

"New human," she said. "Oz emailed. He gave me contact for David's daughter. She grew up on stories about 'the boy from the vineyard named

Joseph Durand.' Her father was the David. He told her if that French boy hadn't come back for him, she wouldn't be here."

Eric's eyes widened. He sat back so fast the chair creaked. "Oh."

"Yeah." She tapped her pen against the table. "Oh."

"So your 'representative courier' now has a daughter in America and an innkeeper in Normandy," he said slowly. "That's... a lot of singularity for a composite."

Ruth let out a breath that was almost a laugh. "You're the one who wanted more data. Congratulations."

He rubbed a hand over his face. "I was hoping for cleaner data, not data that proves you right in a way that makes everyone's life more complicated."

"Welcome to history," she said.

He glanced at the grant letter. "How are you doing with all this?"

She stared at him. "You really want to know, or is this the part where you ask how I plan to phrase it in my abstract?"

"I really want to know," he said. "Abstracts come later."

She hesitated, then nodded once. "The department wants me to pick a category," she said. "Composite, cautious singular, or sharp singular with the moral stakes on the table. They want a neat two-page statement that says 'this is what kind of thing Joseph is' so they can decide how much they can afford to stand next to him."

"And you?" he asked.

"I thought I could live with cautious singular," she said. "Enough hedging to keep everybody from having a heart attack. Enough specificity to keep him from becoming a teaching aid." She gestured toward her laptop. "Now I have a woman whose father named Joseph, whose entire life exists because of him."

She met his eyes. "Calling him representative now feels like telling her she's hypothetical."

Eric was quiet for a long moment. "That's not a methodological problem," he said finally. "That's a conscience problem."

"Exactly," she said, the word coming out sharper than she meant. "And the committee is going to want me to pretend it's only the first one."

He opened the folder on his lap, then paused. "I brought you something," he said. "It's not an answer. But it's... me trying not to duck the conscience part."

He slid a thin draft across the table. She glanced at the title and had to blink.

"'Ordinary as Camouflage: Reading Anonymity and Responsibility in Resistance Diaries,'" she read. "You stole my line."

"Borrowed," he said. "With attribution. Check the epigraph."

She flipped to the top of the first page and saw a quote from her conference paper staring back at her.

"You're... writing on my argument," she said.

"I'm trying to," he said. "I've been replaying that colloquium. The way I used 'replaceable' sounded very clever in my head and very ugly when you answered me."

He took a breath. "I still think we have to be careful about what we claim. If you walk into the committee and declare Joseph fully proven with no gaps, I'll push back. That's my job. But I'm not comfortable anymore with 'composite' as the safe option. And 'representative'..." He shook his head. "I'm starting to see how much that word lets people like me off the hook."

Ruth stared at him. "You're actually admitting that out loud."

He gave a crooked half-smile. "Don't get used to it. But yes."

She skimmed a paragraph in the middle of his draft. One sentence snagged her eye.

"To label such a figure 'replaceable' is not a neutral act; it redistributes responsibility from specific hands and institutions onto a faceless many, offering safety to those who prefer abstraction over accountability."

She looked up. "You wrote this?"

"With your voice heckling me over my shoulder," he said. "And Oz, weirdly. I keep thinking about your line—'If you strip him of authorship because he succeeded at erasing himself, you're completing the regime's work'—and his about institutions polishing away the edges. It's... hard to unhear."

Ruth swallowed against the burn in her throat. "You know the committee is going to assume you're on their side."

"I know," he said. "And I'll tell them what I'm telling you. You can't pretend there's more evidence than there is. But you also can't pretend that being vague is neutral. If they want someone to argue that 'representative' is the only respectable stance, they're going to have to find a different Eric."

She let out a slow breath. "Why?" she asked quietly. "You could have stayed the skeptic and looked very respectable."

He looked down at his hands. "Because I don't want to be the guy David's daughter reads someday and thinks, 'That's the man who turned my father's story into a category,'" he said. "And because... I'd like you to still want to work with me when this is over."

Her heart gave a disconcerting little stutter. "Work with you," she repeated.

"On the project," he said quickly. "On Joseph. On the bigger questions. I know I've made this harder. But if you decide to go with the sharp version, you're going to need someone in the boring rooms saying you're not just a zealot with a pet source."

"You're offering to be my boring-room person," she said.

"I prefer 'methodological ballast,'" he said. "But yes."

She looked back down at his draft, then at Oz's email on her screen, then at the grant letter. The triangle they formed felt suddenly, terrifyingly real.

"I don't need you to agree with me," she said. "I need you to understand why this can't just be another case study."

"I do," he said. "More than I did at the start of the semester, that's for sure."

He stood, gathering his folder. "I'll let you get back to your vortex," he said. At the door, he hesitated. "Just... don't forget you're allowed to admit what you want, too. Not just what you can defend."

She frowned. "What do you mean?"

"You want Joseph to be real," he said simply. "You want David's daughter's story to line up. You want Oz's stone to be the right one. That doesn't disqualify you. It just means you're honest about what's at stake for you."

She felt her throat tighten. "I hate it when you sound like my conscience."

"Good," he said, a small smile tugging at his mouth. "Means I'm doing my job."

The moment between them wasn't awkward, exactly—just unexpected. She'd never planned for this version of Eric, the one who could interrogate his own language and hand her a draft that echoed her arguments back to her.

He shifted his folder under one arm. "Well," he said softly, "see you later."

When the door clicked shut behind him, the room didn't feel calmer, exactly. But the chaos had a new axis. Oz's email, David's daughter, Eric's reluctant solidarity, the committee's deadline—they all pointed toward the same question.

She turned to a clean page in her notebook and wrote, under "Project Statement – Sharp Version":

Not neutral. Not safe. But honest.

For the first time, the words felt like something she might actually be able to sign her name under.

29

Chapter 29

The room felt smaller than usual. The low drone of the air ducts, the muffled voices in the hallway, the click of the clock over the door—all of it just made the quiet inside her head louder. Some days a packed classroom was easier than this; noise gave her somewhere to put her attention. Silence left too much space for the three men crowding her thoughts to jostle for position.

Joseph, with his careful, limited pages and roads that never seemed to end.

Oz, somewhere on a French cliff with crates and logbooks and emails that landed warmer than they should.

Eric, suddenly less of an adversary and more of a colleague than she was ready for.

Ruth shifted in her chair and stared at the journal on the desk, pretending it was the only one of them that mattered.

On the computer screen, Oz's last email waited, the line from the middle still tugging at her:

My aunt said she'd be happy for you to contact her directly, if you'd like. She remembers more of the "bad years" than she lets on.

Ruth exhaled slowly. That door was open. Now she had to decide what to carry through it.

She clicked Reply.

Email 1 – to Oz

Hi Oz,

Thank you for asking your aunt and for letting me know she's open to talking. I keep thinking about the way you described her, remembering more of the bad years than she lets on, and I want to treat that carefully.

On my end, Joseph's entries around your coast are starting to feel less like "background" and more like a hinge in his story. Your great-grandfather's notes about "the boy from the vines" already changed how I read those pages, and the idea that your aunt might still remember the people who passed through is... a lot. In a good way, but still a lot.

I'm going to reach out to her directly, like you suggested, and frame it as clearly as I can—what I'm working on, what I'd be asking, and how much control she has over what gets used. If at any point you or she feel like I'm pushing too hard, I want you to say so. I'd rather lose a source than mishandle your family's history.

Also, and this is the part I'm less practiced at saying in emails to innkeepers, I'm grateful. For the scans, for the attic crate detours, for trusting me with words that belong to your grandfather and now, a little bit, to both of us.

I'll copy her address into a new message so she has me on record. I promise not to blame you if she decides she's had enough historians for one lifetime.

Ruth

She hovered over that last paragraph, then left it. It sounded like her. Maybe a slightly more exposed version of her, but still her.

Send.

The whoosh felt louder than it should have in the small office.

"Okay," she murmured. "One down."

She opened a fresh draft and pasted in the email address Oz had given her.

Email 2 – to the aunt

Dear Madame Marchand,

My name is Ruth Ward. I'm a historian teaching in Oklahoma, and I'm currently working on a project about ordinary people in northern France who helped others move through the first months of the Second World War. Your nephew, Ozias, kindly shared a few pages from your grandfather's notes with me, the ones that mention "the boy from the vines" and families who arrived at the farm late and left again before dawn.

I'm writing because the journal I'm studying, kept by a young man named Joseph Durand on his family's vineyard inland from the coast, appears to describe some of the same routes and nights from the other side. Joseph writes about leading people through the forests toward the sea; your father's pages show what it looked like when those footsteps finally reached a door.

If you are willing, I would be very grateful to hear anything you're comfortable sharing about:

– What you remember of the inn during those years, or what was passed down to you.

– Stories (in general terms) of families or individuals who came through quickly, especially at night.

– How your father spoke about that time later in life—whether he saw himself as "helping," or simply "doing what had to be done."

I want to be clear that I am not looking for anything sensational. My goal is to understand, as honestly as I can, what it meant for ordinary people to keep their doors open along these paths and to make sure that when I write about men like Joseph, I do not erase the innkeepers and families who made his routes possible.

Anything you choose to share can be anonymized in my work if you prefer. If you would rather I use real names, I will only do so with your explicit permission. You are also very welcome to reply through Ozias if that feels more comfortable.

Thank you for considering this, and for preserving your father's words long enough for them to meet Joseph's on my desk. However you choose to respond, even if the answer is silence, I will try to handle both stories with the care they deserve.

With respect,

Ruth Ward

The second whoosh felt smaller than the first, but it still left a hollow in her chest. Somewhere in a quiet American kitchen, an email would land in an inbox belonging to a woman who had once fallen asleep above a French farm and woken to strangers' footsteps on the stairs.

Ruth leaned back in her chair and let her eyes close for a moment. It was a strange triangle to picture: Joseph walking in the dark toward a house he would never name, a farmer keeping count of beds and boots, and a girl who grew up on those stories and then carried them across an ocean. Now all three of them were meeting on her screen.

Her gaze dropped to the journal on the desk. The leather looked dull in the fluorescent light, ordinary and worn, nothing like the live wire it had become.

"Routes first," she said quietly. "Feelings later."

She flipped to Joseph's next entry and picked up her pen, trying not to think about Oz checking his inbox on the far side of the Atlantic, or about a stranger reading her name and deciding whether to answer.

That night, after office hours and a seminar that left the whiteboard crowded with dates and arrows, Ruth's voice was hoarse from walking her students through why a vineyard boy with a pencil might actually have existed. They'd argued troop movements and parish bulletins and logbooks, stacking evidence until Joseph felt almost solid in the room.

Almost.

The hole stayed anyway, a quiet space under her ribs that no footnote could fill.

In her apartment, the glow of the laptop screen painted the walls a tired blue. Her inbox was still stubbornly unchanged—no new message from Oz, no unfamiliar name that might belong to a woman who had grown up hearing about strangers at her father's farm.

Ruth refreshed the page once, then forced herself to stop. Waiting for email wasn't research. It was just waiting.

She closed the browser and pulled Joseph's journal into her lap, thumb resting on the edge of the next unread page.

"Alright," she murmured. "You first."

The leather was warm under her hand, worn smooth by hours of contact. Somewhere between a French farmhouse, an American kitchen, and this small Oklahoma living room, other hands were deciding which pieces of his story to pass on.

For now, all she could do was keep reading, and make her case that the boy from the vines was more than a rumor, even if, for the moment, it still felt like she was arguing around a missing piece.

30

Chapter 30

You don't need big changes here; Chapter 30 already ties the institutional pressure and Ruth's inner stance together cleanly. Just a few small edits for clarity and rhythm. Here's a polished version:

Chapter 30

The end of the week was rushing at her, and the cursor in her project statement document blinked like it knew she was lying.

By the close of the semester, students will have engaged critically with Joseph Durand's journal as one representative example of civilian experience under early occupation...

The committee wanted something tidy and teachable—an "innovative capstone" that walked undergraduates through a well-framed case study and sent them out with better source-analysis skills. They did not want a semester built around a dead French vineyard son who had somehow become the axis of their instructor's life.

But every time Ruth tried to flatten Joseph back into one representative example, Oz's great-grandfather's logbook and the Rouen archives and the list under the oak pushed back. The more evidence she stacked, the more he stopped looking like a type and started looking like a person.

And people were messy in ways committees did not like.

She toggled to her notes from the meeting:

Provenance and corroboration.

Authorship and attribution: composite vs individual.

Ethics: families, ownership, trauma.

Pedagogy: how she'd framed him for the students.

On her own pad, she'd added a fifth, unspoken category: Collateral damage.

Under it, three names were still written in a vertical line.

Oz.

Eric.

Joseph.

Who was she willing to lose if she chose wrong?

More than that, who was she willing to become in the process?

Her inbox tab blinked with a new, meaningless notification—department listserv chatter—but her hand still twitched toward the touchpad. No matter how often she told herself to focus, she couldn't quite stop checking for an email from Oz's aunt, some line from an American kitchen that might finally tell her whether the boy from the vines had really stood in that farmhouse doorway.

Oz made it too easy to believe Joseph was still in the room. His messages from the cliff—attic crates, oak trees, guests asking about ghosts—kept pulling the past forward. Eric, on the other hand, had walked into office hours two days ago with his revised draft and the accountant-father verdict: Your job is to teach them how to read the source, not resurrect the guy.

The committee would love that line.

Ruth dropped her gaze back to the blinking cursor and forced her fingers to move.

In this capstone, Joseph Durand's journal will be presented as a single, deeply textured example through which students can explore broader questions of anonymity, ordinary courage, and the limits of archival evidence...

She stopped there, the word limits humming under her skin.

Limits were exactly what she was supposed to be drawing. Limits between past and present. Between subject and scholar. Between the dead boy in the vines and the living men who had slipped, almost without her consent, into the spaces around him.

For a moment she hovered over the word representative, then backspaced it and typed particular instead.

It wasn't the bolder choice she wanted to make. But it was closer to the truth than the committee's first draft, and for now, that would have to be enough.

She read the paragraph twice, then copied it into the official template, filling in the boxes for "Project Description" and "Pedagogical Outcomes" with language that sounded just cautious enough to pass. Each time she typed Joseph's name, she felt the urge to add more—a line about the oak, about the list, about the way his routes had started to feel like a second spine in her own body—and each time she swallowed it back.

When the last field was finally populated and the spell-check had finished scolding her for accent marks and French place names, she attached the document to a new message.

To: Dr. Singh, Dr. Peters

Subject: Project Statement - Durand Seminar

She let the body of the email stay simple.

As requested, I've attached a draft project statement outlining my framing of the Durand journal for both the current seminar and future work. I'm happy to revise as needed for the committee.

Thank you again for trusting me with this,

Ruth

Her finger hovered over the trackpad for a beat longer than it needed to. Then she clicked Send.

The email vanished into the outbox, leaving the document behind like a shed skin. For the first time all afternoon, the room felt very quiet.

Ruth opened a fresh document and stared at the blank page. No headers. No boxes. No committee.

On the top line she typed, without overthinking it:

The Boy from the Vines - Notes Beyond the Syllabus.

Beneath it, she wrote the sentence that wouldn't fit anywhere in the proposal.

Joseph Durand is not just an example. He is a man I met too late, and I am trying very hard not to lose him twice.

She sat back, heartbeat loud in her ears. It was ridiculous, maybe, to admit that out loud even in a file no one else would see. But it felt like sliding a pin into the right spot on the map. At least here, in this small, unsanctioned corner of her hard drive, she didn't have to pretend the work and the man were separable.

Her inbox icon pulsed again. This time she didn't look. Committee statement sent. Private truth saved. Somewhere between a French farm and an American kitchen, an older woman still hadn't decided whether to answer a stranger's questions about the boy who came out of the vines.

Ruth closed the laptop before she could hit refresh and reached instead for the journal, letting the familiar weight settle into her hands.

"Alright," she murmured. "Particular it is."

She opened to the ribbon and began to read, the glow of the screen fading behind her while the ink on the page pulled her back toward 1940, and whatever waited there next.

Ruth had just set the journal down again when her laptop chimed.

New email. Subject line: Re: Project Statement – Durand Seminar.

That was fast.

She flipped the screen back open.

From: Singh, Anika

To: Ward, Ruth; Peters, Daniel

Subject: Re: Project Statement – Durand Seminar

Ruth,

Thank you for this. I've read through your statement once and appreciate the care you've taken with framing, particularly your emphasis on ethics and on presenting Durand as a particular, deeply textured case rather than a generic type.

From my perspective, this is sufficient for us to move forward with the internal committee. I'll circulate it to the members ahead of Monday's meeting.

One additional request: the committee will want to see not only how you're structuring the seminar, but also a preliminary sense of where you see this going in your own scholarship. In other words, if we support this with a course release and travel funds, what is the likely "end product" and over what timeline? Article? Book proposal? Digital archive?

You don't need a full publishing plan yet, but please come to Monday's meeting prepared to speak to:

– Your best current sense of how and when you will be able to make a firm attribution claim (composite vs individual) about Durand, based on the evidence you expect to gather.

– A realistic timeline for an initial publication (even if that's framed cautiously).

In plain terms: we're willing to invest. We just need to know when you expect to be ready to say, publicly, what you are willing to claim.

Best,

Anika

Below it, Peters had already replied all.

From: Peters, Daniel

Subject: Re: Project Statement – Durand Seminar

Ruth,

Nicely done. This is strong, and I think the committee will respond well to your emphasis on particularity plus caution.

I agree with Anika's note about the next step. Between the seminar, the Rouen archives, the Marchand materials, and any additional family contacts, you're approaching the point where "I don't know what he is" will start to sound less like prudence and more like hesitation.

That's not a criticism; it's simply the clock we all work under.

Let's talk before Monday about what feels honest to you in terms of attribution and timeline. You don't have to promise a monograph on the spot, but you should have an answer more specific than "eventually."

– D.

Ruth stared at the screen, the phrase the clock we all work under echoing louder than the rest.

They were moving her forward—that was the good news. Support, course release, travel. The part her CV needed. The price was a deadline on something she still wasn't sure a deadline could touch.

When will you be ready to say, publicly, what you are willing to claim.

She glanced at the journal on her desk, then at the empty inbox where Oz's aunt still hadn't appeared. Somewhere out there were pages she hadn't read yet, memories she hadn't heard. Somewhere in the binding there might even be words she didn't know existed.

And now the committee wanted a date by which she would decide who Joseph was.

Ruth opened her calendar and created a new event on Monday: Committee – Durand (Attribution / Timeline). Then, almost without thinking, she dragged a second, private reminder into the week after and labeled it, Aunt? Oz?—a quieter clock only she could see.

For the first time, the two deadlines sat side by side on the screen: the university's patience, and whatever time the past would take to answer.

31

Chapter 31

Ruth noticed the shift in the air before she saw the subject line.

Her inbox had been a low-grade hum all morning—students, library notices, a reminder from facilities about hallway painting—none of it important enough to drag her away from the open sprawl of journal, grant letter, and half-edited project statement on her desk. But when the new message slid into view, the name on it straightened her spine.

Subject: Project Statement – Committee Review & Next Steps

She clicked before she could talk herself out of it.

From: Singh, Anika

To: Ward, Ruth; Peters, Daniel

Subject: Project Statement – Committee Review & Next Steps

Ruth,

Thank you again for the revised project statement and for your patience while the internal committee reviewed it this week. After our meeting this morning, I'm glad to say we are unanimously in favor of moving your Durand work forward with departmental support.

Specifically, the committee has approved:

– One course release for the coming academic year (spring),

– A modest research travel budget (France and domestic archives), and

– Continued use of the library research room as a dedicated Durand workspace through next summer.

All of this is contingent on your submitting a short follow-up plan addressing two items we did not have time to resolve fully in the meeting:

Publishing trajectory. A 1–2 page outline of your current best sense of "end product(s)" and chronology (e.g., article draft by X date, book proposal by Y, digital component on Z timeline).

Attribution stance. A concise statement of how you intend to frame the journal in any early publications (individual author; probable composite; deliberately unresolved) and why that framing is the most ethical and sustainable given the evidence you have and expect to gather.

This does not require you to commit to final answers, but it does require you to choose a working position that you are prepared to defend publicly in the near term. A draft along these lines by the end of next week would allow us to finalize the internal paperwork before the dean's funding calendar closes.

Please let us know if you have questions or need clarification.

Best,

Anika

Below it, Peters's reply was already waiting.

From: Peters, Daniel

Subject: Re: Project Statement – Committee Review & Next Steps

Ruth,

This is very good news. It also means the clock we talked about is now official.

I'd urge you not to treat Anika's request as a trap. Use it as a chance to say what you already know: that you cannot yet "prove" Joseph in the way some people would like, and that you also cannot, in good conscience, flatten him into a generic composite.

A clear interim stance—"particular case, open attribution" or whatever language feels honest—will serve you better than another six months of "it's complicated."

I'm free Thursday afternoon if you want to talk through drafts before you send them on.

– D.

Ruth let her hand fall from the trackpad, the words the clock we talked about is now official ringing louder than the offer of a course release.

Approved. Contingent. End product. By the end of next week.

They'd given her exactly what she said she wanted—time, money, institutional cover—and wrapped it around the one thing she still didn't know how to do: pick a box for a boy who had spent his life trying not to fit in one.

For a moment she just stared at the screen. The journal lay open beside the keyboard, ribbon marking a page where routes and rations had taken precedence over everything else. Across the table, the grant letter sat under her pen, REPRESENTATIONAL FRAMING underlined so many times the paper had begun to pill.

"Congratulations," she murmured to the empty office, not sure whether she meant it for herself or for the committee.

Her calendar pinged in the corner. Monday's event—Committee – Durand (Attribution / Timeline)—glowed in university blue. Next to it, the smaller, private reminder she'd dragged into the following week—Aunt? Oz?—still waited in softer gray, quiet as a second heartbeat.

Two clocks. Now both of them were ticking.

Ruth dragged the cursor to the reply button and hovered. Anything she sent to Singh and Peters would live in her file, quoted in memos, folded into budget justifications and tenure dossiers. She could already hear the future versions:

As Dr. Ward herself has stated, her position on the Durand journal is...

She closed the draft unsent and opened a new document instead.

Working Notes – Durand Plan (Not for Committee)

At the top of the page she wrote:

What kind of thing is Joseph?

Under it, two columns.

Left: Evidence.

– Journal (dates, routes, names).

– Rouen archives, Marchand logbook, bishop's letter.

– David's daughter's email waiting to exist.

– Oz under the oak, saying if that boy hadn't come back for my father, I wouldn't be here.

Right: Cost.

– If I call him representative, I lie to her.

– If I call him singular, I can't "prove" him on paper.

– If I stay undecided, they'll decide for me.

She tapped the keys once, twice, then added, almost in spite of herself:

I want him to be real.

I want him to stay particular.

I want to keep my job.

The last line sat there, painfully ordinary beside the others.

"That's the problem, isn't it?" she said aloud. "Ordinary is where things disappear."

Her inbox chimed again.

This time the name at the top of the screen was unfamiliar.

Subject: Re: Inquiry re: cellar, vineyard, 1940

Her stomach dropped and rose in the same motion.

Madame Marchand.

She opened it.

Dear Ruth,

Ozias asked whether it was alright for you to contact me, so I was expecting your message. I am also curious how you came to have the journal he mentioned. Thank you for being interested in a story like this, and maybe helping us see it more clearly.

My father, David, did not say very much about those years. Mostly he would add Joseph's name to my mother's version of how they met and escaped France.

"We left the farm in a hurry, always listening for boots on the road," my mother would say. "With at least twenty other people, we were sent across the Channel in the dark." Somewhere in there my father would say, "and Joseph did all the hard work to protect us."

I don't remember my grandfather well. He never left France, and I only visited when I was very young. My father came with us once. I think I may have heard the name Joseph then, but I am not sure. My mother and my aunt almost never talked about anyone from before the farm.

My father always said he was not a hero for escaping, and that the ones who stayed behind suffered too much for him to take any praise.

I hope this answers a few questions. Please feel free to ask more.

Respectfully,

Marie Marchand

Ruth read the email a second time, then a third, eyes catching on different lines each pass.

My father, David... my mother and my aunt almost never talked about anyone from before.

It wasn't much, not compared to what she wanted, but it was enough. Enough to confirm that the cellar boy had lived long enough to become a man who insisted he wasn't a hero. Enough to put one living voice between Ruth and the night at the farm.

She clicked into her notes and added a new line under Evidence.

– Email from David's daughter (Marie): confirms Joseph's role in "hard work" / protection, farm, Channel crossing. Memory transmitted through her mother's story.

Her fingers hovered, then moved to the other column.

– If I smooth the family tree to make it elegant, I lie about what she doesn't know.

The thought that had sparked on the third read tried to push its way back in. If Marie's mother had been one of the farm girls, then somewhere in the next generation Oz's mother could be the other. Two girls, two daughters, two lines running out from the same night.

It was neat. Too neat.

Ruth sat back and pinched the bridge of her nose.

"This is exactly how people turn lives into charts," she muttered. "Convenient guesses that make better narrative than evidence."

In the Working Notes document she typed:

Temptation: map "two girls" at farm directly onto (1) David's wife, (2) Joseph's future partner → ties both family lines back to single scene.

Problem: neither Marie nor Oz has actually said this. Their silences and gaps are as real as what they remember.

She stared at the words until they steadied her.

The clock in the corner of her monitor rolled five minutes forward. Monday's committee meeting didn't care how many unnamed girls she could balance on the head of a pin. It cared whether she would stand up and say, out loud, what kind of thing Joseph was, and how much of that claim she could actually support.

Ruth clicked back to her inbox and hit Reply.

Dear Marie,

Thank you so much for taking the time to write. I'm grateful you were willing to put even this much into words. I promise I will not turn your father into something he said he was not.

I would love, whenever you feel ready, to hear more of your mother's version of that night at the farm—the details she chose, and the ones she avoided. Those choices are part of the history, too.

Please know that if there are things you choose not to say, I will treat those limits as part of the story rather than holes to be filled in.

Warmly,

Ruth

She sent it before she could start editing herself into a grant-proposal tone.

For a moment the office was very quiet. The journal lay where she'd left it, a thin ribbon marking August 1940. On the screen, her two clocks still glowed: Committee – Durand (Attribution / Timeline). Aunt? Oz?

Between them, now, was a third, invisible one: how long it would take for an older woman in an American kitchen to decide whether she wanted to say the boy's name out loud to a stranger.

Ruth turned back to the document she owed the committee and moved the cursor down to the heading she'd already typed.

Durand Project – Publishing Trajectory & Interim Attribution Stance

Underneath, she wrote:

Interim attribution: I will treat the journal as the work of a single, particular voice whose exact legal identity remains incompletely documented. I will not retroactively assign him "representative" status or tidy family lines in ways that contradict what surviving witnesses are willing or able to say.

Her heart kicked once, hard, as she added the last sentence:

In other words, I am choosing the messier truth over the cleaner story—for my students, for the committee, and for the families who have already lived with its consequences.

She sat back, listening to the faint tick of the hallway clock through the door.

"Particular," she said, more firmly this time. "Even if it doesn't come with a perfect family tree."

She reached for the journal, thumb finding the worn groove near the spine, and opened it again to where she'd left Joseph, counting steps between trees and pretending routes were easier than faces.

32

Chapter 32

The final day of class was approaching, and the room felt more like a pressure chamber than a seminar.

The essays were in, read, and annotated within an inch of their margins; now the final exam waited, a last assignment that didn't ask the students to agree with Ruth so much as to plant their flag somewhere visible. She'd built the rubric herself and told them, three times in three different ways, that she didn't care which position they took on Joseph as long as they could defend it.

Supported argument. That was the phrase on the syllabus.

On paper, it sounded simple: choose a stance—Joseph as singular actor, probable composite, or deliberately unresolved voice—and make a case from the sources they'd spent the semester wrestling. In practice, she knew exactly how loaded the choice had become. Every bluebook on her desk would be a small referendum on the question she was still answering for the committee: What kind of thing is this boy from the vines?

She sat at her office desk, the final prompt open on her screen:

By drawing on Joseph Durand's journal, corroborating documents (archival, parish, military, family), and our class discussions, argue for the most responsible way to frame Joseph's authorship and role in early 1940. Your answer may defend him as a singular figure, a representative composite, or an intentionally unresolved case—but you must demonstrate why that framing is ethically and historically sustainable.

At the bottom, she'd added one more line in a weaker moment:

Note: "Because Ms. Ward believes it" is not an acceptable source.

She smiled despite herself, then underlined ethically and historically in her own printed copy, as if she were the one taking the test.

Stacked beside the keyboard were their essays—narrative analyses, map work, arguments about routes and ration lines and what it meant for a seventeen-year-old to start sounding like a professional courier. Some had surprised her. Malik's meticulous cross-referencing of troop movements with Joseph's dates. Jenna's close reading of where feelings stopped getting full sentences. Even Eric's grudging concession that "if this is composite, it is a composite built so precisely it teaches us more about erasure than invention."

She'd circled that line. Twice.

On the whiteboard in her mind, the course was already divided into three arcs: discovery, disruption, and whatever this last week would be—reckoning, maybe. The final would be the hinge between her classroom and the committee room. Between what twenty undergraduates were ready to claim and what the department wanted in a neat, fundable paragraph.

Her inbox pinged. A new message slid into view.

Subject: Re: Attic crate, part three

Ruth didn't open it yet. Not Oz, not now. She dragged the cursor back to the grading window and forced herself to focus on the line she'd written months ago in the syllabus, when the journal was still mostly hers:

By the end of the semester, students will be able to articulate and defend a position on Joseph Durand's status as a historical actor, using primary and secondary evidence to support their claims.

They were there. Or close enough to pretend.

The question that hummed under her own skin was uglier, and not one she could put on an exam: when she read their arguments, whose verdict would she be grading—her students', or the one she already half-feared from the committee?

She closed the laptop, reached for the journal instead, and let the familiar weight settle into her hands.

"Alright," she murmured to the worn leather. "One more round. Then we see what they do with you."

Outside her office, the hallway clock ticked toward the last day of class, steady as ever, unconcerned with whether the boy from the vines ended up singular, representative, or simply refused to fit in any box at all.

The final class was spent in silence.

The usual shuffle of backpacks and whispered side comments had burned off in the first five minutes; now only the wall clock spoke, its steady tick cutting through the room as pencils moved across paper. Twenty bluebooks lay open on twenty desks, each page slowly filling with the same question Ruth had been rewriting in her head for months.

What kind of thing is Joseph Durand?

From her spot at the front, she'd resisted the urge to pace. Instead she sat on the edge of the table, exam copies stacked beside her, watching as students frowned, paused, flipped back through their packets of excerpts and photocopied maps. Every so often someone glanced up at the projected images she'd left on the board—vineyard, oak, church at Houppeville—as if they might offer one last hint.

Malik wrote in short, intense bursts, hand cramping, then stopping to shake it out. Jenna chewed her lip, flipped to the page with August 19th underlined, and underlined it again, harder. Even Eric, chronic eye-roller, was hunched over his desk, lips moving silently as he counted off points on his fingers.

The tick-tick-tick of the clock grew louder as the hour wore on, a small, relentless percussion behind their arguments.

Ruth let her gaze move once, slowly, around the room. She knew some of what they were going to say already—she'd seen it in their essays, heard it in their debates.

Joseph as singular: a particular boy whose routes matched too precisely, whose handwriting shifted in ways composites rarely did.

Joseph as composite: a carefully curated voice carrying the weight of many unnamed helpers.

Joseph as deliberately unresolved: a case where the ethical choice was to leave some questions open, because the living people tied to the story were still deciding how much of it they could bear to name.

She'd promised herself she would accept any of those if the evidence was there. The rubric in her hand said as much.

Supported argument, she reminded herself. Not right answer.

"Twenty minutes," she said quietly.

Chairs creaked, but no one looked up. The pencils kept moving. One student in the back flipped to a clean page and started over, the first answer apparently not good enough even for themselves.

Outside, the late-semester light was beginning to flatten, the afternoon fading toward evening. Inside, for the length of one exam period, the war summer of 1940 lived again in the scratches of cheap pencils on university-issue paper.

When the clock finally clicked over to the end of the period, Ruth stood.

"Time," she said. "Please finish your sentence and close your book."

There was a collective exhale as blue covers snapped shut. For a moment, no one moved.

Then, one by one, they stood and filed down to the front, stacking their answers on the desk beside the journal, as if they were offering up verdicts to the boy whose voice had carried them here.

The class had spent the last hour writing about who or what they thought Joseph was.

When the door finally shut behind the last student, the room stayed quiet, as if the silence had decided to linger. The stack of bluebooks sat in the center of the front table, a squat, uneven tower between the journal and the dry-erase markers.

Ruth didn't reach for them yet. She just stared.

Each one of those thin cardboard covers held a version of the question she still hadn't answered to her own satisfaction. Singular. Composite. Unresolved. Particular. Representative. The words felt heavier now that twenty undergraduates had tried to live inside them for an hour.

Behind her, the floorboard near the door creaked.

She turned to see Dr. Peters leaning against the back row, arms folded loosely, gaze on the stack rather than on her. He must have slipped in during the last ten minutes, quiet enough not to disturb the concentration.

He watched for several moments before he spoke.

"Feels a little like grading verdicts, doesn't it?" he said.

Ruth let out a breath she hadn't realized she'd been holding. "Something like that."

He nodded toward the bluebooks. "You going to read them now or let them cool?"

"I haven't decided," she said. "Part of me wants to know what they did with him. Part of me would rather keep not knowing for a few more hours."

Peters pushed off the row and walked down toward the front, the old lecture hall steps amplifying each footfall just enough to break the spell.

"You gave them a fair question," he said. "You told them any position was acceptable if they could support it. That's more honesty than most historians get when we inherit sources."

"Doesn't feel fair," Ruth said. "They get to turn theirs in and walk away. I still have to hand mine to the committee."

He smiled, not unkindly. "True. But you've had more time with Joseph. That's the trade."

He rested a hand lightly on the stack, as if testing its weight. "Whatever they wrote, it's not the last word on him. It's just where they landed this semester."

Ruth glanced at the journal lying open beside the exams. "And me?"

"You're not at the last word either," he said. "You're at the first one that's going on record."

He looked up at her, eyebrow lifting. "How's your own answer coming?"

She thought of the document on her laptop waiting under the title Interim Attribution, of the line she'd typed about choosing the messier truth over the cleaner story.

"I think," she said slowly, "I'm about to grade a roomful of arguments for and against calling him particular. And then I'm going to walk into your committee meeting and say it out loud anyway."

Peters's mouth tilted. "Good," he said. "Then these"—he tapped the bluebooks—"are practice. Not verdicts."

He stepped back, giving the table a little nod. "Close the circle with them. Then send me your draft. The clock's ticking, but it's not a firing squad."

Ruth huffed a soft laugh in spite of herself.

When he'd gone, the room slipped back into quiet. She pulled the first bluebook off the top of the stack, thumbed it open, and saw Joseph's name on the first line in a student's wavering hand.

"Alright," she murmured. "Your turn to read them."

33

Chapter 33

Eric waited for Ruth in the hallway, slouched against the wall in a way that tried very hard to look casual and not at all like last-day loitering.

Students trickled past him in twos and threes, still buzzing about the final, about whether Joseph was more scout or courier, singular or composite. Their voices faded as they turned the corner, leaving the stretch of corridor outside her office oddly quiet.

He checked his phone, then shoved it back in his pocket. The bluebook he'd just handed in felt like it was still vibrating in his hand, even though it was now somewhere on Ruth's desk beside the journal.

This was probably the last chance he'd get to talk to her before the break. The next time he saw her, she'd be a line on his transcript and a name on a letter of recommendation if he ever worked up the nerve to ask.

The door opened.

Ruth stepped out, a half-stack of exams in one hand, the journal in the other. For a second they just looked at each other, both of them seeming to realize at the same time that the semester had run out.

"Hey," Eric said, pushing off the wall. "Do you—uh—have a minute?"

Her shoulders tensed for a heartbeat, the reflex of someone braced for one more argument, then eased. "Sure," she said. "No more bluebooks, though. I'm at capacity."

He huffed a laugh. "No, I'm tapped out on bluebooks. I just..." He scratched the back of his neck, eyes skimming past the journal to her face. "I had some questions. About you. Not Joseph."

That earned him a small, wary smile. "That's a first," she said. "Most people lead with the dead Frenchman."

"Yeah, well," he said, shifting his backpack strap. "I already yelled everything I could think of about the dead Frenchman into seventy-five minutes of exam. I figured maybe I could use my indoor voice on the living historian before you disappear."

She tipped her head toward the open door. "Five minutes," she said. "Then I really do have to go argue with a committee."

He followed her in, suddenly more nervous than he'd been in front of the exam. The combativeness that had carried him through arguments about attribution and authenticity had nowhere useful to go now. What he wanted to ask didn't fit in the language of footnotes.

He sat when she gestured to the chair, watching as she set the journal down with the same careful touch she used at the front of the classroom.

"So," she said. "You survived the semester. And made my life difficult in interesting ways."

"I could say the same," he said. "About the difficult part."

She waited.

He cleared his throat. "I guess I'm just trying to figure out how someone ends up... like this."

"Like what?"

He flailed for neutral words. "The person who takes a random journal out of a drawer in Paris and turns it into a year of their life," he said. "Who fights a whole committee over whether a vineyard kid gets to be particular. Who assigns a final exam that's basically 'tell me what you think I believe, and then tell me why you disagree.'"

Ruth blinked, then let out a small, surprised breath. "I didn't realize I was that transparent," she said.

"You're not," Eric said quickly. "That's kind of the problem. You argue like it's all about the evidence, and then you talk about him like..." He broke off, searching for a less loaded word than love. "Like you know him," he finished. "I guess I just wanted to know where that line is. For you."

For a moment she didn't answer. Her gaze dropped to the journal, then to the stack of bluebooks.

"The line keeps moving," she said. "When I started, I thought this was just a good story. Then a good thesis. Then a good case study. Somewhere along the way, he stopped being any of those things and became... a responsibility."

"That's what I thought," Eric said quietly. "I just wanted to hear you say it. Without the footnotes."

She looked up at him, eyes softer than he'd seen in class. "What about you?" she asked. "You came into this wanting to kill him. Now you're sitting in my office asking about lines."

He snorted. "I never wanted to kill him," he said. "I wanted to make sure you weren't getting killed by him. Or by what people would do with him."

"That's... oddly considerate," she said.

"Don't spread it around," he said. "I have a reputation."

She smiled, really smiled, then sobered. "You did your job," she said. "You pushed. Hard. You made me make the case I needed to make before I walked into that committee room. I'm... grateful. Even if I didn't look like it at the time."

"Yeah, well," he said, standing before he could say anything more dangerous. "For what it's worth, I'm still not sure what I think he is. Singular, composite, whatever. But I'm a lot more sure about what I think you are."

She raised an eyebrow. "Should I be worried?"

"A historian," he said. "Not a fangirl. I figure you should have at least one student on record saying that out loud."

Something in her posture loosened at that, like a knot pulled free.

"Thank you," she said.

Eric stood there a moment too long, the air between them filling with all the words he hadn't planned well enough to say.

Ruth tilted her head, waiting. "Was there something else?"

He opened his mouth, then shut it again. Every version of the question that had seemed almost casual in his head—coffee sometime? could I pick your brain about grad school?—sounded, in this office with the journal on the desk, like something else entirely.

"I—" He shifted his weight, fingers tightening on the strap of his backpack. "I was going to ask if you ever... you know... talk about this stuff outside class. Like, over coffee or something."

Her expression flickered, just for a second. Not anger, not discomfort exactly—more like a quick inventory of lines: teacher and student, past and present, Joseph and the rest of her life.

"When you're not grading our verdicts," he added, trying to make it lighter. "Or fighting committees."

Ruth let out a slow breath. "I do," she said. "Talk about it outside class, I mean. With colleagues. With my advisor. With friends who didn't sign up to hear about Nazi patrol routes and still listen anyway."

He managed a crooked smile. "Sounds like a fun crowd."

"It is," she said. Then, gently, "And it's also... a different crowd."

The meaning landed. He looked down, then back up, forcing himself to meet her eyes.

"Right," he said. "Lines."

"Lines," she agreed. "Not because you did anything wrong. Just because part of the responsibility is knowing which worlds don't get to overlap. Yet."

The yet surprised him more than the rest.

"So when I'm not the name on your roster anymore..." he began.

"Then, if you still want to talk about Joseph—or about grad school, or about why we do this to ourselves—send me an email," she said. "From the other side of the gradebook. We can see what makes sense then."

It wasn't what he'd hoped for, but it wasn't nothing. It was, he realized, exactly in character: a boundary drawn with the same care she used on footnotes and families.

"Okay," he said. "Deal."

He stepped back toward the door. At the threshold he paused, looking once more at the journal on her desk.

"For what it's worth," he said, "if he really is just 'representative,' he got insanely lucky. Most of us don't get historians like you."

Ruth's mouth curved, something complicated passing through her eyes. "Most of us don't get students like you, either," she said. "Go enjoy your break, Eric. You earned it."

He nodded and slipped out into the hallway, heart thudding a little too fast. Behind him, he heard the soft click of the door and pictured her turning back to the stack of bluebooks, to the boy from the vines, to the committee clock ticking down.

He walked away still infatuated, but with the odd sense that, for now, wanting more of her time would have to count as its own kind of answer.

When the door shut behind Eric, Ruth stared at it for half a beat longer than she meant to.

Then she set the journal down, dug her phone out of her bag, and thumbed open her messages.

To: Lena

omg, Eric all but asked me out.

She watched the three dots appear almost immediately.

Please tell me you said "ask me again when you're not my student" and not "let's unpack your feelings about early resistance over wine," Lena shot back.

Ruth huffed a quiet laugh, the tension of the last hour unknotting just enough for her shoulders to drop.

I drew a line, she typed. Professionally. Ethically. All the -lys. But still. It was... a moment.

A second later:

Of course it was, Lena replied. You spent a semester teaching him how to care about one complicated man on paper. Now he's noticed the complicated woman holding the paper. Human nature, babe.

Ruth's gaze slid back to the stack of bluebooks and the open journal beside them.

Yeah, she wrote. Lines everywhere.

Then, before Lena could turn it into a full debrief, she set the phone face down, pulled the next bluebook from the pile, and let herself fall back into the one relationship she was allowed to obsess over on university time: her students' arguments with a boy from the vines.

34

Chapter 34

It was two days later. Ruth had spent the entire weekend in the bluebooks. The second requirement from the committee still waited, blinking on her to-do list, and she kept half-hoping time would stretch long enough for another message from Oz or Marie—something that might be the last piece she needed to fix her stance on who Joseph was.

Sunday afternoon, just as Ruth had given up hope, the ding came in.

Ruth,

I'm sorry I didn't get back to you sooner. I wanted to make sure we were all on the same page. I talked with my sister and with Oz, and we finally had the conversation that has been in the air for years but never really discussed. My mother's story, and the story about Oz's grandmother, who is also my aunt, are really the same story told from two kitchens.

My mother was the girl who left the farm with my father, David. Oz's grandmother was her younger sister, the one who stayed behind longer and later married the boy from the vines. We grew up knowing that if Joseph had not come back for my parents, I would not be here, and if he had not kept going back to that farm, Oz would not be either.

Oz always knew about his grandfather's stories, but for him "the boy from the vines" was almost a legend, not a full name. It did not really click for any of us that the Joseph in your journal could be the same Joseph my grandfather talked about, until this weekend.

It's been very enlightening.

We still cannot give you every proof the committees might want or need, but for us he has always been one real man, not a made-up type. I hope you can say that in whatever careful way your work requires.

Love,

Marie

Ruth sat in silence, unable to move.

The glow of the screen washed the rest of the room flat, everything else reduced to gray while Marie's sentences burned sharp and specific: my mother was the girl who left the farm with my father, David... Oz's grandmother... later married the boy from the vines... for us he has always been one real man, not a made-up type.

She read it again, slower.

Two sisters at the farm. One followed David into the woods and onto the boats. One stayed, opened her door to a young man who kept coming back with dust on his boots and other people's fear still clinging to his clothes. Out of that tangle of routes and ration lines had come two grandchildren on opposite sides of an ocean—and both of them were in her inbox.

Her cursor blinked in the half-finished committee document on the other side of the screen, still waiting for a sentence that hadn't quite been brave enough to land.

Interim attribution: I will treat the journal as the work of a single, particular voice...

Until now, that had been a historian's hunch, an ethical stance more than a provable fact. With Marie's email, it was something else: a family's lived position, spelled out in plain words. One real man, not a made-up type.

Ruth let out a breath that was almost a laugh.

"Of course," she whispered. "Of course he is."

She copied one line into her notes under Evidence:

– Marchand email: two sisters at the farm; David's wife and Joseph's wife both trace their lives to "the boy from the vines." For the family, Joseph is a single, real man, not a type.

Then, under Cost, she added:

– If I soften that into "representative," I erase exactly what they're trusting me to carry.

Her calendar reminder for Monday's meeting blinked in the corner of the screen. The clock hadn't stopped. But for the first time all weekend, the ticking felt less like a countdown and more like a signal.

She clicked back into the committee document and finished the sentence.

Interim attribution: I will treat the journal as the work of a single, particular voice whose legal identity can be traced to a real family but remains imperfectly documented in the archival record. I will not frame him as a "representative type" when the people whose lives he altered insist he was one man.

Her fingers hovered for a moment, then added:

This is not the kind of proof that will satisfy every skeptic. It is, however, the most honest alignment of written evidence and living memory I can offer.

Ruth sat back, the words settling into place like pins on her map.

Joseph was still, in many ways, a boy walking through fog. The archives were still incomplete. The committee would still have questions.

But now, between a vineyard in Normandy and a suburban kitchen in America, between a grandson under an oak and a granddaughter at her laptop, a line had been drawn.

Particular, she thought. And not just because I want him to be.

Ruth had held back on reading forward, afraid of more than just how Joseph's war ended.

The pages beyond her ribbon didn't just hold the risk of death; they held the possibility of absence—of the journal simply stopping with no neat conclusion, no final entry to tell her whether the boy from the vines had made it through or simply vanished into the fog of 1940. She was already too far in, already carrying him into committee rooms and classrooms and family conversations; to push past that point and discover either his last breath on the page or his silence would mean grieving him twice.

She glanced at the closed half of the journal, its unread weight heavier than the part she already knew.

"Particular," she thought again, fingers resting on the cover. "But not yet finished. Not for me."

For now, she would walk into the committee meeting with the Joseph she had—vineyard son, courier, boy from the vines who became a line between two families—and leave whatever waited in the unread pages for another day.

Ruth took a breath and started a new reply.

Dear Marie,

Thank you for this. I know it must have been a lot—to talk all this through with your sister and with Oz, and then put it into words for a stranger. I'm very aware that what is "evidence" for my work is family history, and pain, for you.

Hearing that your mother and Oz's grandmother are the two sisters from the farm, and that both of your lives trace back to "the boy from the vines," is more than I ever expected you to share. It confirms some things I had begun to suspect, but it also does something the archives can't: it lets me see Joseph as you have always seen him, as one real man rather than a type.

I will honor that in anything I write. If I describe him as "particular," it will be because your family insists on him that way, not just because I prefer the story.

I have two questions, and you should feel completely free to answer only what you are willing to.

First, do you know how Joseph's story ends, as far as your family has told it? I don't mean official documents—just what your parents and grandparents said (or chose not to say) about what happened to him after the farm.

Second, are there any parts of that story you would not want me to repeat in writing, even without names? Your limits matter as much to me as the details themselves.

Thank you again for trusting me with so much already. Whatever you choose to share or keep, I will treat it as part of the responsibility that comes with carrying his journal forward.

Warmly,

Ruth

Ruth hit send on the email to Marie and, for the first time all weekend, closed her inbox without waiting to see if anything new appeared.

The cursor in her committee document blinked like it had been holding its breath.

Durand Project – Publishing Trajectory & Interim Attribution Stance

She scrolled back to the top and started turning scattered sentences into something that looked like a plan instead of a confession.

Under End Products, she typed:

Article-length case study on early 1940 refugee routes and improvised courier work in the Pays de Caux region, centered on Joseph Durand's journal as a particular voice, submitted to a peer-reviewed journal within 12–18 months.

Book-length project (monograph or hybrid narrative history) in development over 3–5 years, integrating the journal with parish records, military reports, and family testimony.

Potential digital component (interactive map / document dossier) in collaboration with the library once core archival and interview work is complete.

Under Timeline, she blocked off semesters and summers in neat, institutional phrases:

Spring–Summer: complete full transcription and translation, finalize initial article, conduct second research trip to France (Rouen, Pays de Caux, interviews).

Following academic year: revise article based on feedback, draft book proposal, continue archival work as needed.

Then she turned to the part that mattered most.

Interim Attribution Stance

She read the lines she'd drafted after Marie's email and began to shape them into the answer Singh and Peters had asked for:

In forthcoming work, I will treat the Durand journal as the writing of a single, particular author whose actions can be partially corroborated in the archival and family record, but whose legal identity remains incompletely documented. I will not frame him as a generic or "representative" type when the available evidence—including multi-generational family testimony—insists on him as one man.

She added, more bluntly:

This stance is provisional in the scholarly sense, but not neutral: it is a deliberate choice to align my public claims with both the limits of the sources and the way the families whose lives he altered understand him.

Finally, she opened a new subsection: Research Travel and Interviews.

Here, the frantic part began—figuring out what she could ask for without sounding like she'd slipped from historian into evangelist.

Planned second trip (Year 1): 10–14 days in France

– 3–4 days in Paris (archives and legal questions about ownership of found manuscripts).

– 3–4 days in Rouen and regional archives (further work on parish records, diocesan correspondence, and wartime reports).

– 4–6 days in Normandy countryside (Pays de Caux area), including additional on-site work at the former Durand vineyard and surrounding villages.

She hesitated, then added a separate line:

Interviews: I plan to conduct recorded oral history interviews (with consent) with descendants of those involved, including members of the Marchand family. I would like to allocate travel support to make it possible for at least one family member (e.g., Marie Marchand) to join me for part of this work, so that the building of the narrative is not something done to them but with them.

She stared at that sentence, imagining Singh reading it, Peters underlining it, some dean asking whether "inviting family members along" was scholarship or sentiment.

Then she added one more, quieter explanation:

Including a Marchand family member in part of the fieldwork will help ensure that I do not turn their memories into a story that is convenient for the archive but false to the people who lived it. It also reflects best practices in collaborative, trauma-adjacent historical work.

Her calendar alert flashed: Committee – Durand (Attribution / Timeline) – 24 hours.

Ruth saved the document, sat back, and rubbed her eyes.

It wasn't perfect. It wasn't finished. But it answered the questions they'd put to her:

What is this going to be?

When will you say it?

And who, exactly, do you think this boy from the vines was?

She glanced once at the closed half of the journal, then at the sent folder where Marie's name now sat beside Oz's.

"Particular," she said under her breath, letting the word settle over the screen, the map, the bluebooks piled on the floor. "And not alone."

35

Chapter 35

This chapter is pivotal: it crystallizes Ruth's "particular, not representative" stance and shows the committee taking her three-legged case seriously. It's already strong; it mostly needs light tightening and a clean landing for the scene. Here's a polished version with your beats preserved:

Chapter 35

Ruth hadn't slept.

She'd proofread her statement to the committee until the words stopped meaning anything—particular voice, provisional stance, collaborative fieldwork—and still managed to find one more adjective to second-guess every time she reached the bottom of the page.

Lena's name sat at the top of her text thread like a small, insistent light. Three messages, all from the night before:

You alive?

Nazis or not, people need sleep.

Do I need to come confiscate the journal again?

Ruth had seen them as they came in, watched the bubbles appear and disappear while she told herself she'd answer after she fixed just one more sentence. Then after she checked one more citation. Then after she reread Marie's email one more time.

She hadn't answered at all.

Now, in the thin gray of early morning, the apartment felt as over-marked as her draft: mugs on the counter, articles spread across the table, the journal lying closed but not far enough away. The only thing untouched was Lena's thread.

Ruth thumbed the phone awake, stared at the unread messages for a long moment, and finally typed:

Still alive. Committee today. Will explain after I survive telling three tenured historians that I'm betting my career on a boy from the vines.

She hovered, then added:

Thank you for checking. I'm sorry I went dark.

Send.

The whoosh sounded too loud in the quiet room. She set the phone face down, picked up the printed pages of her project statement, and smoothed the top sheet with a palm that wouldn't quite stop trembling.

Three pages. One argument. No sleep.

She slipped them into a folder beside Joseph's journal.

"Alright," she said to the empty room. "Let's see if they buy 'particular' before the coffee wears off."

Ruth hit the automatic door button with her elbow, both hands full—a worn leather journal in one, the blue-backed committee packet in the other.

The hallway outside the conference room smelled faintly of burnt coffee and floor wax, the institutional scent of decisions no one quite wanted to make. Through the narrow glass panel she could see them already in place: Dr. Peters, arms folded but expression open; Dr. Singh, glasses low on her nose, pen already poised; and the third member—a political historian Ruth barely knew—scrolling something on his tablet with the distracted air of a man who hadn't yet decided how much he cared.

She checked the time on her phone: three minutes early. Early enough to look prepared. Not so early she'd have to make small talk in the doorway.

"Committee – Durand (Attribution / Timeline)," the printed agenda taped beside the door read. Underneath, in smaller type, her name.

For a second she let herself lean back against the cool cinderblock wall, folder clutched to her chest.

This is not about whether you love the story, she reminded herself. This is about whether you can carry it without dropping the people inside it.

She thought of Marie's email—one real man, not a made-up type—and of Oz under the oak, brushing moss off stones he hadn't put there but still tended. Of Eric in her office, insisting on calling her a historian instead of a fangirl. Of twenty undergrads hunched over photocopied pages, arguing about whether "plenty of lamb" counted as resistance.

Evidence. Cost. Responsibility.

Ruth straightened, slid the journal into her bag, and kept only the packet in her hands. She didn't trust herself not to hold the leather like a talisman once she stepped inside.

At 9:59, she pushed the door open.

"Morning, Ruth," Peters said, with a quick half-smile that didn't quite reach his eyes. "Thanks for coming in."

"Would've been hard to stand you up after all those emails," she managed, aiming for light and landing somewhere near steady.

Singh gestured to the chair opposite them. "Have a seat. We've all read your materials." Her finger tapped the top page. "We'd like to hear, in your own words, who you think this young man is and what, exactly, you intend to do with him."

Ruth sat, laid the packet on the table, and folded her hands on top of it to keep from fidgeting.

She could feel her pulse in her throat, but when she spoke, her voice came out clearer than she felt.

"His name is Joseph Durand," she said. "He was a vineyard son in 1940, a reluctant guide who became an intentional courier. His journal is the only reason any of us are in this room."

She let that hang for a beat, then added, "And I'm here to argue that he's one particular voice we can't afford to flatten into a type, even if we can't yet footnote every step he took."

Peters's mouth twitched—the slightest encouragement. Singh's pen stilled.

"Alright," Singh said. "Walk us through it."

Ruth slid a second, thinner stack of papers out of her folder and laid it beside the formal packet.

"I didn't include full translations in what I sent you," she said. "But I brought a working set of pages I use in the seminar. I'd like to anchor what I'm saying in his actual voice, not just my summaries."

Singh nodded once. "Go on."

She turned the first sheet so it faced the committee, her finger resting near the top.

"This is an early vineyard entry," she said. "Weather, vines, Mass in Rouen, dinner with David's family. Ordinary, almost boring. You can hear the cadence of a kid who still believes the world is stable."

She flipped to the next.

"Then this one—after the executions. Same hand, same boy, but the register shifts. He describes burying his family and neighbors in three lines, then spends twice as much space listing where each grave is, who lies where. He's already thinking like someone who expects to be asked for proof later."

Another page.

"Here—August 5th. He notes a man in the market who says, 'I'm with a group that may be able to help.' He writes down the phrasing, the meeting place, the fact that the man doesn't want the group to see him. It's the first time he moves from reactive guiding to something like contact."

She slid forward to the Cauville entry.

"August 9th. 'We have plenty of lamb.' He records the code phrase, David's explanation, the logistics of the boats, the numbers—twelve per crossing, thirty who 'want, or rather need, to get out.' That's not the language of a composite; it's one set of eyes, making sense of one set of days."

Finally, she put her hand on the page she'd nearly memorized.

"And this one—August 19th, back at the farm. He describes standing outside with coffee on the stove and choosing the fields over Kate's kitchen. 'For now, it is easier to think about routes and rations. Feelings can wait until after the war, if there is an after for any of us.'"

She looked up.

"These aren't just colorful anecdotes," she said. "Taken together, they show a single consciousness moving from son to helper to courier—changing how he sees the same places as his role shifts. That arc is what I mean by 'particular.' It's not something I can reproduce by stitching together three or four different men."

Peters leaned forward, eyes on the pages.

"And your claim," Singh said slowly, "is that treating him as one voice is not just narratively satisfying, but the most accurate way to describe what we're actually reading."

"Yes," Ruth said. "And I want to be upfront that I recognize my own bias in that. From the moment I started reading, I connected with Joseph as if he were one person talking to me. That's not an argument; that's just where I started."

She tapped the packet.

"The classroom forced me to separate that attachment from the evidence. When students pushed—especially Eric—I had to prove, to them and to myself, that 'particular' wasn't just my favorite version of the story, it was the reading best supported by what we actually have."

She slid a clipped bundle of printouts across the table.

"I've included translated excerpts of two email threads. One is with Ozias, whose family runs the inn near the former vineyard. The other is with Marie Marchand, David's daughter. Oz is Joseph's grandson; Marie is David's. Their mothers were the two sisters at the farm—one who left with David, one who stayed and later married 'the boy from the vines.'"

She indicated a highlighted paragraph.

"In Marie's words: 'We grew up knowing that if Joseph had not come back for my parents, I would not be here, and if he had not kept going back to that farm, Oz would not be either... for us he has always been one real man, not a made-up type.' They did not know about the journal when those stories were first told. When they read the entries I sent, they independently recognized details that match what their parents and grandparents passed down."

She let that sit, then added, more quietly, "I can correlate their claims with parish registers, wartime notes, and postwar sacramental records from Father Laurent's church. I can't yet produce a birth certificate stamped 'Joseph, courier.' But I can show a continuous line from the boy in these pages to the families who insist they owe their existence to him."

Peters glanced at Singh. The third committee member, who had been silent so far, leaned in over the emails.

"So your evidence," Singh said, "is textual consistency in the journal, converging family testimony from both branches, and church records that place those families and a Joseph Durand in the same places at the right times."

Ruth nodded. "Exactly. It's not ironclad in the legal sense. But for the purposes of how I talk about him on the page, it's enough to say: this is one voice whose ripples we can still see."

Peters cleared his throat, tapping the edge of the emails with one finger.

"What you're really giving us here are three legs of the same stool," he said. "The internal voice of the journal, the external documents—parish and wartime records—and the living testimony from both branches of the family."

He glanced at Singh, then back at Ruth.

"Any one of those could mislead you on its own," he went on. "A single diarist can exaggerate. Families can smooth their stories to fit what they want to believe. Archives can be incomplete or wrong. Even two of the three can line up by accident or because people, consciously or not, bend toward a good story."

He tapped again, more firmly.

"But when all three point in the same direction—the same places, same sequence of events, same 'boy from the vines'—you're no longer just confirming what you want to be true. You're showing convergence."

Ruth felt some of the tightness in her shoulders ease.

"That's what I'm arguing," she said. "Not that any one piece is enough to close the case, but that together they justify treating Joseph as one particular man in my work, while being honest about the gaps."

Singh nodded slowly.

"Alright," she said. "Then the question for us isn't whether you've eliminated all doubt. It's whether your three legs make a stool solid enough to sit a thesis on without it collapsing under scrutiny."

Ruth managed a small, wry smile. "That's the hope," she said.

36

Chapter 36

The committee meeting could not have gone better.

They had not waved away her worries or handed her a blank check, but they had done something almost better: they'd listened, asked hard questions, and then put their signatures under a document that said, in careful, institutional prose, we believe this is real enough to back you if you carry it well. Dr. Singh had even used the word "thrilling," albeit with the qualifier "for historians."

By the time Ruth stepped back into the humid Oklahoma air, the exhaustion of the last week had been pushed aside by a sharper, unfamiliar energy. It felt like walking out of a storm cellar after the sirens stopped—everything the same and different at once.

She sat in her car, committee packet on the passenger seat, and stared at her phone.

There were two people she owed first: Lena, whose texts had been the only thing pulling her out of the 1940 fog some nights, and her parents, who had been quietly terrified that "this journal thing" might derail the stable life they'd hoped grad school would guarantee.

Her thumb hovered over Lena's name, then over the family group chat.

Family first, she decided. This needed a table, not a text.

Hey, she typed into the thread. Any chance we can do dinner at Grandma's again this week? I have big news, and it's easier to explain over pot roast.

The typing dots appeared almost instantly.

You bringing home a French husband? her dad wrote.

Lena, who was apparently still on silent-observer mode in the thread, chimed in before Ruth could answer: If she is, I call dibs on godmother of the first bilingual baby.

Ruth smiled, then shook her head.

Not a husband, she replied. A thesis. And maybe a book. The committee signed off on the Joseph project today. They agreed to back me on treating him as "one particular voice" and even approved a second trip to France—with interviews.

There was a pause long enough for her to imagine them all looking at their screens, putting pieces together: Paris, the vineyard, the late-night calls from Rouen and Tahlequah.

Her mom responded first.

Dinner. Thursday. Your grandmother will make enough food for an army of unknown heroes.

Her dad added: Proud of you, kiddo. Also terrified. But mostly proud.

Lena broke out of the group thread and sent a separate text.

Alive and victorious? she wrote. I demand details and carbs.

Ruth leaned her head back against the headrest and let herself feel it for a full thirty seconds—the strange, fizzy mix of relief and fear and something that felt almost like joy.

The committee hadn't just given her permission to keep going. They had given her a bar to reach: a finished article, a mapped timeline, documented interviews, a second research trip with the Marchands folded in as partners, not props. If she cleared it, they would stand behind her when the time came to argue, in print, that a boy from the vines had changed what historians thought they knew about 1940.

Ruth started the engine, almost oblivious to the way the December air cut through the thin seal of the door. The adrenaline did more to keep her warm than the heater ever could.

Before she put the car in gear, she pulled her laptop bag into her lap and balanced it against the steering wheel long enough to open her email.

New message

To: Ozias, Marie

Subject: Committee news and next steps

She hesitated for only a second, then began to type.

Dear Oz and Marie,

I wanted you both to hear this as soon as possible: the committee at my university met with me today about the Joseph project, and they have formally approved it as my thesis and potential book.

They have agreed that I can treat Joseph's journal as the work of one particular voice, with the necessary caveats about gaps in the record, and they have authorized a second trip to France that will include time for interviews with your family and others connected to the vineyard and the farm.

None of this would have been possible without your trust and your willingness to share what your parents and grandparents told you. I will send more detailed information soon about the timeline, what I hope to do on the next visit, and how we can make sure your perspectives are part of the work rather than something I simply write about from a distance.

For now, I just wanted to say thank you, and to let you know that a room full of historians on the other side of the ocean has just agreed that the boy from the vines matters enough to build a whole project around.

With gratitude,

Ruth

She read it once, resisted the urge to over-edit, and hit send.

As the message slipped off toward Normandy, Ruth set the laptop aside and finally eased the car into reverse.

For the first time since she'd opened that dusty drawer in Paris, it felt like she wasn't carrying Joseph alone.

Ruth barely remembered the drive home.

By Thursday evening, the committee packet had migrated from her bag to the dining table at her grandmother's house, joining the pot roast, mashed potatoes, and a sheet cake someone had decorated with uneven blue frosting: CONGRATS, DR. FUTURE.

The scene felt like an echo played in reverse.

Last time, she'd walked in with jet lag and a journal, trying to translate three weeks in France for a roomful of people who still thought of Normandy as a word from history class. Now, she was walking in with a plan to go back—and with a roomful of people who had met Joseph already, who could say "boy from the vines" without needing the whole prologue.

"Okay," her dad said, when the plates were finally full and the first wave of chatter had died down. "You promised us big news that was not a French husband. Floor's yours."

Ruth glanced around the table: her parents, her grandmother at the head with her hands folded, Lena at her elbow, already watching her with that mix of pride and worry she reserved for Ruth's riskier decisions.

She rested her palm lightly on the folder beside her plate, the way she'd rested it on the journal months before.

"So," she said. "You remember how last time I sat here and told you about finding a journal in a drawer in Paris, and you all thought I'd maybe lost my mind a little?"

A ripple of laughter went around the table.

"This week," she went on, "I sat in another room—with three historians instead of cousins—and told them the same story. Only this time, I asked them to let me build my whole thesis, and maybe a book, around that journal. Around Joseph."

Her grandmother's eyes sharpened. "And?"

"They said yes," Ruth answered. "With conditions. I have to finish an article in the next year, do more archival work, and go back to France to interview the families. But they signed off on treating him as one particular person, not just a composite. They're willing to stand behind me when I publish, if I do the work."

For a moment, no one spoke. Then her mom reached across the table and squeezed her hand.

"So you're really going back," she said softly.

Ruth nodded. "If the funding comes through, yes. Paris, Rouen, the vineyard. And this time, not as a tourist with a Eurail pass, but with questions—and with Joseph's granddaughter and grandson agreeing to meet me there."

Lena let out a low whistle. "Act Two," she murmured. "Same cast, bigger stakes."

Her dad leaned back, a familiar look settling over his face, the one he wore when he was both proud and trying not to imagine worst-case scenarios.

"You know we're going to worry," he said. "About money. About travel. About you spending the next few years living half in 1940."

"I know," Ruth said. "I worry about all of that too. But I also know what it would feel like not to do it. And now I'm not the only one who thinks he's worth the risk."

Her grandmother nodded once, decisive.

"Then we feed you," she said. "You can't argue with committees or ghosts on an empty stomach."

Lena bumped her shoulder.

"And after dinner," she said, "you're going to tell me every word Singh used, and exactly how you convinced them, so I can quote it back at you the next time you decide you're not qualified."

Ruth laughed, the sound looser than it had been in weeks.

The first time she'd sat at this table with Joseph's story, it had felt like introducing a stranger to the family. Tonight, as the conversation spilled out into questions about flights and French phone plans and whether Oklahoma girls needed special coats for Normandy in winter, it felt less like an introduction and more like a send-off.

Last time, she'd come home carrying an unknown man's voice in her bag.

This time, she would leave carrying a whole table's worth of expectations—and, for the first time, their blessing to go find out how his story ended.

37

Chapter 37

Ruth went back to work.

The little glass-front room off the quiet floor became her whole world again—pins in the map, color-coded threads, Joseph's tight handwriting under the fluorescent lights. Days collapsed into each other, measured less by class periods than by how many pages she could translate before her eyes blurred.

Lena started showing up with to-go coffees and contraband snacks, claiming the spare chair by the wall.

"This is getting ridiculous," she said one afternoon, watching Ruth flip between the journal and a spreadsheet of dates. "You live in here now. I should start having your mail forwarded to the library."

"Rent's cheaper," Ruth murmured, not looking up. "And the neighbors are quieter."

Lena rolled her eyes, but she stayed—reading, grading her own students' papers, occasionally tossing out a question that forced Ruth to explain some piece of 1940 aloud instead of just in footnotes. It was, Ruth realized, the only way she saw her in person anymore.

When Lena wasn't there, the room was quiet enough that the ping of new mail sounded almost loud.

The last thread with Ozias sat near the top of her inbox, its subject line—Re: Committee news and next steps—no longer an unread flag but a kind of emotional bookmark. Their messages had shifted since the first cautious "Made it home okay?" and "I'm still thinking about the oak and the graves."

Now they ran longer. Practicals threaded through with something else.

He sent scans of his grandfather's notes, scribbled in the margins of an old missal, about "the boy from the vines" and the sisters at the farm. She sent photos of her map wall and described how her students argued over whether plenty of lamb counted as code or coincidence.

In between, there were lines that were not strictly necessary for the project.

If you come in March, the fog will still be on the fields in the morning. It makes the vines look like they're floating.

You will hate the jet lag, but I will try to make sure the coffee at the inn is good enough to compensate.

She found herself rereading those as often as the attached documents.

The last email currently open ended with his response to her committee news:

I'm glad they see what you see. Grand-Père would have been amused that a room of professors is arguing about whether he was "particular." If the funding comes through, tell me your dates. I'll clear the rooms and make sure my aunt doesn't try to feed you to death. Again.

Then, beneath it, a line that made her pause every time she saw it:

It will be good to have you back here—not just as "the historian," but as Ruth.

She hadn't answered that part yet.

Every draft she started read either too formal for the warmth he'd offered, or too warm for someone she'd technically only spent a handful of hours with in person. The anticipation of seeing him again sat somewhere between her ribs, tangled up with flight schedules and interview questions.

Lena caught her staring at the screen one evening and raised an eyebrow.

"Planning your archival strategy?" she asked. "Or practicing your French?"

Ruth closed the laptop a little too quickly.

"Both," she said. "Apparently I'm bad at compartmentalizing when everything hurts and matters at once."

Lena smiled, recognizing her own words thrown back at her.

"Welcome to being human," she said. "Now, do you want to rehearse your questions for the Marchands, or your hello for Oz?"

Ruth reached for the journal instead, but the flush in her cheeks gave away the answer: as winter edged toward spring, the trip ahead was no longer just a return to sites on a map.

It was a return to people, some living, some long gone, and to a story that was pulling her in from more than one direction at once.

She started the practical prep with Marie first: dates, train times, a running list of what absolutely had to happen before Ruth flew home and what could wait for a second visit. They traded bullet points and attachments—museum-quality scans, rough layout sketches for the exhibition, a shared spreadsheet labeled, in Marie's quick English, "Stories We Cannot Leave Out."

In between, there were shorter lines that weren't strictly about vitrines and wall text.

If you stand them in front of the oak, you must tell them he chose to be ordinary. Otherwise they will only see a tree.

Also, my aunt is already planning what cakes to make. Consider this fair warning.

Ruth smiled at that one longer than she meant to. There was a comfort in how easily Marie moved between the gravity of 1940 and the domestic details of 2026, as if the family had learned, over decades, that you could not live on ghosts alone. It made the whole thing—funding, flights, an exhibition with her name on it—feel less like a test and more like joining a line of people who had been carrying this longer than she had.

Lena, reading over her shoulder one afternoon under the pretense of grading, snorted.

"Of course she's in on it," she said. "Classic aunt-with-nephew behavior. 'Come see our historical artifacts, also have you met our very nice innkeeper who definitely has both a pulse and wi-fi?'"

Ruth tried to glare and failed. "We are planning an exhibition," she said. "And fieldwork."

"And feelings," Lena said. "Don't leave out the third F."

By the time the department finally approved the internal travel form and the last piece of funding cleared, Ruth's inbox looked less like a correspondence file and more like a net: Marie on the exhibit layout, Oz on the attic crate and guest rooms, Father Laurent with a brief note promising time in the cathedral's side chapel if she needed the archives again. The March calendar on her wall filled up in layers—colored blocks for interviews and site visits, smaller penciled reminders that simply read things like Oak, Cliff, Market road.

The night before she booked the ticket, Lena showed up at the apartment with popcorn and a stack of sticky notes.

"Last chance to back out," she said, dropping onto the couch. "We can repurpose all this emotional energy into a case study on archival burnout."

Ruth opened her laptop instead. "I need to give them dates," she said. "Oz can't 'clear the rooms' indefinitely."

"There it is," Lena murmured. "The real reason we're doing this tonight."

Ruth ignored her, mostly. She typed out the practical email first—arrival time, rough outline of the first week, the list Marie had asked for detailing which journal entries she wanted to anchor in which rooms. Her fingers hesitated only once, over the last line.

Looking forward to seeing all of you again—in the archives, and under the oak.

She left it. Hit send. Closed the lid before the reply could land and make it realer than it already was.

"Okay," Lena said quietly. "You're going."

Ruth let herself lean back into the couch cushions, the exhaustion and anticipation finally landing in the same place. "I'm going," she said. "For the exhibit. For the interviews. For—"

"For you," Lena finished. "And maybe a little for the innkeeper who writes about ordinary men like they're miracles."

Ruth didn't argue. There didn't seem much point.

They sat in silence for a few minutes, the low hum of the fridge and the tick of the hallway thermostat filling in where words didn't. The journal lay on the coffee table between them, a familiar rectangle of leather and paper that had somehow rearranged her entire life without changing its own shape at all.

Lena's gaze kept drifting toward it, then away. Finally, near the bottom of the popcorn bowl, she spoke.

"I've been thinking," she said slowly, "that I should probably meet him."

Ruth blinked. "Oz?"

"Yes, Oz," Lena said. "Unless there's another French man with an inn and an oak you've been hiding from me."

"You don't speak French," Ruth said automatically.

"I grade freshman reflection papers," Lena countered. "I can handle a language barrier."

Ruth huffed a laugh, but Lena's expression had gone oddly serious.

"Okay," Ruth said carefully. "Why the sudden determination? Besides your lifelong dream of embarrassing me on foreign soil."

Lena shrugged, fingers worrying the edge of a sticky note. "Because I've watched this whole thing happen from one side," she said. "You and Joseph. You and your students. You and your family. You and this man who lives on the other end of your inbox. And at some point, if I just keep cheering from the bleachers, I'm going to look up and realize you built a bridge I never walked across with you."

Ruth stared at her. "You don't have to—"

"I know I don't have to," Lena said. "I want to. I keep telling you not to let the work swallow the rest of your life, but the truth is, I've been letting you do all the crossing. If this guy is going to be part of the orbit you live in when you're not in 1940, I'd like to at least shake his hand before he gets away with being a disembodied email."

Her eyes dropped, finally, to the journal. She reached out, then stopped just short of touching it.

"And," she added, quieter, "I think I want to see what he sees when he looks at this. I don't speak French, and honestly half the time I barely keep up with your theology-meets-history brain. But this"—her fingers hovered a breath above the worn leather—"this is what pulled him into your world. I've been sitting beside it for months without ever asking to hold it."

Ruth swallowed. "You could have asked."

"I know," Lena said. "I didn't feel like I had the right. Like I was... interrupting something."

She looked up, meeting Ruth's eyes.

"But I don't want to wave you off at the airport and then watch from Oklahoma while you stand under that tree with him and talk about a man whose handwriting I've never actually seen for myself. So." She exhaled, a little laugh escaping with the breath. "Maybe toward the end of this semester, before you go, you let me pick it up. Even if all I can do is trace the ink and pretend I understand."

Ruth reached for the journal, thumb resting on the familiar groove where the cord used to sit. For a long moment she just held it, feeling again that first shock of recognition in the Paris shop, the way Joseph's voice had threaded itself through vineyards and classrooms and committee rooms until it was woven into every part of her life.

Then she turned it and laid it gently in Lena's hands.

"You're not interrupting," she said. "You're the reason I'm still here to carry him at all."

Lena's fingers curled around the leather, careful and reverent, as if it might splinter under the weight of being shared.

"Bonjour, Joseph," she said softly, the accent terrible and the sentiment sincere. "Nice to finally meet you before I meet the guy who won't stop writing about you."

Ruth laughed, the sound breaking something open in her chest that had been tight for too long.

"Fair warning," she said. "Neither of them is going to know what hit them."

"Good," Lena replied, eyes still on the page as she carefully opened to the first line. "It's about time the future showed up in this story on purpose."

Lena turned the book over in her hands, testing the weight, running her thumb along the softened spine. The leather was smoother in some places, rougher in others, worn by years of someone else's grip long before it ever sat on Ruth's desk.

She flipped carefully through a few pages, not lingering on the words she couldn't read so much as on the way the ink sat on the paper, darker in early entries, paler where the pen must have been running dry. Her thumb found the back cover almost by accident.

There, along the inside edge, the paper caught slightly. A tiny dog-ear, no bigger than a fingernail, folded into the binding.

"He was rough with it here," Lena murmured, more to herself than to Ruth. "Or somebody was."

She slid her thumb under the crease to smooth it—and felt the whole last leaf give a fraction of an inch, as if it weren't as firmly married to the leather as it looked. The corner of the page pulled away from the cover with a soft, dry whisper.

"Careful," Ruth said automatically.

"I am," Lena replied. But she had already lifted the edge just enough to see that something else was there, pressed flat between the back page and the board. Not new paper—a continuation. A seam that had never quite torn open.

She eased it back another millimeter. The binding flexed. A narrow strip of writing appeared, cramped and angled to fit the hidden space.

Lena squinted. She didn't speak French, but even she could read the first two words.

"Dear Kate," she whispered.

38

Chapter 38

There was a new weight in the journal that had nothing to do with paper. Somewhere between the last dated entry and the back board, a seam had opened. Lena had seen the first two words; Ruth had closed the cover before either of them could read the rest. There'd been an unspoken truce in that silence: they would not pull the page loose until Ruth decided what kind of knowing it would be.

The decision not to read it left a tension in the air as the travel dates approached. It tightened with the first class session of the next semester. Eric was back. So were the board members who caught her in the hallway between meetings, asking if anything new had come up, any developments in "her" case.

She gave them the same answer each time, a careful neutral. Nothing that changes the core structure. Small confirmations, a few more parallels. Things that join the argument, not the kind of discovery that needs a memo.

It was true, as far as it went. It just left out the part about a page pressed into the spine, beginning with a name that could reorder everything.

By the end of the day, Ruth wanted nothing more than the solitude of the library. The glass-front room felt safer than the hallways full of questions, safer even than her own inbox. She spread out her notes instead of the hidden page: travel dates, interview lists, a column of questions for Marie and another for the Marchands.

If she kept her hands on itineraries and consent forms, she could almost ignore the pull to give up "Dear Kate" in an email—attach a scan, let someone else tell her what it meant, surrender the choice of when and how to let anyone know it existed at all.

Instead, she opened a draft to Marie.

They were well past the polite stage now. The subject line read simply: March schedule + one big question.

Ruth laid out the practicals first: arrival in Paris, the train north, which days she hoped to spend at the inn and which at the vineyard, a tentative block for recording Marie's mother and aunt together if they were still willing. She attached the same spreadsheet they'd been passing back and forth, now annotated with colored flags—oral history, artifacts, liturgy, routes.

Then she paused over the empty line at the bottom.

There was no way to ask about David that didn't feel like prying. And yet, if the exhibit was going to be honest, it couldn't stop with a boy from the vines vanishing into the dark and a friend on a boat to England. Families had lived with the after for eighty years. She was walking into their house with a journal that had never heard it.

She typed, deleted, tried again.

One thing I'm still not sure how to handle well is the "after" for your side of the story. I know from you that your father made it out, married, raised you with Joseph as a fixed point. What I don't know—and don't want to assume—is what you grew up hearing about those years between Cauville and America. If there are pieces you'd be open to sharing (or that you'd rather keep in the family), it would help me know how far the exhibition should follow his line forward on the wall and where it should stop.

She read it twice. It still felt like reaching across a boundary, but at least it named the line instead of pretending there wasn't one.

She hit send before she could soften it, then went back to the calendar to color in "Oak" and "Cathedral" and "Inn" on the weeks ahead.

Marie's reply came faster than she expected.

You are not prying. If anything, you are the first person outside our family who has asked the question and not assumed the answer. We grew up with stories, but they were small ones, told in pieces. My father did not give speeches. He fixed things. He built a business. He took us to the temple. Only sometimes, when he thought we were asleep, he would sit under the oak and talk to someone we could not see.

She stopped there, breath held, then kept reading.

I can tell you what I know. My mother can tell you what she remembers. There are also things I have only guessed, and I think you will help us name which is which. For the exhibit, I agree with you: it should not become "The Life of David Marchand," but it also should not pretend he disappeared once he reached the boat. Maybe we let the wall follow him as far as the first safe house in England and then use the rest of the space for what the two families tried to build after. You and I can talk more when you arrive.

At the bottom, Marie had added a single line, almost as an afterthought.

Also, there is a question I have for you: if Joseph wrote about my father so much, did he ever write anything only for the woman he married? Or did he keep all of that off the page?

Ruth stared at the sentence until the words blurred.

She did not answer that part. Not yet.

Her hand drifted to the journal on the desk, to the place where the back cover flexed just slightly if you knew where to press. Somewhere between the last entry and the board was an answer she hadn't let herself read—a piece of the "after" that belonged to Kate as much as David's did to Marie's family.

For now, she wrote back about train times and recording consent and how grateful she was that they were willing to let her step into the middle of their story at all.

The rest would have to wait until she was standing under the same sky they were.

Ruth had just closed out her thread with Marie when another notification slid across the corner of her screen.

Ozias St. Pierre

Re: Attic crate, part seven

She opened it, expecting another set of scanned pages or a photograph of his grandfather's cramped handwriting. There was an attachment, but the body of the email ran longer than usual.

I thought I was finished sending you things, but apparently the attic disagrees.

This time it wasn't just "boy from the vines" notes. Oz had attached a photograph of a different page, the ink fainter, the lines more halting.

Grand-Père writes here about "the boy" coming back after the boats left, about one evening when he stood at the edge of our cove and refused to come in for supper. I will send you the full page, but what struck me is not what he says about 1940. It is what he doesn't say about what came after.

Ruth scrolled.

He never writes, even in private, what he thought happened to Joseph in the end. He only notes that the routes changed, the uniforms changed, and the work of keeping people alive did not. For a man who could not stop cataloguing tides and patrol schedules, that silence feels deliberate.

There was a line break, then:

It makes me wonder about the "after" for both of them. You have asked my cousin about her father. I find myself asking what Grand-Père did with his own ghosts once the war finished using them. He took us to temple, he repaired boats, he taught us to look at the water and see more than waves. But he never once told me whether he thought the boy from the vines survived.

Ruth felt the familiar tightness settle between her ribs. Marie on one side of the Channel, Oz on the other, both circling the same missing years from different directions.

At the bottom, Oz had added, almost shyly:

When you come in March, I would like to show you a place I have never taken guests. It is not far from the inn—a small rise above the cove where he used to sit when he did not want to be found. I think it may have more to say about both of them than the attic does. If you think that belongs to your work, I will take you. If not, I will still make sure the coffee is strong.

Ruth's fingers hovered over the keyboard.

She could feel the old instinct rise up—the one that wanted to paste in a translation of some familiar entry, to answer with evidence instead of herself. Instead, she typed:

I think places like that are exactly where this work lives now. And I think your grandfather's silence is part of the story, even if we never fill it in.

Her hand drifted, almost without thinking, to the back cover of the journal on her desk.

She did not mention the words Dear Kate. Not yet.

Lena appeared in the doorway before Ruth could talk herself out of hitting send, balancing two coffees and a stack of ungraded essays.

"I brought fuel," she said. "And a reminder that sunlight exists somewhere outside this room."

Ruth took the cup with a grateful noise. "I'm scheduling fieldwork," she said. "Sunlight is on the March itinerary."

"Fieldwork," Lena repeated, dropping into the spare chair. "Is that what we're calling cliff walks with the innkeeper now?"

Ruth's fingers tightened around the cup. "He's a community partner," she said. "And a primary conduit for family testimony."

Lena stared at her. "Did you just call the man who writes you about fog and coffee a conduit?"

"He runs the inn," Ruth said, hearing how stiff it sounded even as she said it. "He scans his grandfather's notes. He's—he's part of the archive."

"Uh-huh." Lena set her essays down and swiveled the chair just enough to face the map wall, where Ruth had added a new sticky note near the coast that simply read Cliff. "Do your other community partners get their own post-it with no call number?"

Ruth felt heat creep up her neck. "It's a location," she said. "Sites are labeled by function."

"And what's the function there?" Lena asked lightly. "Source evaluation? Oral history? Checking whether the coffee is strong enough to compensate for jet lag?"

Ruth busied herself straightening a stack of interview questions. "We're meeting to talk about his grandfather," she said. "And about how to frame the cove in the exhibit. It's important to keep the categories clear. He's not—"

"—your boyfriend," Lena supplied. "I know. You keep telling me. That's why you keep calling him 'the innkeeper' and 'the conduit' instead of Oz."

Ruth opened her mouth, closed it again.

"You're allowed to have a category that isn't on the IRB form, you know," Lena said more gently. "He can be a source and a person. A partner and a man you might actually like, in that order or the other."

Ruth stared at the journal on the desk, at the travel calendar on the wall, at the inbox where Oz's name sat in bold above Marie's.

"If I start calling him anything else, it'll change the way I write about all of this," she said quietly. "About Joseph. About Kate. About what it costs to love someone and still walk back into the fire."

Lena's expression softened. "Or," she said, "it might make you more honest about the fact that you're already doing that, and that you're not the only one."

Ruth didn't answer. Instead, she picked up a pen and, in the margin of her questions list, wrote:

Ozias – interview: grandfather, cove, postwar silence.

Oz – coffee, fog, ordinary life.

Two lines. Same man. Both true.

Lena leaned over just far enough to read it, then sat back with a small, satisfied noise.

"Progress," she said. "I'll take it."

39

Chapter 39

The weeks between "Progress" and departure blurred into lists.

There were the visible ones: packing lists taped to the fridge, a class-coverage chart on her office door, a shared document for her students outlining what they'd read while she was gone and when their drafts were due. There were the quieter ones only she saw: questions for Marie's mother and aunt, asterisks beside the dates in Joseph's entries that overlapped with coastal notes from the crate, a single line that just read Dear Kate? with no box beside it yet.

Her parents hosted one more Sunday dinner "before you disappear into Europe again," her dad said, carving roast as if he could pin her to Oklahoma with a serving fork. Her mom slipped an envelope with euros into her hand "for emergencies or pastry, whichever finds you first." Lena commandeered a grocery-store run for plane snacks and a new neck pillow "because one of us should at least pretend we've learned from last time."

Ruth smiled and nodded, answering the same questions—Yes, they're expecting me. Yes, I'll email. No, I won't go wandering alone at night near the cliffs—without mentioning that the heaviest thing in her carry-on was still a page she hadn't read.

The journal stayed on her desk until the last possible morning. Only when the suitcase was zipped and the apartment plants were watered did she slip it into her backpack, wrapped in the same scarf she'd worn the day she first stepped into the vineyard fog. Her thumb found the soft give of the back cover, the place where the binding flexed.

Not yet, she thought. Not on this side of the ocean.

The hop to Chicago was short enough that she could pretend it was any other conference trip. She graded a few paragraphs, half-watched the safety demonstration, let the steady engine noise drown out the part of her brain that wanted to script every conversation waiting across the Atlantic.

By the time the plane rolled to a stop at O'Hare, she was more tired than nervous.

The terminal, however, had other plans. Voices overlapped in a dozen languages. Rolling suitcases clipped her ankles. Screens blinked departures and delays in neat, indifferent columns. Somewhere in that controlled chaos was Gate K12 and a woman who had grown up with Joseph as a fixed point instead of a professional question.

Her phone buzzed as she cleared the concourse.

K12. Blue jacket, too much coffee. I'll wave.

Marie.

Ruth tightened her grip on the backpack strap and followed the signs toward the K gates. Each turn felt like a small crossing: out of her home airport, out of the semester's routines, out of the careful distance that had separated her from the families whose lives she'd been diagramming in chalk and marker.

She saw her before she saw the gate number.

Marie stood near a row of connected chairs, travel bag at her feet, hands wrapped around a paper cup. The blue jacket was exactly as advertised. So was the way her face lit up when she spotted Ruth, as if relief and recognition had arrived at the same time.

"Ruth?" she called.

Ruth lifted a hand, suddenly aware of the journal pressing between her shoulder blades, the weight of all the unanswered afters they were carrying between them.

"Hi," she said, stepping into the open patch of floor between strangers and departure boards. "We made it."

"For once," Marie said, smiling, "we get to start a chapter together instead of trying to read each other's margins."

They stood there for a moment, two women from opposite sides of a war's echo, sharing the same recycled airport air, until the speaker crackled.

"Final boarding call for Flight 184 to Paris. Passengers Ruth Peters and Marie Marchand, please proceed to Gate K12."

Marie glanced at the screen, then back at her.

"Ready?" she asked.

Ruth thought of the oak, the cliff, the hidden page, the students waiting to see how this would end.

"Not entirely," she said. "But I'm going anyway."

They picked up their bags and walked toward the gate together.

There was supposed to be plenty of time on the flight. Eight hours, give or take, suspended between continents and time zones. Ruth had imagined herself sleeping through at least some of it, saving her strength for the days ahead.

Instead, she spent the first hour with the journal open between them.

They'd barely leveled off before Marie unbuckled, turned in her seat, and nodded toward the backpack at Ruth's feet.

"Do you mind?" she asked. "Seeing it—not just the scans?"

Ruth hesitated only a second. Then she slid the bag out, unwrapped the familiar scarf, and laid the book carefully on the tray table between their armrests. The overhead light caught the softened leather, the faint ghost of the name on the cover.

Marie's breath hitched. "I've seen that script in your emails," she murmured. "It's different when it's... there."

Ruth found herself explaining before Marie even turned a page. She traced the routes on the map in the front flyleaf, pointed out where Joseph's dates crossed the notations from the crate, tapped the margins where her students had argued over code words and coincidences. The path from the vineyard to the Green Forest. The nights at the cove. The first time his line intersected a note from a man on the cliff.

It felt, she realized halfway through, a little like an ambush—Lena at one elbow in memory, Oz's questions in Marie's inbox, and now Marie herself bracketed between Ruth's commentary and the weight of her family's own stories.

Somewhere over the dark of the Atlantic, Marie's thumb found the back cover.

"What about the end?" she asked quietly. "You told me the entries themselves stop before the war does."

Ruth's hand shot out before she could think, catching the edge just as the binding flexed.

"There is... something else," she said. "But we haven't read it yet."

Marie looked up, brows drawn. "Haven't?"

Ruth exhaled. This, at least, she owed her.

"A few weeks ago, Lena found a seam in the back," she said. "The last page isn't as fixed to the board as it looks. When she lifted it, we saw a strip of writing hidden inside. Just enough to make out the first two words."

She eased the cover back herself this time, only far enough that the narrow line of cramped script appeared.

Marie leaned in. Even without French, she could read the opening.

"Dear Kate," she whispered.

Ruth let the cover fall shut again, gently, as if closing a door.

"I wanted you to know we found it," she said. "And that we haven't gone any farther without you. I've been trying to hold off until he was back in France. It feels... wrong to open that kind of letter anywhere else."

Marie sat back, eyes still on the closed leather. She looked at Ruth then, something like gratitude and grief braided together.

"Thank you for waiting," she said. "Kate should be the first to hear it. She's waited this long to hear it; we can wait a day or two."

Ruth nodded, the resolve settling more solidly than it had in weeks.

"There's plenty on these pages to argue about in the meantime," she said, turning back to the routes and dates and crossings. "We'll let the last word wait for the land that wrote it."

After almost another hour of Ruth pointing out crossings and patterns, she finally just let Marie go with the journal—quiet now, answering only the few questions Marie asked before the lull of the engines pulled her eyes closed.

She woke to the soft chime of the intercom and the rattle of carts in the aisle.

Outside the oval window, the world had reshaped itself into the gray-blue smudge of early morning over northern France. Clouds thinned, tore; patches of fields showed through—rectangles of winter earth, thin rows of trees, the silver thread of a road she could not name but Joseph might have walked.

"Cabin crew, prepare for landing."

The last time she'd flown into Paris, she'd pressed her forehead to the glass and tried to picture banners hanging from the balconies, boots on cobblestone, uniforms spilling through streets that now held tourists and food trucks. It had been an exercise of imagination then, an overlay from books and films and a handful of journal pages.

Now the picture sharpened.

She could see, in her mind's eye, the mairie wall from Joseph's October entry, the way he'd described bodies hanging beside a plaster Christ, signs shouting justice and order over a town taught to look at the ground. She could see the truck checkpoints he'd timed in careful loops, the farm roads where he'd chosen to keep moving instead of staying at the kitchen table. The approach path below the plane wasn't just countryside anymore; it was a lattice of possible routes and patrol lines and hiding places.

Beside her, Marie had the journal closed in her lap, fingers resting lightly on the cover as if she, too, felt its pull grow stronger with every mile.

"Almost there," she said quietly.

Ruth nodded, swallowing against the pressure in her ears and somewhere deeper.

She'd left France carrying a story that might have been one man or a composite, a question more than a life. This time, she was bringing him back, with his routes mapped, his silences named, his unseen afters brushing up against temple pews and a cove above the sea. And somewhere in the spine, a letter that began with a woman's name and waited for the right ground to open on.

As the plane dipped toward Charles de Gaulle, the city began to take shape beneath them: ring roads, rail lines, the faint glint of the Seine curling through it all. Ruth let the view blur, not into abstraction now, but into layers—occupation and liberation, then all the lives that had stacked themselves over those years without erasing them.

They were putting death on the walls and asking us to learn from it, Joseph had written once. I will. Just not what they want.

Ruth closed her eyes for a moment, feeling the wheels extend beneath her feet.

"Okay," she thought, not sure if she was answering Joseph, Kate, David, or herself. "We're back. Let's see what the land remembers."

40

Chapter 40

The three of them spilled out of customs into the Paris evening, the air thick with jet fuel and rain left over from an earlier shower. Fluorescent light gave way to the softer glow of the arrivals hall, a blur of signs and reunions and drivers holding cardboard placards.

Lena slowed, fingers tightening on the strap of her carry-on as she squinted ahead. Then she caught Ruth's sleeve and tugged, hard enough to make Ruth stumble a step.

"Seriously," she hissed, nodding toward the far end of the barrier, "you slow-played how cute he was."

Ruth followed her gaze. A few yards away stood a tanned man in a worn jacket, dark hair pushed back by travel wind, holding a hand-lettered sign with the inn's name and, beneath it, her own.

He saw them at almost the same moment. For a heartbeat his eyes went to Marie, his face breaking into an easy, familiar smile.

"Aunt Marie," Oz called, lifting the sign in greeting. "It's so good to see you."

Lena huffed out a laugh, not one to be shy.

"Very well played, man behind the curtain," she murmured. "Make him charming to the family first. Smart. Now Ruth's definitely going to overthink every word she says to him."

The easy pleasantries after Lena's joke came out a shade stiffer than usual, everyone suddenly a little too aware of themselves as they shook hands and traded first hellos. They followed Oz out to the car park, the automatic doors sighing shut behind them, and loaded bags into the back of the van in a choreography of wheels and lifted handles that didn't require much conversation.

By the time they pulled onto the périphérique, the sky had settled into full dark. Ahead, through the streaked windshield, the Eiffel Tower rose out of the city glow, and as they curved along the river it burst into its first shimmer of the evening, a sudden scatter of light that chased itself up and down the iron lattice.

Oz let them sit with the lights for a minute, the city slipping past in gold and shadow. From the back, Lena pressed her forehead to the glass, muttering something about postcards and how real life shouldn't be allowed to look that staged.

"So," Oz said at last, flicking a glance at the rearview, "did the flight treat you kindly, or do I need to stop for industrial-strength coffee before we hit the ring road?"

"Coffee is never a bad idea," Lena said. "But we survived. Mostly because Ruth refused to let us sleep until she'd finished turning my tray table into a crime board."

Ruth made a noise of protest. "It was not a crime board. It was context."

Marie's smile warmed in the dim light. "You should have seen her," she said. "She gave me a guided tour of half the journal before we were over Iceland."

Oz's hands tightened just slightly on the wheel. "You read more?" he asked. "Together?"

"A bit," Marie said. "Enough for me to see how your grandfather's notes cross my dad's." She hesitated, then added, "And something else."

Ruth shifted in her seat, feeling the journal's weight against her feet. "You don't have to—"

"It's part of the story now," Marie said gently. She looked toward the front. "Lena found a page hidden in the binding. It's not an entry. It's a letter."

Oz went quiet. Even the hum of the tires on wet asphalt seemed to drop a register.

"A letter," he repeated. "From him."

Ruth cleared her throat. "We've only seen the first two words," she said quickly. "We stopped there on purpose."

"Dear Kate," Marie supplied. "He wrote to my aunt."

Oz let out a low breath that sounded like it had been trapped for years. "You're sure?"

Ruth nodded, though he couldn't see it. "Same hand. Same ink, same paper. Someone pressed it into the spine. We found it by accident."

Lena, for once, stayed quiet.

"We promised not to read it until we were here," Ruth went on. "It felt wrong to open that kind of letter over Oklahoma or the Atlantic. So the page is still folded. Waiting."

For a few miles, the only sound was the indicator ticking as Oz changed lanes.

"My father used to say," he murmured finally, half to the windshield, "that some stories won't speak until the land is ready to hear them. Maybe that's what he meant." He cleared his throat, then added, softer, "Thank you. For waiting for her."

Marie's fingers brushed Ruth's sleeve. "We decided Kate should be the first to hear it," she said. "She's waited this long. We can wait another day."

Ruth watched the towers and rooftops thin as the city gave way to darker stretches of road, the headlights catching only brief flashes of signs and trees.

"In the meantime," she said, grasping for steadier ground, "we were making a list on the plane. Places Joseph mentions that we haven't stood in yet. The cove. The Green Forest. The village where the shopkeeper took his note. I thought we could start by lining those up with what you and your grandfather knew."

Oz's shoulders eased a fraction at the return to routes and maps. "Good," he said. "We'll have time tomorrow, before we go out to the cliff or the graves. You can spread him out on my kitchen table and tell me where you've walked with him so far."

"And you," Marie added, "can tell us what your family remembers that he never wrote."

The van merged onto the highway north, Paris shrinking in the mirrors.

Between Ruth's shoes, the journal shifted with the turn, paper and leather and a thin, hidden page holding its breath for the first full day back on French soil.

The rest of the drive blurred into rain-slick asphalt and the soft rise and fall of Lena's commentary as she tried, and failed, to stay awake. At some point the highway narrowed, traded sodium lamps for pockets of dark, then gave way to smaller roads that curled through fields and sleeping villages. Headlights caught the edges of stone walls, the flash of a wayside crucifix, the brief gleam of a church spire before it slipped behind them.

By the time Oz turned onto the lane that led to the inn, the world had gone quiet. The gravel crunched under the tires, a familiar rhythm that seemed to loosen something in his shoulders. Ahead, a low stone house emerged from the dark, its windows lit with a warm, amber glow. A hand-painted sign swung gently in the night breeze, the inn's name picked out in fading script.

Inside, the transition felt almost indecently soft. The entry smelled of coffee and wood smoke and whatever herb had been tucked into the bowl of lemons on the sideboard. A narrow staircase climbed to the rooms above. Somewhere in the back, pipes hummed as someone ran water.

Oz gave them the quick, practical tour, his voice dropping to that late-hour gentleness that comes from long practice: keys on hooks, breakfast times, how to jiggle the old latch on the back door if it stuck. Lena's second wind had burned off somewhere on the last roundabout; she yawned her way through the explanations, shouldered her bag, and mumbled something about setting three alarms before vanishing up the stairs.

Marie lingered just long enough to squeeze Oz's arm and murmur a quiet "Merci" that carried more than travel in it. Then she, too, disappeared down the hallway, her door clicking shut with a soft finality.

Ruth's room was small but clean, sloped ceiling angling down over a narrow bed. The window looked out over the dark suggestion of fields and, farther off, the faint rise of a line of trees she knew would resolve into hedgerows and vines by morning. She set her bag down and, almost automatically, unwrapped the journal, placing it on the small desk by the window.

For a moment she just stood there, fingers resting on the cover, listening to the inn settle around her—the distant creak of floorboards, a door closing, the muted thump of footsteps below. France sounded different from Oklahoma even when it was quiet.

"Tomorrow," she whispered, thumb brushing the place where the back cover flexed. "You'll have her name back tomorrow."

She washed the airplane from her face in the tiny bathroom, changed into the softest shirt she'd packed, and slid between the cool sheets. Jet lag and adrenaline warred for a few minutes, thoughts skittering between routes and cliffs and the oak, between Kate's waiting letter and the first conversations to come.

Sleep won.

She surfaced to pale light pressing at the edges of the curtains and the soft patter of rain easing off the roof. For an instant she felt that familiar, disorienting jolt—the sense of waking somewhere that wasn't home, her body insisting she should be in two places at once.

Then the smell of coffee drifted up from below, threaded with something yeasty and warm, and the memories snapped into place. Paris. The drive north. The inn. The journal on the desk.

She swung her feet to the floor, padded to the window, and pulled the curtain back.

Outside, the first light had turned the world to grayscale. Fields rolled away in soft, damp folds. A line of trees marked the start of the path toward the sea. Somewhere beyond that, cliffs waited, and a cove, and an oak that held three families' dead and one letter's first two words.

Behind her, on the desk, the journal lay where she'd left it, the leather dark against the pale wood.

"First light," she murmured, more to Joseph than to herself. "Let's see what today asks of us."

41

Chapter 41

The smell of coffee reached her before the sounds did.

For a moment, Ruth just sat on the edge of the bed, toes curling against the cool floorboards, listening to the inn wake up beneath her. A cupboard closed, the murmur of a voice down the hall, the low scrape of a chair. It sounded like any other morning in any other house—and nothing like one.

She dressed quickly, fingers clumsy on the buttons, and hesitated just long enough to lay her hand on the journal where it sat on the desk.

"Day one," she whispered. "No running ahead."

Downstairs, the kitchen was already warm.

Marie sat at the long table with her hands wrapped around a mug, hair pulled back, a faint crease between her brows that relaxed when she saw Ruth. Lena was perched on a stool at the counter, methodically dismantling a croissant.

Oz moved between stove and sink with an easy efficiency—mug in one hand, spatula in the other, bare feet silent on tile. He looked up as Ruth stepped through the doorway, and for a split second she saw the same flicker from the graveyard in his face: recognition, sharpened now by the emails and the airport reunion.

"Morning," he said. "You made it down before the second pot. I'm impressed."

"Jet lag," Ruth said. "My superpower."

"Coffee?" he offered.

"Yes, please," she and Lena said at the same time. Marie's mouth twitched.

They ate in a rhythm that felt both new and oddly familiar: plates passed, questions asked and half-answered, small talk stitched around a weight in the center of the table none of them named yet.

It was Marie who finally nudged them toward it.

"Today," she said, setting her mug down with a soft click, "we should choose where to begin. We cannot touch every place at once." Her gaze moved between Ruth and Oz. "But there are some we cannot delay."

Ruth glanced at Oz. "I promised her," she said quietly, "that the letter would wait until we'd been to the graves. To the oak. I'd like to keep that."

Oz nodded once, serious. "Then the cemetery first," he said. "This afternoon, when the light is softer. This morning..." He gestured toward the other room. "We spread him out on the table. See where you and he have already walked together, and where the gaps still are."

Lena raised a hand. "For the record, 'spread him out on the table' is a deeply unsettling phrase for someone who hasn't had enough sleep."

"You volunteered for this trip," Ruth said.

"I did," Lena agreed. "Which means I get to watch you two make obsessive map faces while I pretend to be a normal tourist for at least twenty minutes."

Oz pushed back from the counter and wiped his hands on a towel. "Come," he said to Ruth and Marie, inclining his head toward the adjoining room. "The kitchen has fed you. Now we let the papers do their part."

Ruth stood, nerves prickling just beneath her skin. The journal suddenly felt heavier under her arm than it had in the classroom or on the plane.

The inn's small sitting room had been transformed. A wide wooden table stood in the center, cleared of everything but a neat stack of enlarged maps, a roll of tracing paper, and a battered cardboard box she recognized from one of Oz's photographs.

He caught her glance. "The attic was generous again," he said. "I thought you'd like to meet your footnotes."

Ruth set the journal down as carefully as if it were glass.

"Alright," she murmured, more to Joseph than to anyone in the room. "Let's see where your world and theirs line up when they're finally in the same place."

Oz's mother—Elise, as she'd insisted at the door—appeared halfway through the mapping, wiping her hands on a dish towel and eyeing the table with open curiosity.

"So this is the famous journal," she said in English tinged with Normandy vowels, nodding toward the leather. "I have heard about him for months and only seen him on a screen."

Ruth glanced at Marie, then at Elise. "If you'd like to look through it, you can," she said. "Most of what I need is in my notes now. I just... ask one thing."

Elise tilted her head. "Of course."

"Please don't tug at the back binding," Ruth said. "There's a loose page tucked in there we've promised to open at the graves first. Under the oak."

Understanding flickered across Elise's face, something like respect layered over curiosity. "Some things need the right ground," she said. "I will be careful." She rested her fingertips lightly on the cover, as if greeting an old neighbor. "I will sit with it later, when you are out making trouble with my son."

"Research," Oz muttered.

"Trouble," Elise repeated, amused, and left them to their maps.

By late morning, their lines had begun to converge: red for Joseph's routes, blue for the Marchand notes, green for the gaps Ruth had brought with her like open questions. Houppeville. The Green Forest. The first safe house. The cove.

"The church should be next," Marie said at last, tapping a finger against Rouen on the map. "Before we go to the oak, I want you to see where his mother's name is still written. And where some of it has burned away."

Ruth felt a small, anticipatory knot form beneath her ribs. "Father Laurent?"

"He will be there," Marie said. "He has been waiting for this as much as we have."

They left the journal on the inn's sideboard when they went—a deliberate act of trust Ruth felt between her shoulder blades as the door clicked shut. Elise stood beside it, dish towel still in hand, as if keeping watch.

The drive into Rouen was shorter than Ruth remembered and longer in all the ways that mattered. The closer they came to the old quarter, the more the streets narrowed, pressing them toward the cathedral spire that needled up into a sky the color of pewter.

Inside, the air was as she remembered it: cool, dim, smelling of stone and wax and the faint tang of incense that seemed baked into the walls. Light fell in fractured shafts from the high windows, dust motes drifting like slow, deliberate snow.

Father Laurent emerged from a side aisle almost before they had fully stepped past the narthex, cassock whispering against the floor. His face broke into a smile that folded lines deeper at the corners of his eyes.

"Ruth," he said, taking her hands in both of his. "You found your way back."

"With reinforcements," Lena murmured under her breath, glancing up at the vaulted ceiling.

Introductions were made: Marie as niece of the boy from the vines; Oz as grandson of the man on the cliff; Lena as the friend who had stumbled on "Dear Kate" in the spine. Father Laurent's gaze sharpened at that, but he only nodded once.

"Come," he said. "The books are waiting."

The parish office was small and cluttered, a low room off the transept lined with shelves that sagged under the weight of registers and boxes. A single window let in an anemic wedge of light. On the central table lay three ledgers, already open, their pages a fan of cramped script and ink that had browned with age.

"I pulled the volumes we spoke of," Father Laurent said, gesturing to each in turn. "Baptisms, marriages, burials. There are gaps, of course. Bombs do not respect filing systems." His mouth twisted briefly, then smoothed. "But some things survived."

Ruth stepped closer, pulse prickling in her fingertips. The first book crackled softly when she touched the edge of a page.

"There," Father Laurent said, tapping a line near the margin of the baptismal register. "His mother."

Ruth followed his finger. The name was simple in ink that had bled but not broken: Lisette Durand. Next to it, the date of birth, the priest's attest, a godmother's name Ruth recognized from Joseph's early entries as a woman who brought bread when times were lean.

"She was born in this parish," Ruth murmured.

"And married from it," Father Laurent said, turning to the slim, carefully penned column that held Étienne and Lisette's wedding. "Here. 1915. Before the last war had finished making widows."

The marriage entry was neater, the ink darker, as if the hand that had written it had not yet known how many names would need to be fit into so little space.

Ruth traced the line without quite touching it. "He must have stood here," she said softly. "Watching them. The same font, the same stone."

Marie's hand found the back of a nearby chair, knuckles whitening. "And here," she said, her voice thinner, "where they stopped."

The burial register for 1940 was a different creature entirely. The pages were singed at the outer edges, blackening into nothing halfway down some columns. Names were half-missing, dates truncated. In one place, the ink bled into a smoky blur where water had hit fire.

Father Laurent pointed to a tight cluster of entries that had survived near the top of one page.

"You see?" he said quietly. "June twenty-fourth. Three names, consecutive."

Étienne Durand. Lisette Durand. Lucie Durand.

Someone's hand—another priest, another time—had drawn a small cross beside each where the fire damage crept close, as if guarding them from vanishing a second time.

Ruth's throat closed. The list Claire had shown her at the farmhouse flashed in her mind—the same names, the same date, the note about the oak. Here, the church's record stopped with the fact of their deaths. In the vineyard, Joseph had written where he'd laid them down.

"They were buried," she whispered. "Not just gone."

"As much as we could say so," Father Laurent replied. "There were days we knew bodies had been laid in earth and we did not know where. Your Joseph gave us back the 'where.'" He looked at her over the register's edge. "You give us back the 'who.'"

Silence pressed in around the tiny room. Even Lena looked stripped of words, her usual quips burned off by the names inked on the page.

Oz cleared his throat. "Is there anything here about... after?" he asked. "About Kate?"

Father Laurent turned a few more pages, slower now, scanning the entries with a practised eye.

"Not under her maiden name," he said. "War years are... untidy. People married in cellars, on farms, under trees, with no paper, only witnesses. But—" He tapped a later volume, thinner, its cover newer. "There is a note, after Liberation, about regularization of certain unions. If we are patient, we may yet find the day the Church admitted what the vineyard already knew."

Ruth let out a breath she hadn't realized she'd been holding. Somewhere in these cramped lines, or in a gap between them, was the formal acknowledgment of Joseph and Kate's vow—a bureaucratic echo of a decision made in secrecy and fear.

She stepped back from the table, letting the room widen around her again.

"Thank you," she said. "For keeping them. For letting us see them."

Father Laurent closed the burial register with a careful hand. "This is your work," he said. "And theirs. I am only the caretaker of the ink."

Marie looked at Ruth, a question in her eyes.

"Next?" she asked.

Ruth thought of the oak, the graves, the letter in the spine. Of Elise at the inn, the journal under her hand. Of Maman upstairs at the farmhouse, still offstage but moving closer in the story's orbit.

"Next," Ruth said, "we go back to where he wrote what the books can't."

42

Chapter 42

The inn felt different when they came back from Rouen.

The light had shifted, slanting low through the front windows, and the air carried the layered smells of something slow-cooked and finished with butter. Low light pooled over the long table. Elise moved between kitchen and sideboard with the calm focus of someone who had spent a lifetime feeding people through every kind of day.

Another woman sat near the far end, back to the door, dark hair twisted into a knot. She turned at the sound of their steps.

"Claire," Marie said, her face breaking into something that was half smile, half relief.

Claire stood, wiping her hands on a folded linen napkin. Her work jacket was gone; in its place a simple blouse and cardigan, but she still carried the vineyard in the set of her shoulders.

"You made it," she said, eyes moving from Marie to Ruth to Oz. "I was beginning to think Father Laurent had stolen you for the night."

"He tried," Lena said, dropping into the nearest chair. "The man has the energy of a grad seminar and a youth pastor combined."

Claire's mouth curved. "That sounds like him."

Elise appeared from the kitchen with a pot in her hands and nodded toward the empty chairs. "Sit, sit. You can be historians after you are human again."

They gathered around the table with Ruth between Marie and Oz, Lena opposite Claire, Elise at the head like a quiet anchor. Bowls and plates made a small geography between them: stew, crusty bread, a salad that tasted like it had been cut from the garden that afternoon. A bottle of red Claire uncorked with the ease of muscle memory followed.

For a while, the talk stayed on safe ground: the drive, the weather, the way Lena had nearly walked into a bicyclist staring up at the cathedral façade.

"How was the flight?"

"Crowded."

"And Rouen?"

"Exactly as stubborn as I remembered," Marie said.

It was Claire who steered them back to the land.

"Tomorrow," she said, tearing a piece of bread in half, "I would like you to come out to the vineyard. Properly this time. Not just the oak."

Ruth looked up. "If you're sure," she said. "I don't want to... intrude."

Claire shook her head. "Intrusion was last time, when you arrived with a journal and no warning," she said, not unkindly. "This time, you come as guests. As family, if you will allow it." Her gaze softened. "You have seen where the Church wrote their names. You should see where they walked before there were registers."

Marie's fingers tightened around her glass. "And Maman?" she asked quietly.

Elise and Claire exchanged a glance Ruth couldn't quite read.

"She is... awake more, lately," Claire said. "Some days better than others. I think she knows you are here." Her eyes flicked to Ruth. "I think she has been waiting for this as much as we have."

Ruth felt the words settle like a stone in her chest.

"We won't bring the letter into her room without you," Elise added, as if she'd heard the unspoken fear. "But the land is hers as much as Joseph's. She would want you to see it in the morning light."

Oz cleared his throat. "We can go early," he said. "Walk the rows first, then the oak, then the house. Let the ground introduce itself before the walls do."

Lena nodded slowly. "Field trip to the origin story," she said. "Got it."

Claire smiled at that, a quick flash of amusement. "Bring good shoes," she said. "And whatever courage you have left after the archives. The vines are forgiving. The memories, less so."

The conversation drifted to logistics after that—times, directions, whether to take one car or two—but underneath it all Ruth felt a quiet, insistent pull. Tomorrow wouldn't just be a visit to a vineyard. It would be a return to the place where Joseph had stopped being theory and become soil and stone and a girl named Kate.

Claire's attention swung back to Ruth.

"So," she said, looking at her over the rim of her glass, "tell me how you plan to explain him to a room of strangers. The boy whose journal you carried into my kitchen. If I am going to let you loose on the vineyard again, I would like to hear the story from the beginning."

Lena leaned back, interested. "Oh good," she said. "The montage. I've only seen the director's cut."

Ruth swallowed a mouthful of stew that suddenly felt too thick. The table waited.

"Alright," she said. "From the top, then."

She set her spoon down and folded her hands, more out of habit than piety.

"I found the journal in a little shop in Paris," she began. "Bottom drawer of a bureau that didn't want to open. The first pages were what you'd expect—vines, weather, gossip from town. A boy in northern France who still believed the war might pass him by."

Claire's mouth twitched. "We all thought that, once."

"Then," Ruth went on, "the handwriting changes. The ink digs deeper. He starts talking about Norway, Denmark, the gray spreading over the map. About ghettos. About plans for a cellar, just in case the Germans don't stay on the radio."

She sketched the arc with words, each beat like a pin on the map they'd left in the sitting room:

The cellar plans behind the vineyard house.

The march west with David and the families, threading between Rouen and Barentin under the cover of the Green Forest.

The nights at Cauville, the boats slipping into the Channel, the boy on the cliff timing tides and patrols.

Le Berger and the pivot—the moment Joseph stopped being just a helper and started thinking like a courier, looping back alone to scout routes and plant information in confessional cracks and shop counters.

Lena watched her with an expression that was part pride, part quiet alarm. She'd heard versions of this before, but not like this, not with the registers and the graves now layered in.

"And in the spaces where the ink stops," Ruth said softly, "you all pick him up."

She nodded toward Claire and Oz.

"Claire's grandfather buying what was left of the vineyard, finding that burial list in the cellar wall, starting the cemetery under the oak. Your family keeping the Durand photo and the names when no one came back to claim them. Oz's grandfather mapping routes from the cliff. Father Laurent guarding the registers through fire and water."

Claire's fingers tightened around her glass. "And Kate," she said. "Do not forget her."

"I couldn't," Ruth said. "Even if I tried."

She spoke of Kate the way Joseph had written her: the farm girl who waved him in from the barn; the woman whose kitchen smelled of coffee and onions while the world burned beyond the hedgerows; the presence he stepped away from to keep doing the work.

"And somewhere," Ruth finished, "between the last dated entry and the back board of the journal, there's a letter that begins with her name. 'Dear Kate.' We haven't read the rest. We've been waiting to bring him back here first."

The room settled around the words. Even Elise, who had heard most of this in fragments over months of emails and late-night phone calls, stood still by the sideboard.

Claire exhaled slowly. "So," she said, "to a room of strangers you will say what, exactly? That he was a boy who became a courier? A farmer's son who buried his own family and walked into the dark anyway?"

Ruth considered.

"I think," she said, "I'll say he was someone who refused to let the official record have the last word. That he wrote the names and places the ledgers couldn't hold. And that your families kept those pieces safe when the rest of the world moved on."

Lena's voice cut in, softer than usual. "And I'll tell them," she said, "that my friend fell in love with a dead guy's handwriting and let it rearrange her life."

Oz huffed a quiet laugh. "That part is obvious," he murmured.

Marie's eyes shone in the half-light. "Tomorrow," she said, "you will see where he wrote when he wasn't holding a pen."

“The vineyard,” Claire added. “The paths he walked to the oak. The house where Kate still listens for his steps when the floor creaks.” She lifted her glass a little. “Consider this your last calm meal before the land starts talking.”

They ate after that with fewer interruptions, the stew and bread doing their work. Outside, night pressed close to the windows. Somewhere beyond the circle of lamplight, vines waited, and a tree, and an old woman in a farmhouse bed.

Ruth felt it all gathering at the edges of the day, the way a storm builds just out of sight.

“Tomorrow,” she thought, fingers resting on the table near Marie’s, “we stop telling his story and start standing where he did.”

43

Chapter 43

The four of them reached the vineyard just as the light was starting to turn the world gold.

Claire was already at the gate, hands tucked into the pockets of her jacket, watching the sun climb over the rows. The vines caught it first, each line throwing a long, thin shadow across the damp earth. As they stepped through onto the packed dirt lane, Ruth's gaze pulled past the neat geometry to the far corner of the field.

There, the oak rose against the pale sky, its branches spread wide. The new light caught it from behind, stretching its silhouette down the slope—a dark, reaching shape that spilled over the rows and across their path until it brushed their feet.

"Every morning," Claire said quietly, following Ruth's line of sight. "Before the day burns the shadows away, it reminds us where everything ends up."

Ruth's fingers tightened around the strap of her bag, the journal a solid weight at her hip.

"And where it began," she said.

They walked on together, the oak's long shadow leading them toward the heart of the vines.

Beneath the tree, the ground was still damp, the grass flattened in places where feet had stood many times before. The stones Claire had shown her on Ruth's first visit sat in their quiet row, names softened by weather but no longer strangers.

Ruth opened the journal with careful hands. The others gathered close—Marie on her right, Oz on her left, Lena just behind her shoulder.

For a moment she let the breeze ruffle the edges of the pages, then found the last dated entry and began to read.

June 1, 1944

They keep saying something is coming.

No dates. No names. Just a feeling that has settled over the villages like the low clouds on the Channel, heavy and waiting. The men who pass through the farm now are different from the ones I first met in the forest in 1940. Fewer uniforms stolen from dead soldiers, more clothes that do not fit the places they claim to be from. Their French is careful. Their questions are not.

Le Berger sent word last month that the work in our corner will change. Less moving people, more moving information, more making sure the right roads are open—or closed—when the time comes. He did not say when that would be. Only that we should be ready to make noise and then disappear.

My part is simple on paper, complicated in practice. There is a stretch of road east of here the Germans favor when they move men and fuel toward the coast. A bottleneck between hedgerows and a small stone bridge that was old when my grandfather was a boy. If it stands, they can send trucks through for days. If it falls at the right moment, they will have to find another way, slower and narrower.

They want eyes on that road, and someone who can read the pattern of patrols without being noticed. Someone who can walk from the farm to the bridge and back without leaving a mark, who knows which hedges you can slip through and which houses will slam their shutters if they see you.

I told them I already know the paths. I did not say how many times I have walked them in the dark.

For now, my job is to count and remember. How many trucks in a day. How many tanks. How often the officers ride with them instead of in cars. Whether the guards on the bridge smoke, and if they do, what time the glow of their cigarettes appears in the night. Somewhere, someone with a map is marking all this down in neat lines and symbols. I am only the pencil stub in the mud.

Kate pretends not to listen when the men come and go, but I can feel her watching me. She moves between the stove and the table with that same quiet efficiency she had before any of this started, as if nothing has changed and I am still only the boy who came in from the vines with dirt on his boots. Only now, when she sets a cup of coffee beside my hand, her fingers linger for a heartbeat longer, and her eyes search my face as if she is trying to fix it in her mind.

Last night, after everyone else had gone to bed, I heard her father on the porch talking to one of the men from the maquis. They spoke softly, but the walls in this house remember everything.

If he is caught out there, Kate's father said, they will not treat him like a farmer. Not anymore.

The other man answered, He has not been only a farmer for a long time.

I lay awake in the barn staring at the rafters, thinking of the bridge, the road, the gray trucks, the oak in the corner of the vineyard, the cellar wall where I carved the names of the ones we buried. So many pieces of land holding what the papers cannot.

Something is coming. You can feel it in the way the soldiers have started to look over their shoulders, in the way even the bravest old women fall silent when an unfamiliar car passes through the square. The radio spits rumors when we can get to one safely. England. Planes. Landings. No one knows anything and everyone knows more than they can say.

In a few days—maybe weeks—the work will change again. Less counting. More acting. The man from the maquis says they will need someone from here to guide them when the time comes, someone who can move quickly between the farm and the bridge and the church and back without having to stop and ask the way. Someone who can take a message from the fields to the sea without leaving it in ink.

He looked at me when he said it, as if there was no one else he could mean.

I am not afraid of what they are asking. I am afraid of what it will cost Kate if I say yes. And of what it will cost everyone if I say no.

For now, there is still time to walk the road and count the trucks and memorize the rhythm of boots on stone. For now, I can still come back at night and hear the sound of her moving in the kitchen, the low murmur of her father's voice, the creak of the house settling around us as if it believes we will all still be here tomorrow.

If I do what they ask, this place will change again. Maybe for the last time.

They keep saying something is coming.

I think, this time, it is.

Ruth's voice thinned on the last line and then fell silent. For a heartbeat, only the wind in the branches answered.

Just as the quiet settled, the crunch of gravel reached them from behind.

Claire turned first. A slim wheelchair eased into view between the rows, its wheels bumping gently over the uneven ground. Elise walked behind it, one hand steady on the handle, the other shading her eyes from the growing light.

Beneath the oak's spreading branches, they stopped.

The woman in the chair was smaller than Ruth had imagined, folded in on herself by years, but her eyes were clear and sharp as glass. A blanket lay across her knees, the edge of it caught in thin fingers that still seemed capable of work.

"Maman," Marie breathed. "You should have waited. We were coming back to the house."

"Nonsense," Kate said, her voice papery but firm. "If he is going to have his words read under my tree, I will not listen at a window." She looked at Ruth then, gaze dropping to the journal in her hands. "Besides, I have been waiting a very long time to hear how he chose to finish that page."

Elise eased the chair closer to the stones. "Careful," she murmured, but Kate was already lifting one hand, reaching toward the worn leather as if greeting an old friend.

"They told me later," she said, eyes still on the book, "that he was ambushed at a checkpoint. The Germans changed the pattern on the road, moved their men where no one expected. He went out to guide a team bringing decoys—rubber tanks, wooden guns, things meant to confuse them on their maps." Her mouth tightened. "They caught him with lies made of canvas and air and decided that was enough to hang a death sentence on."

Her fingers brushed the edge of the journal. "May I?" she asked.

Ruth stepped forward, throat tight, and placed it gently in her hands.

Kate turned it with the care of someone handling a relic, then thumbed her way to the back. The others held still as she eased the last page away from the board, revealing the narrow seam of paper hidden in the spine. She bent her head and read in silence.

No one spoke. The breeze moved through the oak above them, a low rustle like distant pages turning. The light in Kate's eyes seemed to sharpen with each line, competing with the morning sun.

At last she exhaled, a sound halfway between a sigh and a laugh.

"Eighty years," she said, her voice crackling but steady. "Eighty years I have waited for Joseph. I did not expect to hear from him again before heaven."

No one asked, but everyone wanted to know what the narrow strip of paper said. Kate's thumb rested on the fold, holding the secret a moment longer.

When she looked up, her gaze found Ruth.

"This book is yours more than anyone's now," she said quietly. "You carried him when the rest of us could only remember him. I have been waiting to hear his words. You have been working to share his story. If you are willing, I would be honored to let you be the one who reads this out loud."

She extended the journal back toward Ruth, the hidden page still marked by her hand.

44

Chapter 44

Ruth stood facing them, the stone with Joseph's name at her back, the journal open in her hands where Kate's thumb still marked the hidden page. The air beneath the oak was cool despite the rising sun, carrying the damp scent of earth and leaves and old stone. Somewhere beyond the rows, a tractor started, then fell quiet again, as if the rest of the land were choosing to listen.

The letter had emptied them.

By the time Ruth folded the thin strip of paper back into the spine and closed the journal, no one seemed sure what to do with their hands. Marie knelt for a moment to touch the stone that bore Joseph's name. Claire stood with her eyes on the horizon, lips moving in a prayer too quiet to catch. Elise rested both palms on the back of Kate's chair, as if steadying them both.

Eventually, gravity reasserted itself.

"We should get Maman out of the sun," Elise said softly.

Kate gave a small, resigned huff. "Yes, yes. Before I turn into parchment to match his pages."

The slow procession back through the vines formed almost on its own: Claire leading, Elise pushing the chair, Marie walking close, one hand on her mother's shoulder. Lena hesitated, looking between Ruth and the farmhouse.

"I'll go help inside," she said finally. "Someone needs to make sure they don't feed you all out of grief."

When the sound of their voices and wheels on gravel faded, only two people remained under the oak.

Ruth and Oz stood for a while without speaking, the journal cradled against her chest, the stones at their feet.

It was Oz who broke the silence.

"He would have hated that letter," he said quietly.

Ruth blinked. "What?"

"Not the words," Oz amended, toeing a pebble near the edge of the grave. "The fact that we all just stood here and listened to it like a sermon. He wrote to one person. You turned it into... an audience."

Guilt flared, sharp and stupid. "I shouldn't have read it out loud," she said. "I should have let it stay between them."

Oz shook his head. "That's not what I mean."

He crouched, tracing the carved letters of Joseph's surname with one fingertip, then looked up at her.

"He wrote it to her," he said. "But he hid it where someone like you would find it. In a book meant to outlive him. In a place where paper and memory overlap." He straightened. "I think he trusted that if anyone ever stood here with both the letter and the journal, they'd know how to carry him forward without turning him into a statue."

Ruth looked down at the leather in her hands. The weight of it had changed. Or maybe she had.

"I keep thinking," she said slowly, "that I'm trespassing. That I've walked too far into someone else's life and started rearranging their furniture."

"You thought that in my inn, too," Oz said. "And at the cove. And in the archives. Joseph's whole world was other people's rooms. Farms. Churches. Cliffs that didn't belong to him." His mouth curled. "He didn't wait to be invited. He just refused to forget what he saw."

The wind stirred, lifting a loose strand of hair across Ruth's cheek.

"You're not him," Oz added. "But you're doing the same thing in a different war. Walking through other people's stories and insisting they don't disappear into footnotes." He nodded at the journal. "That's not trespassing. That's... continuing."

She let the idea sit, uncomfortable and oddly right.

"Being his voice," she said, tasting the words as if they might bite. "That's not what I set out to do."

"No," Oz said. "You set out to write a thesis."

She huffed a laugh that felt too big in her throat.

"I don't want to turn him into a monument," she said. "Or myself."

"Then don't," Oz replied simply. "Tell it the way you read it the first time. With all the gaps and wrong turns left in. Remember that he was scared and stubborn and sometimes wrong about people. That he loved badly and bravely at the same time."

He glanced toward the farmhouse, where a thin column of smoke rose from the kitchen chimney.

"And when it gets to be too much," he added, "remember that he also went home for soup."

Ruth smiled, small but genuine.

"The exhibit," she said after a moment. "The book. The classes. They're all going to want answers. Timelines. Clean arcs."

"And you," Oz said, "know where the story refuses to be clean."

She looked down at Joseph's name one more time, then at the line of stones beside it, then out over the vines.

"I can live with that," she said. "With being the one who keeps saying 'we don't know' out loud."

"And with being the one who keeps saying his name," Oz added.

The words settled in the space between them—not a vow, exactly, but something close.

Ruth slid the journal back into her bag, the hidden letter now part of a whole that felt less like an artifact and more like a conversation she'd walked into halfway through.

"Come on," she said. "If we stay out here any longer, your mother will assume I've defected to the cemetery."

They started back toward the house, the oak's shade falling away behind them. The path between the rows narrowed, vines brushing their sleeves. Somewhere ahead, a door opened, distant voices rising and falling over the clatter of plates.

Halfway up the slope, Ruth slowed.

"I should write this down before it blurs," she said. "The letter, what Kate remembered about the checkpoint, the way the light—" She broke off, shaking her head. "If I don't, it'll all turn into something tidy in my notes, and it wasn't tidy."

Oz watched her for a moment. The way her shoulders had crept up again. The way her hand hovered near her bag, already reaching for pen and paper like a reflex.

"You will," he said. "You always do."

She nodded, gaze drifting back toward the tree. "This is the part where I go home and turn someone else's life into paragraphs."

"And conference papers," he added. "And exhibits. And students who leave your class seeing more than maps and dates when they hear 'Normandy.'"

"I don't know how to be anything else anymore," she admitted. "Some days it feels like all I'm good for is translating other people's ghosts."

She took another step toward the farmhouse.

He didn't.

"Ruth," Oz said.

Something in his tone made her stop.

She turned back. He stood in the narrow lane, hands loose at his sides, the lines of vines running away on either side of him like rails. For a heartbeat, he looked very much like his grandfather might have: rooted and tired and still unwilling to let someone walk into danger alone.

"You're not a ghost," he said quietly. "And you're not only a voice for the dead."

She opened her mouth to argue, but he went on.

"You came here," he said, "and you made my family remember things we'd turned into habits. You made Marie ask questions she'd stopped asking. You made me look at this place and see more than guests and invoices and weather reports." His mouth quirked. "You even made my mother admit she likes having strangers under her roof."

The corners of Ruth's eyes tightened, a laugh and a warning both.

"Oz," she began.

He stepped closer, closing the last of the distance between them in two careful strides.

"You carried Joseph across an ocean," he said. "You read his last words under an oak he never planned to be buried under. You are going to go home and tell his story, and you're going to do it well." He paused. "But you don't have to vanish into it."

She swallowed. The bag strap creaked under her fingers.

"What does not vanishing look like?" she asked, and there was more fear in the question than she wanted him to hear.

He didn't flinch.

"It looks like you coming back when this is over and there's no exhibit deadline," he said. "It looks like you walking these rows without a notebook, just to see how the vines look in a different season. It looks like you sitting on my kitchen counter complaining about my coffee instead of my citations." His smile turned softer. "It looks like you letting yourself have a life that isn't only other people's wars."

She stared at him, the cracked earth and green leaves and gray stone all blurring at the edges.

"And if I don't know how to do that?" she asked.

"Then we figure it out," he said simply. "Slowly. Like everything else."

The wind lifted again, carrying the smell of damp soil and distant smoke.

"You know I live on another continent," she said, because someone had to say it out loud.

"I've noticed," Oz said. "There are also planes. And email. And the miraculous invention of sabbaticals." He hesitated, then added, "I'm not asking you to move here and become a full-time inn mythologist."

She huffed a wet laugh at that.

"I am asking," he said, "that when you write this, you leave a line somewhere that points back to us. To now. To the fact that you were here and you mattered to people who are still breathing."

He let the words hang between them for a beat, then, very gently, reached out.

Her hand was still on the bag strap. He curled his fingers around hers where they gripped the worn canvas, not tugging, just covering, steadying.

"You don't have to answer today," he said. "You don't have to answer at all. But don't walk away from this field thinking the only thing you changed was a footnote."

For a moment, she couldn't speak. Her mind skittered to all the things waiting back home—classes, committees, drafts. To all the reasons this was complicated and impractical and exactly the kind of thing she'd told herself she didn't get to have.

And then, underneath all of that, to the simple fact that she didn't want to walk back to the farmhouse alone.

She turned her hand in his until their fingers threaded properly, the gesture as tentative and deliberate as a first line on a blank page.

"I can leave a line," she said, voice low. "Maybe even a paragraph."

His answering grin was quick and startled, like he hadn't quite let himself hope.

"Good," he said. "Historians need evidence."

They stood there one heartbeat longer, the oak's shadow still touching the backs of their shoes, the farmhouse waiting ahead.

Then Ruth squeezed his hand once.

"Come on," she said. "If we're late to lunch, your mother will blame me. I'd rather save that for when she reads the book."

They started toward the house together, step for step this time, not a march away from the past, exactly, but something that felt, for the first time in a long while, like walking toward a future that had room for both history and whatever this was becoming.

Epilogue

Dear Kate,

I am sitting beside you, watching you sleep and trying to imagine what our lives might look like when this is over. I picture a small house that does not have to hide anyone, a baby crying in the next room and that being the worst trouble we have. I try to hear that cry so loudly in my mind that it drowns out the guns and the boots and the stupid orders of men who have never seen this valley at dawn.

But even with all of that, I cannot shake the feeling that I may never live long enough to see it with you. Maybe it is simply that it has been too long, or the weight of the nights and roads behind us, or the faces of friends who will not be coming back. War makes a man practical about his chances. It does not make his heart any smaller.

If I have never found the words while sitting across from you, let me try now, on this page that may outlive us both. I will never be able to express how deep my love for you runs. You have been the center of every step I have taken since the day your hair blew across your face in the yard and you scolded me for tracking mud into your mother's kitchen. You carried bread to the barn as if it were nothing. You carried my courage without even knowing it.

When I leave you for these trips, I do not walk away from you. I walk because of you. Every family I lead through the vines, every child who falls asleep on a wagon instead of in a ditch, is my way of insisting that you and our child will someday live in a world where no one has to whisper their own name. If there is any sense to this madness, it is that the fear stops with us and does not reach your doorstep again.

I am afraid, Kate. More often than I have ever admitted. I am afraid of the checkpoints and the men who are beginning to recognize my truck, of the wrong face in the wrong doorway, of a knock on this door when I am not here to answer it. But I am more afraid of doing nothing. Of standing still while others disappear. You once told me you would rather be a widow than the wife of a coward. I hope, if it comes to it, that you will not have to be either.

If I do not come back from one of these roads, know this: I did not gamble lightly with what we have been given. I measured every path against your face, every risk against the feel of your hand on my sleeve, every night away against the sound I have never yet heard, our child crying in the next room. I go because I want that sound to exist in this house, in a France that can breathe again.

Take care of our little one in whatever world is waiting. Tell them I loved you both as fiercely as I knew how. Tell them their father once walked these rows in the dark and believed, stubbornly, that light would return to them. If there is anything left of me in this place, let it be in the way you laugh without listening for boots on the road, in the way our child runs through the vines without looking over their shoulder.

If by some mercy I do grow old and foolish at your side, you can take this letter out and laugh at how serious I was. You can remind me that we did, in the end, get nothing more dramatic than a baby crying and soup cooling on the stove. That is all I am fighting for now. That is all I want.

You are the center of why I do this, and the home every road leads back to in my mind. Whatever happens to my body, remember that the best part of me has already been given to you.

Your Joseph

www.ingramcontent.com/pod-product-compliance
Lightning Source LLC
LaVergne TN
LVHW100524110826
845146LV00002B/764
* 9 7 9 8 9 9 9 1 0 6 0 5 6 *